BLOOD AND CHOCLATE

Judith Cranswick

www.judithcranswick.co.uk

Novels by Judith Cranswick

For more information, please visit
www.judithcranswick.co.uk

Prologue

He laid the gun on the table beside the photograph. The Browning PRO-9 pistol was not his weapon of choice. He much preferred a long-range rifle, but the location meant that there was no chance of that. The target would be surrounded by crowds and there were no high vantage points in the vicinity.

It would not be an easy operation and would involve more risks than usual. Why the client had insisted that it take place in such a public area he had no idea, not that it concerned him. As long as the man had been prepared to pay, that was all that mattered. It wouldn't be the first time he'd wormed his way into a crowd, killed the target then made his escape in the ensuing panic. It just took careful planning. There was one advantage. The security men wouldn't fire back even if they saw him. Too many innocent civilians in the way.

He wrapped the pistol in the cloth and returned it to its hiding place between the joists underneath a loose floorboard. He picked up the photograph and looked at it for the last time. He'd have no trouble recognising the target. Placing the photograph on an old foil tray, he set light to it and watched the yellow, red and orange flames dancing over the fast disappearing picture. Once he'd let it cool down, he picked up the tray and carried it to the open window gently blowing the ashes out into the empty backstreet below.

The Treasures of Flanders

Belgium may be famous for its chocolate, beer and lace but there is so much more to this fascinating country. The rich cultural past of Flanders is reflected in the magnificent architecture of Brussels, Bruges and Antwerp, three of Europe's greatest medieval cities, and in the Rubens, Breughel and Van Eyck masterpieces that can be seen in its museums and cathedrals.

Throughout this wonderful holiday, your expert Tour Manager will be on hand to guide you through some of Belgium's most beautiful towns and ensure that you have a truly unforgettable experience.

Super Sun Executive Travel
Specialists in luxury Breaks and Continental Tours

The Treasures of Flanders Passenger List
* Members of Swanley Association
with Fiona's added comments

Tour Manager…Mrs Fiona Mason
Driver…Mr Winston Taylor

Mr Noel Appleby* – *Group treasurer. White curly hair & moustache*
Mrs Charlotte Appleby* – U*ntidy swept-up hair, vague, disorganised*
Miss Peggy Brent* – *'Margaret Rutherford' no nonsense type*
Mr Patrick Cahill – *Late 40s*
Mrs Joan Cahill – *Vegetarian*
Mr Aubrey Diamond – *Intent on inflicting his cold on everyone else!*
Mrs Glenda Diamond – *Large lady difficult to miss*
Miss Dee Foley – *Broad, butch, v short fair hair, wears plain clothes*
Mr Robert Heppell* – *Chinstrap beard, short, likes sound of own voice*
Mrs Janice Heppell* – *Statuesque, glasses, confident, bit intimidating*
Mr Malcolm Kennedy – *40s amiable Scot,*
Mrs Liz Kennedy – *Fair curly hair, soft Scottish accent*
Mr Simon Lithgow* – *Big, broad-shouldered, dark hair grey at temples*
Mrs Gina Lithgow* – *Mid 30s, odd hairdo*
Rev. Nicholas McArdle* – *Tall, stooped, reserved, wears glasses*
Mrs Barbara McArdle* – *Late 60s, short and plump, motherly*
Mr Felix Navarre* – *Quiet, seems pleasant*
Mr Austin Pilkington* – *Tall, distinguished, well-spoken*
Mr Jeffrey Prior – *Beer belly*
Mrs Eleanor Prior – *Loves to gossip*
Miss Olive Scudamore* – *Fussy, knitted cardigans*
Miss Hazel Tonkin – *Dee's pretty, slim, somewhat 'dizzy' partner*
Mr Bernard Western* – *Thinning on top. Much older than wife*
Mrs Philippa Western* – *Tall, willowy, handsome, designer clothes*

Day 1 Friday

*Our feeder coach will bring you from your chosen
pickup point to Dover where you will board our luxury
Platinum Class coach in time for a lunchtime ferry
crossing to Calais.*

*Our journey takes us through France and into
Belgium to the superbly appointed Hotel Leopold in
Brussels, within walking distance of Grand Place,
justly claimed as one of the world's most beautiful city
squares.*

Super Sun Executive Travel

Chapter 1

Fiona knew the man was going to be trouble from the moment she first clapped eyes on him at Dover. It was all too evident that Robert Heppell was a man who liked to get his own way. Apart from the self-important air, his most distinguishing feature was the inch-wide strip of pure white beard along his jawline, in stark contrast to the dark brown hair only moderately flecked with grey.

The only surprise was that he had waited until now. So much for a quiet drink before dinner! The moment she had walked into the hotel's elegant lounge bar, he was on his feet and striding towards her, chin thrust forward in grim determination.

'Fiona, I need to talk to you about the itinerary.' The chairman of the Swanley Association was primed and ready for battle.

Fiona did her best to smile. 'We'll be going into dinner in a few minutes, perhaps we could...'

'This cannot wait any longer.'

Heads were turning and it wasn't only her Super Sun passengers whose peace was being disturbed.

There was no point in putting it off any longer. 'Shall we find somewhere a little quieter?'

Fiona led the way out into the large foyer area and over to one of the groups of easy chairs in a secluded corner.

Almost as soon as the final arrangements for the tour had been arranged, she'd been warned that Robert Heppell might prove to be a difficult client. The moment he'd received his copy of the details of the "Treasures of Flanders Tour", he'd been on the phone demanding to speak to one of the Super Sun management team.

Having failed to persuade the company to follow the exact itinerary he had originally put together, Heppell had obviously decided to work on Fiona. Forewarned is forearmed and when he'd approached her the moment they'd reached the hotel, she knew she was not to be spared the confrontation. With all the arrangements that needed her attention at the time, Fiona had no choice but to delay their meeting, but with it hanging over her like some sword of Damocles, the sooner it was over the better.

'This is not the programme I asked Super Sun to put together for us,' he said by way of introduction, throwing down the tour booklet on the low table in front of her.

Fiona looked up at the towering figure with a fixed smile and motioned him to the seat opposite.

'No, I do realise that, Robert.' She was not going to start off with a formal *Mr* Heppell. 'However, as I believe the company has already explained, because you were not able to find the minimum twenty passengers necessary to make an exclusive trip for the Swanley Association viable, it was a question of either cancelling the visit altogether or advertising it as part of our general programme to make up the numbers.'

'I know that,' he snapped as he flung himself onto the settee, 'but whoever put this together has changed the whole character of the tour. You've cut out all the Fine Arts museums!'

'That is not true at all, but a week devoted solely to looking at Flemish Masters was felt to be a little heavy for the average Super Sun client.' Best not to let him know that she was the one responsible for suggesting the changes. 'Although we have included visits to some alternative places, the holiday is still very much, as I'm sure you will concede, a cultural tour.'

The hairless upper lip quivered in barely suppressed anger. 'And what about the Musées Royaux des Beaux-Arts in Brussels? That was to be the highlight of the whole trip and you've replaced it with a trip to Waterloo!' The sneer in his voice almost made her recoil.

'We have simply moved that visit to another day and wonderful though its collections might be, it was felt that the majority of passengers would find a whole day in the museum rather too much. However, as I am sure you were told when you spoke to the company, if you wish to spend the rest of the day at the museum there is nothing to stop you or any of the group from doing so.'

She could see his fists clenching. Before he could interrupt, she continued firmly. 'Besides which, I think you will find that the museum is closed on Mondays. We had no choice but to find an alternative venue. I appreciate Waterloo was not on your programme, nevertheless, I think even the members of Swanley Association will find it a fascinating and enjoyable day and it will give an insight into a significant event in European history.' Her smile was becoming more fixed by the minute.

Appreciating that he had lost that particular argument, Robert changed tack. Leaning forward, he jabbed a finger at the booklet. 'What about Antwerp? The Koninklijk Museum has one of the best collections of the full range of early Flemish Old Masters anywhere.'

'That is true, but only because with visits to the Fine Arts museums in Bruges and Brussels it was felt that Plantin's printing workshop with its original Gutenberg bible in Antwerp would widen the cultural horizons.'

'Humph,' he snorted.

Before he could launch into a further tirade, Fiona cut in, 'However, should you or any of your party prefer to go to the Fine Arts Museums in Antwerp instead, there is nothing to stop you. I can look up the cost of the entrance fees if you'd like and you can put it to your members, but if any of them do decide to join you, I will need their names before the day so I can keep track of everyone.'

'Why should we have to pay? It was part of the original negotiations with Super Sun that all entrance fees would be included.'

'As indeed they are for the places on the published "Treasures of Flanders Tour". With only fourteen members rather than the thirty-to-forty you predicted, the cost for the programme you initially outlined virtually doubled. You did accept the company's suggestion to offer a slightly amended itinerary to the general public which allowed the price to be kept at the initial estimate. However, there is nothing to stop you and your party going ahead with your original programme bearing in mind that you will have to make your own way to the various museums and churches and pay the additional entry fees. Obviously that additional expense incurred will still be far short of the amount you would've had to pay for an exclusive tour for so few of you.'

Enough was enough. She gave him the most charming smile she could manage, rose to her feet and walked away before he could find something else to complain about.

Winston was at the bar watching for her. He raised his glass and smiled when she caught his eye. Not for the first time, she thanked her lucky stars that she'd been teamed with the bear-like West Indian driver. As she knew from their previous tours together, he remained calm no matter what the problem and always had a smile on his face. Just the man to have in a crisis.

'Battle over, sweetheart?'

Fiona nodded and climbed onto the bar stool next to him. 'My legs are still shaking.'

'I take it you won.'

'More or less,' she said doubtfully, 'but that was only the opening skirmish in what could be a long war. There's a good chance that Heppell might still try and cause trouble. If he manages to enlist the support of other Swanley Association members, things could turn nasty.'

Winston shook his head. 'Not from what I's been hearin'. From the things they's bin sayin' behind his back most of 'em don't like the man.'

'He *is* their chairman. They must have elected him.'

'Probably 'cause no one else wanted the job, shouldn't wonder,' he chuckled. 'Don't you worry; I's just been chatting to the chap with the white 'tash.'

'That would be Noel Appleby.'

'Well, according to him, there were nearly forty people interested at the start, but they nearly all pulled out when he took charge. That's why the party's mainly only committee members he more or less shamed into coming. By the sound of things, even they is a lot happier with your itinerary than the one he'd got planned for 'em.'

Winston's comments made a lot of sense. It explained why Heppell failed to raise enough people for a full coach at the last minute, but Fiona still had her doubts. 'I still need to keep them happy. Apart from adding a new tour to the company brochure, the top brass see this as a chance to break into a different market offering bespoke itineraries specifically designed to suit the needs of various clubs and groups. If I mess this up, I could be out of a job.'

Winston wrapped an arm around her shoulder. 'The boss man wouldn't have asked you to do the trip if he didn't have every confidence in you, sweetheart.'

Fiona gave him a sidelong look. 'The reason I was asked to do it was because so few of the old hands are prepared to cover tours blind. It involves too much work researching all the places beforehand, especially as this is a brand-new tour. I'm still new so I didn't have much choice.'

The big West Indian gave one of his deep, rumbling laughs. 'You may not've bin with the company long, sweetheart, but you's already got a reputation for being able to handle awkward clients and from all the fuss he kicked up at Head

Office, our friend Mr Nasty was always going to be a challenge.'

'I was warned,' Fiona admitted. 'I may only have been in this job for five months, but I'm already beginning to spot the potential trouble-makers straight away.'

'You look like you need a drink, sweetheart. A strong one. What's your poison?'

'Don't tempt me, I'll stick to my usual orange juice thank you, Winston.' She tilted her head and looked up at the six-foot four gentle giant of a man with shoulders a sumo wrestler would be proud of. 'Have you noticed,' she said conspiratorially, 'how often short men seem to feel the need to assert themselves? Napoleon was only five foot five.'

Winston chuckled. 'So, tomorrow's itinerary stays as is, I take it.'

'It does indeed.' Fiona gave a sigh. 'I was hoping to have a few minutes before dinner to check the hotel arrangements before the briefing. I really ought to go and double check on the breakfast and dinner times before I speak to everyone.'

'Already done, sweetheart.' Winston handed over a slip of paper. 'Had a word with one of the girls at Reception.'

'Winston, you're a star!'

He gave her one of his beaming smiles. 'Want me to come along to the briefing? A bit of backup in case that Mr Nasty starts getting up to his tricks again.'

'There's really no need. It'll only take a few minutes and I doubt Mr Heppell will cause any more trouble tonight. As he has already pointed out, the evening lectures some of his members have prepared are an integral part of the programme. If the essential information I need to pass on to everyone encroaches by as much as a minute beyond eight-thirty when the first talk is timetabled, I shall have another war on my hands.'

Winston laughed. 'No pressure then, sweetheart.'

Fiona glanced at her watch. 'At this rate, I'm going to be late for dinner and I still need to check which tables had been reserved for our group in the restaurant.'

'Before you go, sweetheart. Seems there's some sort of rally in the park tomorrow. Over by the European Parliament Building. Shouldn't be a problem as you won't be taking your lot over that way, but you might find the centre of town a bit crowded.'

Fiona did her best to muster a smile. 'Then I'll just have to make sure I don't lose any of the party. Thanks for the heads-up, Winston.'

She jumped down from the high stool and made for the door. One way or another, this tour wasn't getting off to a good start.

Chapter 2

Fiona could hear Robert Heppell's hectoring tones at the next table even before she had finished her soup. It was evident that she was not the only one to earn the man's disapproval this evening. The argument was becoming more heated and the voices more strident.

'Governments *should* be doing more to ensure affordable housing and decent benefits for the disadvantaged and unemployed. Why should the less well-off in society have to bear all the pain? The Anti-Austerity protesters have a perfectly legitimate grievance,' snapped the round-faced woman with cropped hair and mannish clothes.

'Legitimate my arse!' Robert Heppell banged his fist on the table. 'Most of them have never done a decent hard day's work in their lives. Spongers living on state hand-outs from our hard-earned taxes.'

'Do you know how many thousands of people in Britain are living below the poverty line? Until the basic wage is raised to the level of a living wage, there's no chance of them being able to afford to even feed themselves properly.'

'No, but they have enough for their smartphones, their giant wall televisions screens and their subscriptions to Sky Sports. The reason they eat all this cheap processed rubbish is because they can't be bothered to get their lazy backsides up off the couch and go and cook themselves a decent, healthy meal. These workshy layabouts are bleeding our country dry and it's exactly your kind of woolly-minded liberalism, young lady, that's let them get away with it.' Heppell pointed an accusing finger. 'Your namby-pamby attitude is what got our country into the mess it's in today.'

'As opposed to your right-wing reactionary attitudes, I suppose.'

Their raised voices were attracting attention from everyone else in the restaurant. Things were rapidly getting out of hand. Any more and she would have to intervene.

There was a sudden snort of disapproval from the dowdily dressed woman sitting next to Fiona. 'That young lady is proving to be most disagreeable. It really isn't good enough upsetting dear Robert like that.'

Dear Robert, indeed! As far as Fiona could make out, Robert Heppell was the one provoking all the conflict. They had hardly sat down before she'd heard him sniping at Dee Foley, dismissing her comments as "radical claptrap"; although it couldn't be denied that the dour, masculine-looking woman had not been slow to rise to the bait. Robert Heppell had then tried to involve the gentle Rev. McArdle who was no pulpit-thumping clergyman, in his scathing criticism about her humanist views. Views, which according to Robert Heppell, led to the rejection of all the decent values upheld by society, let alone the established church and thus to the inevitable breakdown of society.

Fiona had little sympathy for the extreme polarised stance of either antagonist. The earnest, dour Dee Foley might possess few endearing social qualities, but the loud-mouthed, opinionated Robert Heppell was proving to be more objectionable the more she got to know him.

'Robert has very strong views about freethinkers,' Olive Scudamore continued indulgently, pulling the edges of her hand-knitted cardigan across her chest.

'Surely everyone is entitled to express their own views?' Fiona tried to reason.

'Not when they blatantly flout the laws of decent morality. Robert takes a very hard line on lesbianism.'

From the disapproving looks she'd been throwing in the direction of Dee and her pretty younger partner Hazel Tonkin all evening, Fiona judged that Olive was also something of a homophobe. Either that or her unswerving devotion to her hero led her to her unshakable support.

'It might be as well for him not to express such sentiments quite so vehemently. It might not prove too popular a stance with his prospective voters. Didn't I hear that he was hoping to stand as a parliamentary candidate at the next election?'

Fiona's sly dig went unnoticed and Olive's moon face broke into a smile. 'He'll make an excellent MP. He's done so much for deserving causes in our area and he's made a considerable impact as Leader of the Council. Many people were surprised when he was elected after so short a time, he'd only been on the council for eighteen months, but that's just the dynamic, farsighted man he is.'

'Really?'

Olive was in her element. 'Without him, we would have lost the Community Centre and the Rainbow School. That whole area was run down and in a very poor way and the Council was all set to sell the site to one of these big out-of-town shopping centres before Robert took over. The developers promised they'd build a new library as part of the complex, but the children would have had to be bussed to other schools right out of the area. That's bad enough for youngsters without problems, never mind disabled ones and those with learning difficulties. Robert led the campaign to fight the proposals. He got all sorts of people involved including several MPs from all parties to come to speak at a protest meeting. There was lots of publicity. It's thanks to Robert, not only that it was saved, but since he was elected Leader, he's managed to get all sorts of grants to regenerate the complex and now the school and the Community Centre have been refurbished and the County have revamped the library.'

'I'm surprised with all the work that such a role must entail, he still has time to act as Chairman for Swanley Association.'

'Well you know what they say, "If you want something done, ask a busy person." Besides,' Olive confided, 'I don't think the rest of the committee would let him retire. They do depend on him so.'

To judge by the attitude of several of the other members of the Swanley Association, Robert Heppell was by no means held in such high esteem as his loyal Group Secretary tried to make out. Quite how Heppell had come to be elected chairman in the first place was a mystery. Apart from the dowdy devoted Olive, few people appeared to be easy in his company. It was a reasonable assumption that the majority of group members opted for a quiet life and chose to accede to his decisions rather than face the man's scathing tongue and bad temper by suggesting alternatives.

Fiona was still relishing the last few mouthfuls of her dessert, a red berry fruit tart in a particularly scrumptious buttery pastry case, when the volume at the corner table rose again. Conversation at the surrounding tables ceased as everyone turned to see what was going on. Dee Foley was on her feet, bright pink spots on her cheeks, tension rippling through her whole frame. With a dramatic sweep, she pushed back her chair and marched out the restaurant head held high, her pretty if somewhat ineffectual partner Hazel Tonkin scurrying in her wake.

The commotion did not end there. Noel Appleby's sterling efforts at trying to keep the peace were no longer having the desired effect.

'No. I will not let it go. The woman needs to be told.' Robert Heppell's strident voice caused heads to turn throughout the room yet again.

Fiona couldn't hear the rest of Robert's diatribe, but from the way the charming, easy-going Noel recoiled and the shocked looks from the others sitting at the same table, the onslaught was not confined to Dee Foley.

Winston ushered the last of the party into the small conference room the hotel had set aside for the evening talks, gave her the thumbs up and closed the door. Fiona looked around at the expectant faces hoping that her bright smile hid the apprehension she was feeling.

'Good evening everyone, and a belated welcome to Brussels and what I know will prove to be a wonderful week visiting some truly memorable towns. We have a very busy schedule for you and I do hope you have all brought comfortable shoes as advised in your tour booklet. It's not that we will be walking any distance, but you will be on your feet for much of the day and as those of you who took the opportunity to do a little exploring before dinner will have already discovered, Belgian cobbles can take their toll.'

There were nods of agreement. Once she'd covered the essentials and reminded them all about the hotel arrangements for meals, pointed out the importance of being on time for the coach and answered a couple of questions, Fiona glanced at the sullen Robert Heppell. He was sitting in the front row arms folded across his chest, legs thrust forward, staring at his feet, resolutely avoiding her glance. Dare she tell the non-Association members of the party that they were free to listen to the presentations? They were about the lives and work of various artists and the different architectural styles that they would all be seeing on the tour. She had hoped that as Chairman of the Association, Robert might invite them to do so.

It was Noel who came to her rescue. As soon as she'd finished, he was on his feet and smiling at everyone.

'Yes indeed, we'd be happy for you all to stay. Tonight's talk is by way of an introduction. Nothing too heavy. Just a bit of background to give you a flavour of what we'll be looking at throughout the week and help put it all in context. We'll take a look at the architecture, from the magnificent Baroque merchant houses we will see in the Grand Place tomorrow morning to the Art Deco Sacré-Coeur Basilica we'll be visiting in the afternoon.' The bright eyes twinkled behind the rimless spectacles and he gave a boyish grin. 'But to put us all in the right mood, there's still time to fetch yourselves a drink from the bar while you listen. An important part of Belgian culture is its beer and the individual glasses they come in. If you haven't already tried it, may I suggest one of the wonderful Trappist ales or I can thoroughly recommend the cherry-flavoured Kriek which I've just sampled.'

Noel's light banter had struck just the right note and although most people got to their feet, Fiona had few doubts that a great many of them would return.

Fiona had been looking forward to Noel's presentation and she was not disappointed. His obvious enthusiasm and the well-chosen pictures that illustrated his commentary appeared to have his whole audience fascinated.

There were several questions from the floor when he finished. There were still a few hands waving for attention when Robert Heppell pushed himself from his chair and turned to face the audience, stilling the general buzz and laughter that had greeted Noel's last reply.

A man near the back of the room was on his feet ready to ask the next question, but before he could speak, Robert flapped a hand for him to sit down.

'Right then, everyone,' Robert announced, 'we promised to limit these sessions to no more than three quarters of an hour and we mustn't tread on the toes of our other speakers who'll be giving us more detailed information on each of the main artists. Thank you, Noel. Tomorrow night, Simon will be talking about Peter Paul Rubens and the rise of the Seventeenth Century Baroque.'

Without even bothering to ask for a vote of thanks for the speaker, Robert turned his back on everyone and proceeded to pack up the equipment. For a moment, there was a stunned silence at the man's rudeness, but it was soon covered by the applause. If Robert had intended to belittle Noel's efforts, the attempt had backfired. In addition to the noisy clapping which continued for some time, a great many of his audience gathered around Noel all pressing to express their appreciation.

'That was absolutely fascinating, Noel,' Fiona said when she was eventually able to reach him. 'And those slides of the Maison du Roi and the Hotel de Ville were wonderful. When we get to the Grand Place tomorrow, I shall leave you to point out all the different guild houses you were talking about.'

'I haven't stepped on your toes, have I?' The poor man looked mortified.

'Far from it, Noel! I hadn't realised that Victor Hugo lived in one of those houses. You really whetted everyone's appetite for our visit tomorrow. Now let me treat you to one of those special beers you were talking about by way of a thank you.'

'I really ought to sort out the projector.'

'We'll see to that, old man.' A much younger, dark-haired man clapped a hand on Noel's shoulder. 'You leave the clearing up to the rest of us and go and enjoy the fruits of your reward.'

'Thanks, Simon.'

When they reached the bar, there were so many of his audience insisting on buying him a drink that Fiona never did get a chance to do so. With the sudden influx of people all trying to catch the barman's attention, Fiona decided to find herself a seat and wait until she could catch the eye of one of the waiters, especially as the easy chairs at the far end of the room appeared to be filling up fast.

'May we join you?' asked the pretty, curly-haired woman in a soft pronounced Scottish accent.

'Please do.'

'That was an excellent talk. I'm glad we stayed. Did you enjoy it?' the woman asked as she and her husband sat down.

'Very much.' Fiona tried to remember her name.

'If they are all like that, they'll be well worth listening too.' Her husband didn't look quite so sure.

'Do I take it you were not so impressed?' Fiona asked him.

'Oh yes. But if there are going to be different speakers every evening, I'm not so sure I'll bother with the one by that chap with the odd beard. Seems a miserable sort. Can't imagine him being that entertaining somehow.'

As he was talking, they were joined by another couple; a good-looking younger man in his early-forties and a much older woman.

'That would be a shame,' said the woman who introduced herself as Peggy. 'Robert can be a cantankerous old curmudgeon at times but give him his due, he is a good speaker, and despite appearances, he can be quite charming.'

'When he wants to be,' muttered her companion.

'I take it you two are part of this group that's travelling with us?' asked the woman whom Fiona now knew as Liz.

'That's right. The Swanley Association.' Peggy eased her not inconsiderable bulk back in her easy chair to get more comfortable.

'Are either of you going to be giving any of the talks?'

Peggy chortled, shaking her several chins. 'Oh no. Austin and I are not on the committee and that thank goodness, is a task reserved for them. Noel's one of the stalwarts of the Association. Been our treasurer for as long as I can remember. Whereabouts in Scotland do you two come from?'

'I'm from Edinburgh,' Malcolm replied, 'and Liz was born in a small town halfway between Edinburgh and Glasgow.'

'You haven't travelled all that way today?'

'No, no.' His pale, freckled face broke into a smile. 'We moved south ten years ago now. We live just outside Cambridge. Had to move with the job. Mind you, we still had an early enough start.'

As the conversation continued, Austin did his best to

attract one of the waiters, but to no avail. 'I think I'll have to get our drinks from the bar myself. What's everyone having?'

As Austin was making his way over, the last few committee members came through after putting away the equipment. Robert Heppell still hadn't arrived although his wife was amongst the group now gathered at the bar. Perhaps he'd gone off to sulk somewhere.

Fiona wasn't the only one to notice Robert's absence because as Janice Heppell passed their table, Peggy stopped her and asked, 'Robert not coming?'

'He'll be along in a minute. Just putting the laptop back up in our room for safe keeping,' she said with a smile. Unlike her curmudgeonly, argumentative husband, Janice appeared to be a friendly, affable individual who got on with most people. A large woman with a matronly bosom, she was a couple of inches taller than her husband, with all the social graces that would make her an excellent politician's wife.

'We were just saying, Noel was in good form tonight,' Peggy continued.

'Wasn't he just.' Whatever her husband's verdict on Noel's performance, to judge from Janice's bright smile, she did not seem to share his judgement. 'Set quite a high standard for the rest.'

'Sorry to interrupt,' Liz leant forward to get Peggy's attention, 'but I think your son is trying to get your attention.'

A look of complete bewilderment crossed the elderly woman's fleshy features as she stared at Liz. 'Pardon?'

Liz pointed towards the bar. Peggy swivelled awkwardly in the chair to look over her shoulder. Austin was waving. When he caught her eye, he lifted up a glass and mouthed exaggeratedly, 'Ice and lemon?'

'Please,' she bellowed across the room, nodding her head making her copious chins wobble. 'Austin is a dear boy, but he's not my son.'

'I see. As you were sitting together on the coach, I just assumed.'

Day 2 Saturday, Brussels

We begin our visit of Belgium's fascinating capital with a short walking tour to the town's central square, the glorious Grand Place. After our guided tour of the magnificent Gothic Town Hall, the opulent Hotel de Ville, there will be free time to admire the spectacular carpet of flowers laid out in the square after and to explore some of the fascinating cobbled side streets and shop for those irresistible handmade chocolates!

After lunch, we drive to the royal estate of Laeken where there will be time to stroll through the beautifully landscaped park. We will see the Japanese Pagoda and visit the Chinese Pavilion with its splendid Oriental porcelain both commissioned by King Leopold II. As part of his great vision, he also commissioned the Basilica of the Sacred Heart whose vast green copper dome can be seen from many parts of the city. After a brief stop at this magnificent Art Deco building, reputedly the largest ever built, we return to our hotel.

Super Sun Executive Travel

Chapter 3

Although they dined in the elegant, silver-service Baudouin Restaurant each evening, the buffet-style breakfast was served in the less formal Terrace Café. Fiona always tried to spend a little time with each of her passengers as soon into a trip as possible and glancing around the room, she spotted the Rev. McArdle and his wife sitting at one of the smaller tables on the raised upper section by the picture windows.

'May I join you?'

The tall, thin, bespectacled man in his early seventies, with a permanently distracted air, peered up at her with a slightly puzzled expression as though he was not quite sure who she was.

'Of course, my dear. Do forgive me. I was miles away.' Half rising to his feet, he motioned her to an empty chair beside him.

Although her husband gave every impression of the archetypal professor, stooped from years poring over his books, Barbara McArdle was warm and outgoing with twinkling eyes and an alert expression. After a few minutes of small talk about how much she and her husband were looking forward to their holiday, the subject came round to the Swanley Association.

'Have you both been members for long?'

'Nicholas was responsible for setting it up, weren't you, dear? That must have been well over thirty years ago now. Mind you, it has changed a good deal since those early days.

It was more of a social club for the parish originally, particularly for our older members and the young mums. But things move on, don't they?' There was no mistaking the tinge of regret in the older woman's voice. 'We still have the monthly talks from outside speakers and visits, but they've become a little more sophisticated since Robert took over as chairman. Our meetings used to be in the church hall at St Timothy's but since we've moved to The King's Head, the Association has grown a good deal. The majority of the members are newcomers to the town and there aren't so many of us old originals left. Peggy Brent and Noel Appleby, of course. He was our treasurer right from the start, but he's kept a good deal busier now.' She gave a girlish chuckle.

'Oh?'

'We did have money raising events right from the beginning of course. Jumble sales, bring-and-buys, summer fetes and so on, mainly for the Old People's Christmas party and a few local good causes, but now the membership includes many more wealthy incomers with all their contacts, the projects have become much more ambitious. Currently, the committee are hoping to raise £25,000 for a new minibus for the disabled children's school.'

'My goodness! That does sound an awful lot of money to find.'

'We have managed almost half of that already.'

'Well done! That must have taken a great deal of work on everyone's part.'

'Robert made a very generous donation of £500 to get the ball rolling,' Barbara admitted somewhat reluctantly. 'Much of the rest came through the auction of promises.'

In the pause that followed, Fiona ventured, 'You must have had some wonderful things to auction to raise that much.'

'Simon Lithgow offered a meal for two in the restaurant at The King's Head; Philippa Western persuaded her father to donate a day's fishing on the trout lake at his country house and Austin Pilkington has an old school friend who plays in the London Philharmonic and he was able to get a couple of seats for one of their concerts.'

'That all sounds wonderful.'

Barbara's smile was somewhat fixed. 'Yes. I'm afraid my offer of babysitting seemed very meagre by comparison.'

'Simon's the younger man with dark hair, isn't he? Broad shoulders, always smiling.'

'That's right. He's the landlord at The King's Head. He and his wife haven't been with us that long, but he's become quite an invaluable member. He's our Vice Chair and most of the actual organisation of the auction fell on his shoulders.'

'And better still, unlike our old fetes and Christmas bazaars, it didn't involve you, my dear, in weeks and weeks of hard work attempting to organise all our band of faithful volunteers.' Nicholas patted his wife's hand affectionately.

'Well yes. I have to admit it was all getting a bit too much for me those last few years. It wasn't so much the physical effort, but the worry. People promise the earth and then fall by the wayside at the last minute.' She took a sidelong look at her husband and added quickly, 'for all sorts of good reasons, I'm sure.'

'People must have bid a great deal of money to reach such a spectacular total,' Fiona said.

'People were very generous, and we did have a great many promises.'

'Mainly through Robert's efforts,' the vicar said quietly.

'Our new chairman has a great many contacts in some very illustrious circles and was very persuasive in getting them to donate all sorts of things.'

Fiona detected a definite coolness in Barbara's voice at the mention of Heppell's name.

'Including the two that brought in the most money.' Barbara McArdle might be harbouring a degree of resentment against the passing of the old order, but from her husband's tone, he at least didn't seem to bear any regrets. 'A fortnight in someone's villa in Tuscany and a tour of the

Williams' Formula One garage in Oxfordshire. I wouldn't have minded bidding for that one myself.'

Fiona found the picture of the vague, gentle man sitting glued to the television watching the thrills and spills of a Grand Prix, enthusiastically cheering on his favourite driver somewhat incongruous.

'Really? I'd have thought you'd be too busy on a Sunday to watch television.'

'The DVD recorder is a wonderful invention.' His pale grey eyes twinkled at her. 'As long as you remember not to listen to the results on the news in the meantime.'

It was time for Fiona to take her leave. There were still things to do before they left for the walking tour.

Friends and family had complained about how much weight Fiona had lost over the last few years when Bill was alive. Lifting her husband's inert twelve stone body from bed to wheelchair and in and out of the car had taken its toll of her petite, five-foot three-inch frame not to mention the lack of appetite that had accompanied his passing almost a year ago. Nonetheless, with all the wonderful food on offer in the quality hotels used by Super Sun Executive Travel, Fiona was all too aware how easy it would be to put on the pounds. From her first assignment back in the spring, she'd tried to use the stairs rather than take the lift whenever possible.

The last half flight was always the worst. She paused for a moment when she reached the fifth floor waiting to get her breath back and for her heart to recover. The door onto the corridor faced the lift and through the glass panel she could see the steel doors slowly slide open revealing its two occupants.

She recognised Robert Heppell immediately. Even through the opaque patterned glass, the white chin-strap beard was unmistakable. He was talking earnestly to a woman who appeared to be trying to put as much distance between the two of them as possible.

It wasn't until they both stepped out of the lift that Fiona recognised the slim, tall, elegant woman as Philippa Western. Few women could carry off that sleek, cropped hairstyle shaped into the neck, but on her the glossy jet-black coiffure served to emphasise the perfect high cheekbones and the flawless translucent skin. Even in her flat, comfortable walking shoes, she was inches taller than Heppell.

He laid a hand on Philippa's arm to detain her. Immediately she batted it away and with a look of pure hatred, snarled some riposte, then turned on her heel and swept down the corridor. Fiona was too far away to hear what Heppell had said to so infuriate Philippa, but the slow, smug smile on his face as he watched her walk away was enough to make Fiona's flesh creep.

Fiona did another quick count of the people gathered in one corner of the spacious foyer. After so short a time, she was still not sure if she could recognise all the members of her party, especially as they were no longer wearing the same clothes as yesterday.

Several of them she had not yet had a chance to chat to, but she reasoned the woman with a grey bun on the top of her head standing next to Noel Appleby must be his wife and the one hovering by Simon's elbow had to be Gina Lithgow. Fiona frowned.

Despite her suggestion about wearing comfortable footwear at last evening's briefing, Gina had chosen to come in high-heeled strappy sandals. Gina's most distinguishing feature was her asymmetrical hairdo cut short into the neck on one side and hanging across her face and almost to the shoulder on the other. Such a style might be all the fashion, but it merely looked odd and out-of-place on Gina. As though she was trying too hard to be noticed.

Fiona glanced at her watch. Still a couple of minutes to go. No point in getting anxious. She was reasonably confident that the couple sitting a little apart, a very overweight woman and her husband, were Super Sun clients; in which case, there were only four more to arrive.

The start of any trip was always a little fraught until the routines were established. Although she no longer felt herself a complete novice as a Tour Manager, this was a new venture for the company. Fiona had been happy to volunteer for what had promised to be a doddle of a job with nothing to do but accompany a group of club members who had organised their own itinerary and ensure the smooth running of the practical arrangements. As her previous visits to Belgium were either so long ago or recent short stops en route to other destinations, she'd seen it as a great opportunity to get to know the country without all the responsibility of hours of work swotting up all the necessary background information to act as 'expert' guide.

The failure of the Swanley Association to come up with the minimum numbers not only meant that Super Sun had taken over the itinerary, it had given her that extra responsibility. Now she felt apprehensive that her charges might tumble to the fact they were in the hands of someone with so little experience and no previous knowledge of the area.

They all seemed contented enough at the moment. Perhaps she should just check that that the couple sitting on the red plush seating encircling the central towering plant arrangement were in her party.

The middle-aged, grey-haired woman looked up with a sunny smile as Fiona walked over. 'Good morning, Fiona. Are we ready for the off?'

Thank goodness. At least she was saved the embarrassment of having to ask.

The lift doors opened, and Dee Foley and Hazel Tonkin emerged and came towards them. As they passed Robert Heppell, his voice rose and the words '. . . empty-headed protesters. All talk and no action,' were clearly intended for Dee to overhear.

Dee Foley stopped and stared at him; eyes blazing, and her

square chin thrust forward.

Fiona felt her jaw tighten, but her attention was claimed by one of her other clients. 'Will we have much free time after the guided walk this morning?'

For the next few minutes, Fiona was so busy answering questions and giving suggestions for possible places the woman might like to see after the visit to the Town Hall that she wasn't aware of trouble brewing until she heard raised voices.

'But I was so looking forward to seeing the inside of the Town Hall.' Hazel's pleading voice rose to a loud wail. 'Everyone says the Council Chamber is an absolute must-see. Not to be missed.'

'I'm not stopping you going. I don't expect you to come with me. It's not your thing.' Dee turned to go but Hazel grabbed her arm.

All conversation had stopped. Everyone in the busy foyer was watching Hazel and Dee including those not in the Super Sun party.

'But it's our holiday. We should be spending it together.' For a moment, Fiona thought Hazel was about to burst into tears. Instead, she took a deep breath and gave a strange squeak – half sob, half sigh.

'For the love of heaven!' Shaking off her friend's hand, Dee stomped off towards the revolving entrance doors.

'Oh dear,' said a sneering voice. 'Lovers' tiff.' Robert gave an unpleasant guffaw and turned to his friends.

The poisonous look Hazel threw at his back would have soured milk. 'You obnoxious little man.'

Robert didn't reply. He simply waved her comment away with the back of his hand over his shoulder, not even bothering to turn to face her.

After a momentary embarrassed silence, the general hubbub of chatter began again.

'Dee! I ask you;' he sneered, 'what kind of name is that?'

Even though the group of committee members were

sitting several yards away, Fiona was still aware of Robert Heppell's jeering voice.

'It could be short for Deirdre,' suggested Noel, always the peacemaker. It was difficult to hear the rest of what the more softly spoken man was saying but Fiona was able to catch the odd phrase. He was evidently suggesting that it might be as well not to antagonise the people with whom they were going to be spending the rest of the week.

'Might've known Mr Nice would stick up for the queers.'

Enough was enough. Time to take control.

'May I have your attention everyone?' Once they had gathered around her, she pulled a passenger list from her tote bag. 'Before we leave for our walk, I need to check who's here.'

To add to her troubles there was no answer when she called Austin Pilkington's name.

'He was here a moment or two ago,' piped up a bemused-looking Peggy Brent. 'I was just talking to him.'

'He's over there with Philippa.'

Fiona looked towards the reception area where the speaker was pointing. The two seemed to be in earnest conversation.

One problem solved, but as it turned out, the Diamonds were missing. Fiona put a call through to their room to discover that Aubrey had a bad cold and they had decided to give the morning's guided walk a miss.

She returned from the reception desk, trying to keep the annoyance from her voice as she announced, 'As I mentioned in my welcome briefing last evening, I'm sure many of you have been to this beautiful city before and are quite familiar with many of its attractions. Should you wish to go off and do your own thing rather than joining the rest of us at any point in our holiday, please feel free. But please do let me know so the rest of us aren't kept waiting for you.'

She forced a smile and continued, 'We are going to make our way to the central square of Grand Place and on the way, we will pass the small statue of the famous Mannekin Pis. I'm sure I don't need to translate that for you or tell you what the little boy is doing,' she paused for the laughter. 'However, he was originally known as Petit Julien. I'll tell you a little more about him when we get there, so if you'd all like to follow me, we'll make a start.'

Despite the poor start to the day, their private tour of the Hotel de Ville had gone well. Their guide had been excellent, and it was difficult not to be impressed by the sumptuous décor. Now that her passengers were free to spend what was left of the morning to do as they wished, Fiona could relax. She had every intention of making the most of the opportunity to see the sights herself. Having seen the tiny Mannekin Pis statue, she'd toyed with the idea of taking a look at some of his six hundred outfits presented by the town's distinguished visitors over the many years which were on display in the City Museum on the far side of the square. But before she made any decisions, it was time for a sit-down and a well-deserved cup of coffee.

Cafés on the Grand Place were notoriously more expensive than elsewhere in the city centre. After the difficult start she was having on this trip, she decided she had earned the right to treat herself and sit and admire the harmonious seventeenth century architecture surrounding the world's most beautiful square at her leisure.

At first it looked as though her plans would be thwarted. Not surprisingly, at midmorning at the height of the tourist season every table at the top of the square seemed to be taken. As she slowly scanned each of the pavement cafés for a second time, she caught the eye of a man in a pale grey and blue argyle sweater. He gave her a warm smile and raised a hand in greeting. The cheek of the man. She glanced away quickly, pretending to check her watch. He might look respectable, but she had no intention of being picked up.

When she looked up again, he was on his feet and walking towards her. Best to pretend she hadn't seen him. There was something familiar about the tall, aristocratic figure but for the moment, she could not place him.

'Fiona.'

She turned and looked at him properly for the first time. 'Mr Montgomery-Jones!'

'Peter, please.'

She smiled and shook his hand. 'I didn't recognise you out of uniform.'

He lifted an eyebrow in mock admonition. 'You have never seen me in uniform.'

She stifled a giggle. 'I meant I am used to seeing you in a three-piece suit complete with watch chain. Do the casual clothes mean you're on holiday?'

He gave one of his slow, enigmatic smiles. 'Not exactly. I have been attending a conference for much of the last week and I decided to use the opportunity to spend an extra day or so to see something of Brussels whilst I am over here. I was about to order some coffee when I saw you and your party coming out of the Hotel de Ville. Do you have time to join me?'

'I'd love to,' she replied after only a split second of hesitation. Although she was never quite at ease with the autocratic Intelligence Chief, she'd had cause to be grateful for his intervention in the past. Their previous encounters had always been as part of his investigations and never purely social. She always felt uncharacteristically gauche and inept in his presence even though she had been instrumental in helping him to solve two of his previous cases.

He led her to the corner table at the front of the café where he'd been sitting. The service in the Maison des Boulangers was exemplary, as was to be expected of one the most expensive of the cafés in Brussels. Even though the place was moderately busy, a waiter suddenly appeared seemingly from nowhere and pulled out a chair for her. But then, Montgomery-Jones was the sort of man whose commanding presence always had people rushing to do his bidding.

Once their order had been taken, Fiona sat back and asked, 'What was your conference about?'

'The international exchange of sensitive intelligence on suspected terrorists.'

'Sounds fascinating,' she chuckled.

For a split second, she wondered if she'd made yet another social gaffe, but the raised eyebrow and imperious glare turned into a slow smile.

'It did prove to be rather pedestrian and predictable. The only reason I did not send someone else in my place is because I was asked to give one of the papers.'

Fiona was spared a reply by the arrival of their drinks.

The coffee was superb. She took a sip and put down her cup with a contented sigh. 'I needed that. It's been a very long day, even if it is only eleven thirty.'

'Do I take it your morning has been somewhat fraught?'

'Let's just say it's had its moments.' This wasn't the time to start pouring out her troubles. Best to make a joke out of it. 'So far, no one's killed anyone. But give it time. Today is only the first proper day and with all the divisions in the camp, events could well turn out in ways that could make the Battle of Waterloo look like a tea party.'

He gave a soft chuckle. Not something she'd heard him do that often. She had always appreciated that Montgomery-Jones, ever serious and remote, was nonetheless one of the most physically attractive men she'd ever met, but without the cool, appraising stare that so often characterised his expression, he'd managed to reduce her to the state of a giddy teenager.

'This trip is something of a new venture for Super Sun,' she rushed. 'There are an increasing number of clubs and societies who are interested in arranging holidays designed to meet their specific interests. Once the programme has been agreed, our company organises the hotels and entrance fees and provides a tour manager to see it all goes smoothly. The last thing I need is it to fail when I'm at the helm so to speak.'

'What's the problem?'

'Swanley Association couldn't come up with sufficient numbers and so there had to be a few changes. Let's just say their chairman is not very happy with the new itinerary.'

'I have no doubt that you will cope.'

'Not if I sit here any longer. Time I was getting on.'

She bent down to pick up the large tote bag propped against her chair leg and hefted it onto her lap.

'Do you always carry half the contents of your suitcase around with you?' he asked with an amused smile.

'Absolutely essential. All my notes and sets of maps. I'm always worried that I might get everyone lost when we're out. Later in the week I shall be leading a walk around this area, so I thought I'd do some preparation and make sure I can recognise all the places I'm due to point out to everyone. I've put in a couple of guidebooks with plenty of pictures which is why it's so heavy today. Most coach companies just drop passengers off to explore for themselves, but Super Sun tries to offer a bit more. Although if the people on my tours realised that their so-called "expert guide" is a raw recruit and has never been to the place before, they might not be so happy.'

'If you are concerned about getting lost, perhaps you should have a satnav.'

'My line manager is happy for me to have one of the latest mobiles with the relevant app, but I keep putting it off. I'm having enough trouble getting my head round technology as it is. I know it's pathetic, but I never needed to use a mobile all those years cooped up in the bungalow when Bill was ill, so it's a question of making time to go up to Head Office for them to talk me all through it.'

Montgomery-Jones was looking over her shoulder. Hardly surprising, he was probably bored with her idle chatter. He frowned suddenly.

She turned to see what he was looking at. Half a dozen policemen were rushing across the square and disappeared down the street in the far corner.

Before either of them could comment, his phone bleeped.

He took it from his pocket and glanced at the caller's name. 'Excuse me; I must take this.'

His face remained impassive as he listened to the message. 'I see. I will be there directly.'

The old Montgomery-Jones was back. Formal, aloof, authoritative.

'I must apologise, Fiona. I am needed elsewhere.' He signalled for the bill and a waiter appeared at his elbow so quickly, it was as if he had been standing ready for the call. She was taken by surprise when he turned back to her with a smile. 'Perhaps you will allow me to make it up to you. May I take you to dinner one evening?'

'That would be very nice,' she stammered.

He was gone. It would probably come to nothing. Perhaps that was just as well. Even if he did, he would never tell her what was so urgent that he had had to rush off so suddenly.

Chapter 4

Fiona felt oddly disconcerted, though quite what had triggered her unease she could not tell. It was not the unexpected meeting with Peter Montgomery-Jones; perhaps it was the policemen dashing off en masse. It played in the back of her mind all the time she was in the museum, so much so that she found herself having to reread many of the information panels on each of the exhibits. She had given up bothering by the time she reached the porcelain room. Only on the top floor did the vast array of costumes for the Mannekin Pis finally manage to gain her whole attention.

On her way back to the hotel, she strolled through the Galeries St-Hubert. She recognised the glass-domed roof of Europe's earliest shopping arcade from the pictures in the Eyewitness Travel Guide straightaway. It was impossible not to linger at the tempting window displays of the artisan chocolatiers, strictly in the interest of finding those essential presents to take home for friends of course, she told herself firmly. She reluctantly pulled her gaze from the silver dishes arranged with pyramids of mouth-watering truffles and moved on to the adjacent lace shop.

The exquisite workmanship of the delicate white blouses caught her eye. There was one that caught her attention, long sleeved with a high neck. Not that she would consider buying it. Beautiful though it was, it would probably sit in her wardrobe from one year to the next waiting for an occasion for her to wear it.

As she turned away, she almost bumped into someone else moving forward to admire the detail on one of the items in the window.

'I'm so sorry, Mrs Appleby!' She recognised the small, rather plain looking woman straight away. Unlike the somewhat dapper Noel, his wife seemed a little dishevelled and preoccupied.

'Fiona! This is a surprise. Do call me Charlotte.' She brushed aside a stray lock of hair that had fallen across her face and tucked it back into the untidy upswept bun on the top of her head.

Fiona looked around. 'Noel not with you?'

'It's our grandson's birthday at the beginning of next month and I wanted to see if I could find something a bit different for a present, but you know men and shops. He claimed he had a bit of a headache, so he's gone back to the hotel. We're meeting up later for a spot of lunch.'

'Have you found anything suitable?'

Charlotte shook her head and gave a deep sigh. 'Boys are so difficult to buy for. Now if he were a girl that dress in the corner would be just perfect. Isn't it exquisite?'

'Adorable. Highly impractical of course, but it would make any little girl feel like a princess. My granddaughter would love it, I know. Becky has just had her sixth birthday, but I might just be tempted to buy it for Christmas. The trouble is I've no idea what size to get. They grow up so quickly at that age and I haven't seen her in a long time. My son and his family live out in Canada.'

A pained expression came over Charlotte's face. 'It is difficult when you don't see them, isn't it? I haven't seen Ben ever since. . . My son and his wife aren't together anymore. Tracy's cut off all contact. We sent cards and presents last Christmas, but we've heard nothing from her or Ben. Not even a thank you letter.'

'I'm so sorry. It must be very hard for your son.'

Charlotte's jaw tightened. 'He only has himself to blame.'

She spoke so quietly; Fiona wasn't sure she had heard correctly. 'Still, I mustn't keep you.'

'Enjoy the rest of your day,' Fiona called out to the woman's retreating back.

She watched the woman bustle away. She wasn't sure what to make of the encounter. It was clear that Charlotte Appleby was nursing some deep hurt and from the abrupt way she had taken her leave, she had said more than she'd intended.

Her musings about Charlotte soon disappeared when Fiona turned off along a street lined with restaurants with outside tables nestling under gay awnings. Caught up in the happy hustle and bustle and the sea of smiling faces enjoying the riot of colour, her spirits quickly rose. A photographer's paradise. She stopped to admire the trays piled high with fruits, vegetables, lobsters and every kind of shellfish that encroached onto the narrow central cobbled passageway. Waiters stood ready to accost passers-by in an effort to entice in customers for lunch.

Fiona glanced wistfully at the all-inclusive menu boards. The company had negotiated a good deal with the Hotel Leopold, but as they were based so near the city centre, Fiona would have much preferred to allow everyone the opportunity to find restaurants of their own choosing where they could sample more local fare. Although the quality of the food at the Leopold was good, like in the majority of city centre hotels, the menus consisted of safe predictable dishes one might find in any city centre hotel catering for visitors from all over the world. It was Robert Heppell's insistence on having the evening talks that necessitated everyone having to eat at the hotel.

When Fiona arrived back at the hotel, she found Winston in the foyer sitting in one of the easy chairs by the lifts. He looked up as she walked over.

'You'll never guess who I bumped into this afternoon.'

She told him all about her encounter with Peter

Montgomery-Jones. He let her natter on for a minute or two, but she soon sensed that he was only half listening.

'Is there something wrong?'

'We could have a problem, sweetheart. You know that big Protest Rally in the centre this morning?' Fiona nodded. 'Seems it turned nasty and they had to bring in the anti-riot squad. Several people got hurt and they's arrested at least a dozen protesters.'

Fiona's heart sank. She knew what was coming next. 'Don't tell me. Dee Foley?'

'Got it in one, sweetheart.' The bear-like shoulders heaved as he gave a sigh. 'Her friend came back in a right old state. Saw the woman bundled into a police van she did, but she's no idea where they've taken her.'

'Where is Hazel now?'

'Up in her room.'

'I'll go straight up.'

Fiona hurried to the lift though quite what she could do was another matter.

Hazel's pretty face was distorted with tears and the hunched figure looked more in need of protection than ever.

'What happened exactly?'

According to Hazel, Dee had simply been an innocent bystander. Even if she hadn't been involved in any of the actual fighting, it wasn't difficult to imagine the belligerent Dee screaming all kinds of abuse about heavy-handed police tactics. Once the woman was roused, she didn't know when to stop.

'There must be something you can do?' Hazel pleaded.

Fiona frowned. 'I think we are just going to have to wait. With the situation as it is and the police force stretched to the limits dealing with all that's been going on, I doubt anyone is going to be available to answer any questions right now, even if we do try ringing the police station.'

Hazel nodded forlornly, pulled another tissue from the box

at her side and snuffled into it.

'I don't like to leave you like this, Hazel, but I need to get things ready for this afternoon's trip. I expect by the time we get back, everything will be sorted and Dee will be here waiting for you.' It was a forlorn hope, but Fiona couldn't think of anything more positive to say.

'I'm not coming. I need to stay here,' Hazel said defiantly.

'If that's what you really want to do, but surely she'll phone you on your mobile. It might be best to be with the rest of us and have something to take your mind off the situation rather than sitting in your room worrying all afternoon.'

Hazel shook her head and like a petulant child, said, 'I'm staying here.'

'If you're sure.'

Fiona left the girl crying softly into her tissue. Obviously, she was justifiably upset, but this wallowing in self-pity was of no use to anyone. Fiona knew nothing about their relationship or how long it had existed, but from what she'd seen, Hazel deferred to Dee at every turn and seemed incapable of doing anything by herself.

At the door, Fiona relented. 'I'll tell you what. I'll go down to reception and ask if they can find out what's going on.'

Hazel frowned and began to flap. 'She won't want everybody knowing. . .'

'I appreciate that. I won't give them any details, just ask if they have any idea of what's happening. Presumably when the police discover where Dee's staying, they will ring the hotel to check.'

The young man at the desk did his best, but all he could tell Fiona was that there had been some kind of disturbance outside the European Parliament building, which was nothing she didn't know already. Fiona informed him that in the resulting chaos, one of her party had become separated and asked him to ring her mobile number if he received any news of Dee's whereabouts.

For the moment, there was nothing else Fiona could do. Right now, there were other things to occupy her thoughts. She would have to keep her fingers crossed that the violence which had broken out at the rally would not cause any difficulties for their afternoon programme. It was a good bet that much of the centre would now be closed off to traffic, but at least they were heading out of the city.

As she turned to go back to her room, Fiona spotted the statuesque figure of Janice Heppell pacing up and down by the glass entrance doors. She was obviously agitated about something and kept glancing at her watch then staring along the road back into town.

Fiona pushed through the heavy door.

'Mrs Heppell, is there anything wrong?'

When she turned to face her, Fiona realised the woman looked more annoyed than anxious.

'Janice, please.' She managed a quick polite smile. 'Robert hasn't returned and if he's not here soon he's going to miss this afternoon's excursion.'

'You weren't together then this morning?'

'Not after our visit to the Town Hall. He decided to go along to that Protest March or whatever it was.' Her disapproval was patently evident in her voice. Whether that was because of her objection to being abandoned or because she had little sympathy with the campaigners, Fiona could not hazard a guess.

'I wouldn't have thought he was a supporter of the Anti-Austerity cause,' Fiona said.

'Oh, he isn't!' Janice gave a bitter laugh. 'He claimed he wanted to hear what the leaders had to say for themselves, but if you ask me, he only went along to heckle the speakers. We were supposed to meet back here for a snack at lunchtime, but he still hasn't turned up. He's probably got himself lost I shouldn't wonder. Like a lot of men, he's far too pig-headed to ask for directions, the silly man.'

'Oh dear.' Should she mention that there had been trouble?

Surely, he hadn't managed to get himself arrested as well!

'I've rung his mobile three times, but he's not answering.' Heaving her not inconsiderable bosom, she took another look at her watch and then turned to face the hotel entrance. 'In any case, I don't intend to waste any more time waiting here. I'm going back up otherwise I'm going to be late. I'll see you in a few minutes, Fiona.'

With that, she marched defiantly to the lift. Fiona decided that if Robert Heppell's wife wasn't worried by his absence neither would she. With one thing and another, she had enough on her plate without adding needlessly to the list. Janice was probably right. If Robert had been one of those bundled into the police van with Dee, Hazel would have mentioned it. Besides, if she didn't get a move on, she'd be late herself.

Chapter 5

As she sat sipping her tea on the café terrace overlooking the royal Gardens enjoying the pleasant warm sunshine, Fiona had a chance to observe some of her charges. The tall, good-looking Austin Pilkington had taken Peggy's arm as they slowly ambled along the path beside one of the wide flower borders. Occasionally they would stop, and he would bend down to inspect the labels on a shrub for her. It seemed a strange pairing. Peggy had been quick to point out that he was not her son, but he was obviously very attentive to her. In his late thirties, early forties at most, he was more of an age with the Lithgows and Philippa Western than the elderly Peggy who was much the oldest in the party.

Fiona glanced across at the Westerns who were seated at a table with Janice Heppell and Olive Scudamore at the far side of the terrace. Bernard Western, currently sporting a floppy sunhat to protect his fair skin and balding scalp, was a good deal older than his wife, Philippa, the svelte stylish woman Fiona had seen arguing with Robert Heppell after breakfast. Philippa lay back in her chair, nonchalantly fanning herself with the table menu card, taking little part in the conversation. Her eyes roved over the rest of the party still strolling around the gardens. Was it her imagination, Fiona wondered, or did the woman's gaze linger over Austin? He was a fine-looking man, with well-chiselled features and a thick crop of wavy light brown hair.

Her husband's absence didn't seem to be bothering Janice.

She appeared perfectly at ease, smiling and talking with Bernard and Olive. If anything, she appeared to be more relaxed than Fiona had ever seen her. Despite the heat, Olive was still encased in a hand-knitted cardigan buttoned right up to the neck. She obviously didn't believe in opening herself up to the elements. Unlike nearly all the other ladies in the party now sporting sandals, Olive was wearing thick stockings and her feet were encased in sensible laced-up walking shoes.

Fiona glanced at her watch. Time to round up the troops. She walked over to the Scottish couple, Liz and Malcolm Kennedy, sitting on one of the benches.

Liz had taken the opportunity for a bit of sunbathing. Her face was lifted to the sun, eyes closed, legs stretched out with her skirt pulled up just above her knees. Caught in the sunlight, her glossy golden curls looked more than ever like a halo framing the pretty heart-shaped face. Not for the first time, Fiona thought how young she looked, but as the Kennedys had a son who had just graduated from Stirling University, she had to be in her forties.

'Are you two ready to make a move?' Fiona asked.

Liz looked up with a big grin. 'If we have to, I suppose, though it is lovely just sitting here enjoying the warm sunshine.' In her pleasing soft accent, the word warm was almost two syllables.

Fiona chuckled. 'So I see.'

'The Chinese House was delightful,' Liz continued. 'Not a bit like I expected. That fabulous staircase and all that beautiful porcelain. It's such a pity that the Glass Houses were closed though. I would've loved to have seen them.'

'They are the private property of the Royal Family,' Fiona explained. 'They are only open to the public for a couple of weeks in April when they're at their best, but if we had come then, you wouldn't have seen the flower carpet in Grand Place like we did yesterday.'

'That's true.'

'Never mind, hen. It's a good excuse to come back another year.' Malcolm's Scottish burr was even more pronounced than his wife's.

Liz laughed. 'I'll hold you to that, Malcolm Kennedy.'

'Although the foundation stone was laid in 1909, the Basilica of the Sacred Heart took fifty years to complete. Smaller than St Peter's in Rome and our own St Paul's, it is nonetheless the fifth largest church in the world. This is the first Art Deco building we'll be visiting, and I believe a member of the Swanley Association will be giving a talk on Art Deco architecture later in the week.' Fiona paused and Bernard Western sitting near the back of the coach waved and gave a nod of agreement.

Fiona helped everyone down from the coach and as they filed through the great door into the Basilica, she found herself standing next to Janice Heppell.

'Impressive, isn't it? All those soaring columns.'

'Quite spectacular,' Fiona agreed.

'Robert doesn't know what he's missing.'

'Have you heard from him yet?'

Janice shook her head. 'I would have thought he would have rung me by now. Either that or he's been arrested, and they've taken his phone. So much for a peaceful demonstration. You heard that the police were called out I take it?'

Fiona nodded.

'You must think me uncaring,' Janice continued, 'but he can be so stubborn at times. Don't misunderstand me, Robert has many admirable qualities. Most of the time you couldn't wish to meet a kinder, more caring, generous man, I wouldn't have stayed married to him for thirty odd years if he wasn't, but I'm afraid so far on this trip you've only seen the worst side of his character. What's got into him I do not know. His behaviour has been quite intolerable.'

'Not to worry. By the time we get back to the hotel, I'm

sure you'll find him there, full of apologies.'

Fiona couldn't help but smile. There was little doubt that Robert Heppell, however much he might like to try to browbeat others, had met his match in his equally forceful wife. Fiona didn't rate his chances when his wife did catch up with him.

As she walked back into the hotel an hour or so later it was not the absence of Robert Heppell that occupied Fiona's thoughts, but that of Dee Foley. Once all her clients had been seen to, she returned to her room, dropped her things on the bed and hurried along to Hazel and Dee's room on the floor below.

There was no answer. Perhaps that was a good sign. There was a good chance that the woman had been released early enough for the two of them to have gone out for what was left of the afternoon; although by now Fiona would have expected them back in time to get ready for dinner. Perhaps they had already changed and had gone down to the bar.

A quick glance into the lounge bar proved otherwise. Her only option now was to ask at Reception. The man at the desk was busy handing out keys to the steady stream of people returning from their various outings. So, when in answer to Fiona's question that he hadn't seen Dee return, Fiona decided not to press for him to see if there were any messages.

Back in her room, Fiona barely had time to kick off her shoes before getting changed when the phone rang. It was far from reassuring to hear that there was a policeman waiting downstairs to speak to her.

The two uniformed officers were standing by the desk when Fiona stepped into the Foyer.

'I am Fiona Mason. I believe you are looking for me?'

'You are the tour manager for the group from Super Sun Executive Travel Ltd?' the older man asked in perfect accented English.

'Yes.' Fiona's stomach tightened.

'Perhaps we could all go somewhere more private.' The older of the two men led the way through a door marked "Staff Only" into a dark uncarpeted corridor. A second door was slightly ajar. He pushed it open and waved her ahead of him.

Once they were all settled, he opened the folder he'd been carrying, took out a pen and began by double-checking her credentials and establishing how long the Super Sun Executive Travel group had been in the city.

'What's this all about?'

The officer was not to be rushed. 'I understand that you took your party on a walking tour of the city this morning.'

'That's correct. Then we had a private tour of the Hotel de Ville.'

'With the whole group?'

'No. One gentleman felt unwell and he and his wife remained in the hotel and another client opted out to do her own thing. But after the tour finished around eleven, everyone was free to explore as they wished until we met back here at the hotel at two o'clock for a coach trip out to the north of the city.'

'Does that mean, you cannot account for the whereabouts of any of your party?'

'Not after they dispersed at the end of the tour.'

'Did you see any of them after that?'

'There were some in the museum and I may have passed a few walking back to the hotel, but that's all.'

'Are you aware that there was a demonstration in the Leopold Park this morning?'

It was obvious now where this was leading. 'I did hear that there was a scuffle of some sort outside the European Parliament building. I understand the riot police were called out and someone said that several people had been arrested. Is this to do with Dee Foley?'

'Could you describe this gentleman for me?'

46

'Dee is female. I would say she is in her early-forties, around five foot six, stocky build, very short haircut. . .'

He shook his head. 'I have no information about this lady.'

Should she feel relieved? 'I see.'

He frowned and after a moment's pause, continued, 'I am afraid the situation was a good deal more serious than you may have been led to believe. At least a dozen people have been injured, some seriously, in the ensuing panic. Are any other members of your group unaccounted for?'

'Robert Heppell wasn't back in time for the afternoon tour although his wife was expecting him.'

'Would you describe him, please?'

'Mid to late-fifties, short with dark grey hair and an almost white chin-strap beard but no moustache.'

'I need to speak with Mrs Heppell. Is she in the hotel?'

'As far as I know. I expect she is in her room. Would you like me to fetch her?'

'That will not be necessary.' He gave a nod to the younger policeman who was on his feet and at the door almost before his superior had finished speaking.

'What can you tell me about Mr Heppell?'

'Very little. I only met him for the first time yesterday.'

'But to the best of your knowledge, he is here in Belgium on holiday?'

'Yes, of course. The whole trip is essentially at his instigation. He put together a cultural tour of Flemish Art for members of his local social group which is the basis of our Super Sun Programme.'

'Has he any connection with the organisers of the Anti-Austerity Rally?'

'I wouldn't know, but I very much doubt it.'

He raised an eyebrow. 'Why do you say that?'

She shrugged her shoulders. 'Only because when the subject of the protest came up last evening, he showed little sympathy. As I said, I have only just met the man. I am not the person to ask about his associations?'

'Did he attend the rally?'

'He was with the rest of the group until we all split up late morning. His wife expected him back at the hotel for lunch, but he never arrived. That's as much as I can tell you.'

He closed his folder and got to his feet. 'Thank you for your time, Mrs Mason?'

'Can you tell me what's happened to him?' She knew it was a pointless question, he wouldn't tell her even if he knew, but she had to ask.

He gave her a polite smile, opened the door for her, and stood back. A clear indication that their discussion was at an end.

Chapter 6

Fiona had reached the second-floor landing when her mobile rang. What now? Surely nothing else could have gone wrong.

'It's only me, sweetheart.'

'Winston!'

'Where are you?'

'On the way back to my room.'

'It's that rally I told you about. It's on the news on the telly. I think you oughta see it.'

Whatever the crisis, Winston was always the one to stay calm. It made her doubly apprehensive to hear the worry in his voice.

'I'll be there straight away.'

Winston's door was already open, and he was waiting for her.

'In case the rest of 'em are watching this, I thought I oughta get you up to speed before you face 'em all at dinner.'

She was only in time to see the final minute or so, but the scenes of screaming protesters hurling bottles, bricks and anything else to hand at the riot shields held high by the solid line of police moving the crowds down the street were frightening.

When the picture switched back to the studio and on to the next news item, Winston switched off the television and turned to Fiona.

'My French's pretty non-existent, but you don't need no CSEs to translate that lot. Seems once the fighting broke out and the police arrived, people started running all over the place, stampeding through the streets. Utter chaos. No wonder folk got hurt. They showed a picture of that politician; the one that's always in the news complaining about the bankers and their million-pound bonuses and all the golden handshakes for the big bosses. You know, the one that was always on the telly when all those protesters camped out in their tents in front of St Paul's that time.'

'Tom Moorhouse, the rebel labour MP?'

'That's the fella. The one that keeps banging on about "stop the cuts" and an increase in the minimum wage. I couldn't understand if they were saying he was just one of the speakers at the demo or if he'd been injured.'

'It was an international rally so it's a good bet he was one of the speakers. He was pretty vociferous as a Union Leader but now he's at Westminster, he never misses an opportunity to get into the limelight.'

Winston's habitually smiling face for once was clouded by a deep frown. 'I could be wrong, but I got the idea the girl on the telly was saying he was dead.'

'Oh, my goodness!' She sank down onto the bed. 'I suppose that's what started the panic. I've just been talking with a policeman and he said at least a dozen people were injured in those riots.'

Fiona told Winston about her interview. 'At first I assumed Robert Heppell had been arrested. He's just the type to start shouting the odds and causing trouble, but now I've this dreadful feeling that he is one of those seriously injured or, heaven forbid, among the dead. The police obviously wouldn't tell me. They said they wanted to speak with his wife.'

It was almost time for dinner. Fiona hurried up to her own room. Even if she hadn't time for a shower, she needed to at least put a comb through her hair. She caught sight of herself in the full-length mirror and bit her lip. Her casual daytime attire was hardly the thing for the sophisticated Baudouin Restaurant. Her party would have to wait while she had a quick wash and change. Besides, she needed to work out what she was going to say to them all. Word would have got round by now about the violence at the demonstration which in itself was unsettling enough. At best, they would want to know if it would affect their itinerary, but it wouldn't take long before they noticed the absence of the Heppells and Dee Foley.

At least everyone knew where they were sitting this evening, so it hardly mattered that Fiona wasn't waiting by the restaurant door ten minutes ahead of time as was her custom. Most of the tables were already occupied, but she was relieved to see that a good half dozen of the Super Sun party were still not down, so she was not the last to arrive.

There was no sign of Dee or Hazel as she glanced round the room. There was still a chance that they might arrive, but somehow Fiona doubted it. It flashed through her mind that she ought to check on Hazel and perhaps arrange for some food to be sent up to her room, an idea she immediately tried to quash. She already had a reputation in the company for being a soft touch and even the ever patient, kindly Winston had told her she needed to learn not to get so involved. Besides, Hazel might prefer to be left on her own rather than have someone fussing over her. She was a grown woman and quite capable of ordering room service for herself if she didn't want to face the rest of the party.

Fiona spotted the tall, slightly stooped figure of the Rev. McArdle walking across the foyer.

'Barbara not with you?' she asked when he reached her.

'No. She's gone with Janice. I don't know if you've been told, but the police came to tell Janice that Robert is in the hospital.'

'I knew the police wanted to speak to Mrs Heppell.' Thank goodness; at least the man was alive and not in some mortuary. If Nicholas McArdle was surprised by the look of relief on her face, he didn't show it. She could only hope that if he had noticed it, he hadn't interpreted as any kind of satisfaction in Robert's suffering. 'But I hadn't appreciated that your wife had gone with her.'

'The police suggested she might like someone with her. Barbara was the obvious choice.'

'One of the duties of a vicar's wife?'

He looked puzzled. 'I suppose so, but I meant because they're such close friends. Always have been. They were at school together.'

'Oh, I see.' Fiona felt suddenly embarrassed. Just because Barbara seemed to have little time for Janice's husband didn't mean the two women had to be at odds. 'I didn't realise. Do you know how Robert is? Was he badly hurt?'

Nicholas shook his head. 'No idea. I haven't heard from Barbara yet. I expect she'll give me a ring later when there's any news.'

'Do let me know, when you hear, won't you?' she gave him one of her most engaging smiles.

As she surveyed the room from the doorway, there was a pause in the low hum of earnest chatter and a sea of faces turned in her direction. It didn't take much imagination to guess the topic of their conversation. The last thing she wanted right now was to be beckoned over for a grilling about what was happening.

She stepped back quickly out of everyone's line of vision, and almost bumped into Eleanor Prior who had come up behind her.

'I'm so sorry. . .'

'Have you seen the news on the television? Tom Moorhouse has been shot! I mean, he was an odious little man. It's not his politics so much as the way he shouted down anyone who didn't agree with him. But you don't expect that sort of thing, do you? I didn't know he was even over here in Belgium but. . .' Eleanor Prior was like a windup toy, whirring away and showing no signs of running down.

'Shot?' Fiona queried. 'Do you mean he's dead?'

'Oh yes. Jeffrey went onto the internet to check, didn't you dear?'

Winston was right, but the confirmation was still hard to take in.

Eleanor's husband nodded earnestly. 'We saw the pictures. It's all over YouTube. He was up on the stage, and a group in the crowd started heckling him. It got so bad, other people started telling them to shut up and that's when the fighting started. A right old punch up.'

'We saw it too.' Aubrey and Glenda Diamond had joined the group.

Eleanor carried on the story, 'The police tried to wade in and there was absolute chaos. People started throwing paint bombs. Moorhouse was shouting, telling everyone to calm down and then the shots rang out and he fell to the ground. Pandemonium broke out, utter chaos, people screaming and running all over the place. They didn't say if they managed to catch the gunman, but I doubt it in all that mayhem. Not nice to think there's a deranged man running about the streets of Brussels waving a firearm.'

It took several minutes for Fiona to calm them all down and persuade them to take their places. The situation was even worse than she'd imagined and if the Priors' and the Diamonds' reactions were anything to go by, she was going to have a job on her hands trying to reassure everyone that things were under control.

When everyone settled down, Fiona looked around for an empty chair. There were only four people at one of the tables near the door so she went to join the elderly Peggy, Felix Navarre, to whom she hadn't yet spoken, and Noel and Charlotte Appleby, the pleasant gentleman who had given the introductory lecture and his wife she had met outside the lace shop earlier in the morning. Was it really only a few hours earlier? So much had happened in the last six or seven hours.

Fiona usually looked forward to the evening meal. It was a good opportunity to get to know her passengers in a pleasant relaxed environment. Tonight, the atmosphere was far from relaxed. News of the shooting and the subsequent riot had spread like chickenpox in a nursery. It appeared to be the sole topic of conversation at every table and not just her own.

'I can't say I liked the man's politics, but I have to admit without Tom Moorhouse's involvement, our Community Project would never have achieved the amount of coverage it did,' Charlotte said, shaking her head. 'It's thanks to him that the Rainbow School was saved. Once the national newspapers published that picture of him in one of the classrooms, laughing with that five-year-old with Downs Syndrome, plus all his comments about putting business interests above the needs of vulnerable children, the council had no choice but to back down.'

'Did you all meet him when he came?' Fiona asked.

'Oh yes,' Peggy replied. 'Trying to save the school and the old Community Centre was the first big project that the Swanley Association undertook. Our committee organised the protest meeting when the developers' plans for redevelopment of the area were first made public. Robert tried to get the local MP and as many influential figures on our side as possible. I'm not sure how Tom Moorhouse came to be involved, but his speech really swayed the audience at the meeting.'

'Being cynical, you could say it did his own reputation no harm to be seen supporting such an obvious good cause,' said Felix.

'Maybe, but you never met him did you, Felix? That was before you joined us, but I have to say, he really was quite charming when he came. He made a point of coming to talk to every one of us. He even went into the kitchens to thank the ladies who looked after all the refreshments.'

Felix chuckled. 'Well, he does have a reputation for sweet talking ladies.'

'He was perfectly affable with all of us,' Noel said. 'I confess I found myself liking the man. Obviously, I don't approve of a great deal of what he stands for, but he did have a point about corporate greed. How it is possible to justify million-pound bonuses to bankers and the like, I really don't know.'

Peggy nodded. 'It really is quite scandalous how these incompetent managers of nationalised companies who lose billions of taxpayers' money can walk off with outrageous golden handshakes.'

'If you believe Moorhouse, it's not only bankers and businessmen. According to him, our government leaders are equally corrupt. Though, if you ask me, they're all on the take. If you can believe what the papers say, the expenses scandal is happening all over again and worse than ever. Become an MP and you can set yourself up for life. Most of them appear to be far more interested in what they can get out of the system for themselves than bothering to listen to the views of the people who elected them,' said Felix.

Peggy leaned forward stretching out her copious chins and said in a mock sotto voce, 'Best not to say too much in Robert's hearing though.'

'Oh?' Felix gave a weak grin. 'Come to think of it, I did hear a rumour about him intending to stand at the next election. I don't suppose he has much sympathy where Moorhouse and his cronies are concerned.'

'I should say not! Did you hear him at dinner last night when he was arguing with that lesbian woman? She was going on about social justice and the exorbitant salaries these city managers earn. I'll admit it was quite a diatribe, but Robert really took her to task. Called her views simplistic and how she obviously didn't understand the basics of economics. How high wages were essential if you wanted to get the right people at the top of major companies. He claimed the money they were paid was a mere pittance compared with billions of profits they made for the business.' Everyone smiled at her clever mimicry of Robert's hectoring tone. 'You know how he gets when he's on his high horse.'

'Poor Noel got his head bitten off when he tried to calm things down, didn't you, dear?' Charlotte Appleby shook her head, which threatened to dislodge the perilously balanced upswept hairdo. 'Just be thankful you weren't at our table, Felix. It was very embarrassing for the rest of us.'

'The two of them were still at it first thing this morning,' said Peggy.

Felix nodded. 'I did notice her storming out.' He looked around the room. 'Neither of them are here now. Too ashamed, do you think?'

'Too stroppy to give in more like! Heaven knows what all the other people on the tour must think.' Charlotte turned to Fiona. 'You must wonder what on earth you've been landed with. Do you often have this much trouble with your passengers?'

If only they knew! Was it pure co-incidence that it was those two who were missing? Fiona forced a smile. 'Travelling does tend to tire people out more than they realise and things can get a little strained on the first evening. Shall we go and get some coffee? After your excellent presentation last night, Noel, I must say I'm looking forward to tonight's talk.'

The unprepossessing entrance to the British Embassy, a double doorway in a block of shops just off a major roundabout, could easily be mistaken for a rundown department store if it were not for the Union Jack and EU flags fluttering half-heartedly above. Like most SIS foreign desks, Brussels Station was tucked away in a few rooms at the end of long corridors in a back corner of the British Embassy. There was little of the towering grandeur of the MI6 headquarters at Vauxhall Cross, but then it was home to only a handful of permanent staff.

Four men sat around the table in the small office. The

Commissioner of Police was on one side of Montgomery-Jones and Ferguson, Head of Brussels Station on the other. The youngest man, an MI5 bodyguard, looked exhausted and was slumped forward on his elbows his head in his hands.

'So, Tompkins, to clarify the order of events. A rowdy group of hecklers interrupted Moorhouse's speech and fighting broke out when supporters tried to shut them up. The officials tried to force their way through and one of the speakers, Giorgos…' Montgomery-Jones ran his finger down his notes, 'Dimitriadis, moved from his seat to the front of the stage to remonstrate and was pulled down into the crowd.'

'Yes, sir.' The young man lifted his head. 'Moorhouse jumped down from the podium to go and help. As he stepped out from behind the bulletproof screen, there was a shot and Moorhouse went down. The bullet had gone straight through his temple.'

'Did you see the shooter?'

Tompkins shook his head. 'He'd melted away into the crowd. I suppose I was distracted by what was happening to Dimitriadis. I should have stopped Moorhouse, but it all happened so fast.'

As the bodyguard slumped forward again, Montgomery-Jones said, 'Thames House [MI5 headquarters] are sending over Andrew Salmon and he will be arriving later this evening to take over the investigation. He will obviously want a full report. So, unless the Commissioner has any more questions,' the Belgian shook his head in answer to Montgomery-Jones's raised eyebrow. 'I suggest you go get your head down until then. It is going to be a long night.'

The bodyguard rose like an automaton and trudged to the door while the other three men shuffled their papers together.

Once the door was closed, the Commissioner said, 'His story confirms that of my officer in charge of the security detail at the scene. Moorhouse stepped down before your man had a chance to stop him.'

He pushed back his chair and all three men got to their feet.

'Thank you for coming here to speak to us, sir.'

The Commissioner tucked his cap under one arm and took Montgomery-Jones's proffered hand.

'Obviously, you have the full cooperation of the Belgian Police.'

The Commissioner's mobile began to ring. The man's face was grim as he ended the short call.

'That was an update on one of the previously unidentified riot victims in intensive care. It now appears he is a British tourist. He is not expected to survive the night. There is some question as to how he came by his injuries.'

'Oh?'

'The concern now is trying to save the man's life, but I will keep you informed.'

'Thank you. Do you know the hotel where he was staying?'

'I could find out. Although I believe his wife has been informed.'

'I would appreciate that, sir.'

If Ferguson was surprised at Montgomery-Jones's gentle insistence, he did not say so.

Chapter 7

Simon Lithgow's presentation provided a welcome distraction. In preparation for their visit to Antwerp, which was planned to include a tour of the artist's house and studio, the evening's talk was on the great master of Flemish Baroque, Peter Paul Rubens. The burly publican may not have had the cultural upbringing of some of his fellow committee members, but he had an easy way of speaking and a flair for engaging an audience and together with an impressive selection of slides, soon had everyone engrossed in the subject.

The talk had just ended, and Noel Appleby was on his feet to give a vote of thanks when Fiona's mobile vibrated in her pocket. It was an opportune moment for her to be able to slip out of her place and take the call outside without disturbing anyone.

Not wanting to delay answering any longer in case the caller rang off, she didn't stop to check who the call was from before picking up. 'Fiona Mason.'

'I am sorry to have to disturb you.' The voice came not only from her mobile but from behind her. She whirled round to face him.

'Peter?'

Switching off his phone and slipping back into his pocket, Montgomery-Jones took her elbow and guided her towards one of the deep plush sofas in a far corner of the foyer where there was no chance of them being overheard.

'I apologise for bringing you out of your meeting, but this is not the social call I was hoping our next encounter would be.'

'The Anti-Austerity rally?'

He nodded. 'Indeed.'

'I thought you were supposed to be taking a break from work for a few days,' she teased in an attempt to break the tension as they sat down.

He gave a wan smile. 'The assassination of a Member of Parliament, especially one so high profile, tends to overrule such arrangements. Although, thankfully, I shall not be heading up this particular investigation. It's an MI5 matter and someone from Thames House is on his way over as we speak, but as I was already on hand in Brussels, I have been asked to commence interviews and collate all the available evidence.'

'I see, but I'm not sure how I can help.'

'I wanted to talk to you about Robert Heppell. You are aware he is in hospital.' She nodded. 'What can you tell me about him?'

'About Robert? I don't understand. Why? How is he relevant to your investigation?'

'Quite possibly, no more than that he was injured in the panic that ensued. However, it was you who said he was a difficult man to deal with. Extremely forceful in his opinions. "A man used to getting his own way with little respect for the view of anyone else," to quote your words.'

She could hardly deny it.

'How did Mr Heppell relate to others in the group?'

'Shouldn't you be putting your questions directly to Robert?'

Fiona felt her jaw tighten. Despite their pleasant interlude of the previous day, there was a history between the two of them. All the old tensions rose to the surface; she had never responded well to Montgomery-Jones's intrusive questioning.

It would serve no purpose to repeat some of the more choice criticisms levelled at Robert Heppell by several of his fellow club members, but she could not deny that he had managed to antagonise nearly all of the non-Association members.

'Mr Heppell is in a serious condition. His wife is with him and I would prefer not to trouble her at this difficult time. However, the more information I can obtain now. . .'

'Is he going to be all right?' Fiona interrupted.

Montgomery-Jones paused for a split second. 'He did require major surgery.'

'What happened? He wasn't shot too, was he?'

'No. He was found unconscious a short distance from where the rally was being held. There were over fifty people who required medical assistance after the trouble broke out. Many were injured when the crowds panicked. Several have been detained in hospital.'

'But I still don't understand. How is what happened to Robert relevant to Tom Moorhouse's death?'

'There may not be a connection.'

'Then why all the questions?'

Montgomery-Jones did not answer straight away, giving himself time to choose his words carefully.

Fiona glared at him. 'If you're suggesting that Robert came to Belgium specifically because of the Anti-Austerity Rally you're way off beam. Robert put together the programme for this culture tour over a year ago. The dates were fixed long before any demonstrations were even thought about. To the best of my knowledge, he had no intention of going anywhere near the rally until much later in the morning after the tour of the Hotel de Ville. I doubt he even knew that Moorhouse was to be a speaker. Robert has no interest in anything to do with anti-austerity measures. He is as far to the right of the political divide as Moorhouse was to the left. The only thing they had in common was an overrated sense of their own importance and a love of hearing their own voices.'

Montgomery-Jones's severe countenance broke into a smile. 'I see.'

'You're not suggesting he was involved in the shooting?' she said crossly. 'That's absolutely preposterous.'

'I agree. It hardly seems to be a credible notion. I am simply trying to establish what happened and how Mr Heppell obtained his injuries.'

'But how does that help your investigation? What possible connection can there be? There is obviously something that you're not telling me.'

'A prominent British politician was fatally shot at the height of a major demonstration. Robert Heppell was found unconscious a few streets away minutes later. As yet, we have no explanation as to how he got there or how he received those injuries. There may be a link between the two, maybe not. Either way, that needs to be thoroughly investigated.'

This was getting nowhere. They were going round in circles.

'I understand Mrs Heppell did not accompany her husband to the rally,' he persisted.

'No. She said she went to the City Museum in the Maison du Roi and I have no reason not to believe her. Several other people headed over there so I'm sure someone will be able to vouch for her.'

'Do you know if anyone else went with Heppell?'

Fiona shrugged. 'I wouldn't know. Everyone went their separate ways after our tour. You were there; you saw us all coming out.'

'Indeed.'

A sudden thought struck Fiona. 'I doubt they would have gone together, but Hazel Tonkin must have headed in that direction because she saw Dee being arrested.'

Fiona explained that Dee had decided to opt out of the morning walk in order to attend the rally.

'Is it possible that Mr Heppell arranged to meet her there?'

'I very much doubt it!' Montgomery-Jones raised an eyebrow at the vehemence of her response. 'They seemed to have little in common.'

A slow smile spread across his face. 'Is that your diplomatic way of saying they argued?'

Damn the man. He always seemed to be able to read her mind. 'Well, yes. But it was hardly a deep-seated enmity. The two of them had only just met.'

'I see.' He looked thoughtful. Had she said more than she should? 'Her friend, Miss Tonkin did you say?' Fiona nodded. 'Was she intending to join Miss Foley at the rally?'

'I really couldn't say. I've no idea.'

'Is it possible to speak to her?'

'I'll ask Reception to ring her room and ask her to come down.'

Not surprisingly, they did not have to wait long. Hazel emerged from the lift and the moment she saw Fiona she rushed over, her eyes wide with worry.

'What's happened to Dee? Has she been released?'

'We don't know what the situation is at the moment, but this is Mr Montgomery-Jones and it might help if you tell him what happened.'

It took a moment or two for Fiona to calm Hazel down and eventually she sat perched on the edge of the armchair opposite them.

'You told me you saw Dee being arrested,' Fiona prompted.

'She was standing with a group of other people and a policeman just grabbed hold of her and pushed her into the police van.'

'But not you?' Montgomery-Jones asked.

She shook her head and her face crumpled as she blinked back the tears. 'I was at the other end of the road. I tried to get through to her, but there were so many people.'

'And where was this exactly?'

'I don't know the name of the road, but we were close to

the park somewhere.'

'Tell me what happened after you left the rest of the party at the Grand Place.'

'I tried to ring Dee. I kept ringing, but she must have switched off her phone. I went to see if I could find her, but when I got to the rally, there were thousands of people. I walked round the edge of the park for a bit, but it was hopeless, so I decided to come back. By then, I'd lost my bearings and I had no idea where I was. None of the road names I could see were marked on my map, so I took the next road and just kept walking. Eventually I saw a sign for a hospital and realised I was on completely the wrong side of the park. There was no way I was going back through those crowds, so I headed north looking for a metro station.'

Hazel gave a little sob.

'And then?'

'After a bit, I heard all this commotion and a load of police vans roared past. They turned into one of the side roads just in front of me. I had no idea what was happening at first, then suddenly all these people came rushing out. There was still a lot of shouting and banging going on, so I went to look round the corner to see what was happening. There was a great crowd of protesters at the far end of the street and the police were trying to herd them back with riot shields. Someone threw bricks and everyone joined in. The police started hitting people with batons. That's when I saw Dee. A policeman had her by the arm and was dragging her to one of their vans. I was about to go and help her, but the police let off these tear-gas canisters and everyone started running towards me. There were dozens and dozens of them. It was a stampede. Some of them fell over in the crush and got trodden on in all the panic. I had to jump into a shop doorway just to get out of the way. It was terrifying.' She put her head in her hands and started sobbing hysterically all over again.

Fiona went over to put an arm around her. Eventually

Hazel calmed down.

'Did you see what happened to your friend after that?' Montgomery-Jones asked.

Hazel shook her head and looked as if she was about to burst into tears again, but suddenly she sat up, thrust her chin forward, fists clenched.

'It's all that dreadful man's fault. If it hadn't been for him going on and on at her last night about her not being prepared to stand up for what she believed in, she'd never have gone to that stupid rally in the first place.'

'Which man was this?'

'That Robert Heppell. He's an evil man. He was goading poor Dee all evening. Making snide remarks at whatever she said. It was nothing less than harassment. He was the one who said if she really believed in the rights of the so-called deserving poor then she should go and join the protesters. Show solidarity.'

'Did you see Mr Heppell at the demonstration at any point?'

'No,' Hazel snapped. 'I'd have punched him in the nose myself if I had. All the trouble he's caused.'

The diatribe went on and on and there was little Fiona could do to stop her. Montgomery-Jones would get completely the wrong idea. Perhaps later she could explain that although there was a degree of truth in Hazel's assertion, from what Fiona had overheard, Dee had given as good as she'd got and needed little goading from Robert Heppell to attend the rally.

Eventually Hazel ran out of steam and once more, the tears ran down her cheeks as she pleaded with Montgomery-Jones to find out where Dee was being held and get her released.

'I will see what I can do, but it may take a while. As I understand it, as many as eighty people were taken into custody and dealt with in various police stations over the city. If it is of any consolation, I doubt they will want to detain so many people in the cells overnight. The most likely outcome is that after a cooling off period the majority will be released with a caution.'

'But she's not answering her phone.'

'I would assume that is because it was confiscated when she arrived at the police station.'

Hazel was in no state to go back up to her room alone and any further questions Fiona had for Montgomery-Jones would have to wait until their next meeting.

Squashing the inner voice that suggested she ought to offer to stay with the overwrought woman, Fiona made her excuses to Hazel and left. There was little she could do in any case, she reasoned in an attempt to ease her guilty conscience at abandoning the woman. The thought of having to field more unwanted questions if she returned to the rest of the party in the lounge was more than Fiona could face. It was almost ten o'clock and after the day she'd had, if anyone deserved an early night she did.

At least there was one thing she could be grateful for. Give him his due; for once Montgomery-Jones had been sympathetic. As she knew from past encounters, his questioning technique could be aggressive and unrelenting. It was kind of him to agree to help find Dee. Especially when he was so busy with the Moorhouse shooting. Perhaps he was just saying that to reassure Hazel, although that wasn't exactly his style. He was not a man to make empty promises.

Those first few hours into an investigation were always the most precious. It did not make sense that he was wasting time with Robert Heppell let alone over Dee Foley's arrest. What was going on?

Had Robert been there when Moorhouse was shot? Had he been seen on CCTV? It was a major international rally. One that would have prompted TV coverage from all over Europe and even further afield. By all accounts, there were also plenty of YouTube videos on the web. Surely there was no way that Robert could have been involved, but why all the questions?

It was a ridiculous idea. Fiona sighed; she was letting her imagination run riot. She was physically and emotionally drained. Time for bed. She would have to wait and see what happened in the morning. She kicked off her shoes and padded through to the bathroom.

Day 3 Sunday, Antwerp

The great Renaissance master, Pieter Paul Rubens spent his last 29 years in Antwerp where he produced some of his best work. We begin our tour with a visit to his house and studio. In the Grote Markt, the town's medieval core, we will see the elegant 16th century Stadhuis or Town Hall, the stately guild houses and the famous Brabo Fountain which depicts the soldier, Silvus Brabo, Julius Caesar's nephew in the act of throwing the severed hand of the evil giant plaguing the city into the river. Supposedly, it is from the word "handwerpen" which means hand-throwing, that the city derives its name.

After lunch, we visit the magnificent Gothic cathedral, which dates from the mid-thirteen-hundreds, and took two centuries to complete. In the 15th and 16th centuries, Antwerp was the centre of printing and our final visit is to Museum Plantin-Moretus, home of Christopher Plantin, the town's most successful printer. This fine 16th century house is on the UNESCO World Heritage List.

Super Sun Executive Travel

Chapter 8

Fiona woke to the sound of the bedside alarm. She checked her mobile but there were no messages. It was typical of Hazel not to think to let her know if Dee had returned as she had promised, but she was surprised that the Rev. McArdle had forgotten to let her know how Robert and Janice Heppell were faring.

It was still too early to ring any of them, besides which, Winston would be worried if she was late for their usual breakfast meeting.

The big West Indian driver was already in the Terrace Café when she arrived.

'Mornin', sweetheart. How's you this fine sunny morning?' He picked up the large silver teapot, poured out a cup and put it in front of her before she had time to settle herself in the chair.

'All the better for seeing you, Winston.'

'How's tricks? What's the latest news on our injured passenger?'

'I have no idea. I was told he was seriously hurt so I don't expect he'll be out of hospital any day soon. And there was no news about Dee Foley by the time I went to bed either. From what Mr Montgomery-Jones was suggesting, there were more people arrested than they could cope with in the cells last night, but what time she got back, if at all, I've no idea.'

'What d'you wanna do about today's programme?'

Fiona shrugged. 'Go ahead as planned I suppose. What else can we do?'

'On the plus side, the weather's fine and there's no traffic holdups reported so it's Antwerp here we come, eh?'

Fiona grimaced. 'It's probably a good thing we'll be out of Brussels for the next couple of days. With everything that's happened I expect there'll be large areas of the city centre cordoned off for quite a while.'

After Winston had left, Fiona buttered herself a slice of toast, but after a couple of bites, decided she had no appetite. She was about to return to her room when she spotted the arrival of the McArdles. Barbara stood in the doorway looking around and when Fiona caught her eye, she hurried over.

'I'm so glad I caught you, Fiona. Nicholas said you were anxious to know how Robert was. We did try to find you when I got back, didn't we, dear?'

She turned to her husband who nodded. 'We tried the lounge and we did try ringing your room, but there was no answer.'

'Not to worry. Do sit down both of you.' It was intimidating having them towering over her. 'How is Robert?'

Barbara frowned. 'Not good, I'm afraid. He has major head injuries and they had to take him back into surgery just before we arrived. I waited with Janice until he came out of theatre, but I didn't see him of course. They let her stay overnight and that's not a good sign, is it?'

'Not necessarily.'

'We rang the hospital just before we came down, but they didn't say much except that he's not receiving visitors. Obviously, we can't ring Janice, so we've just got to wait till she rings me.'

A waitress arrived at the table to ask if they wanted tea or coffee. Fiona decided it was time to leave them to it.

On the way back to the fifth floor, Fiona toyed with the idea of going straight to her room and checking up on her notes for the day's visits as she usually did after breakfast, especially on a tour like this which was new to her. She hadn't seen Hazel or Dee in the café, and she was still feeling guilty about abandoning Hazel when she'd been so distraught the previous evening. When she reached the fourth floor, she pushed open the door from the stairwell with a sigh and made her way to Room 415.

She tapped lightly and waited. No answer. Perhaps she should try again.

Suddenly the door was jerked opened and a suspicious looking Dee stared at her. 'Oh, it's you?'

Forcing a smile, Fiona said, 'I'm glad you're back.'

'Sorry,' the woman said grudgingly. 'Didn't mean to be rude. Come in.'

Hazel was sitting on the stool in front of the mirror brushing her short brown curls. Both women were dressed, but the room was a tip. Not just untidy, it looked as though they'd upended their cases onto the bed and strewn the contents over every piece of furniture in the room.

Dee was happy to recount her experience at the hands of an oppressive bureaucracy that had detained her without just cause simply for expressing her opinions. Because she had refused to give her name, they had detained her in a cell until late into the evening.

'They charged me with a breach of the peace and demanded a bloody great fine. I told them they could stick their fine where the monkey sticks his nuts. Then the sergeant says it's up to me, but they'd confiscated my ruddy bum bag, so they had my damned passport. I could either pay the fine and get it back then and there or spend a night or two back in the cells until they could take me to court and probably extract an even bigger fine. Bloody fascists.'

Fiona had to bite her inner lip to stop herself smirking.

Dee suddenly burst out laughing. 'Yeah, well. I suppose it

was funny really. Believe me I was tempted to have my day in court, but Hazel wouldn't have been too happy would you, sweetie?'

Hazel clearly didn't see the funny side and scowled at Fiona as though it was all her fault.

Time to beat a retreat. 'After all that excitement, I expect you're both starving, so I'd better let you both get yourselves down to breakfast. You are joining us on the trip today are you?'

'Might as well get our money's worth,' said Dee with a beaming smile.

The early morning sun was already streaming in through the windows of the small top floor office and despite the electric fan, the atmosphere was stuffy and tense. All five men had removed their jackets.

'Thank you for your reports, gentlemen.' The short, chubby man at the top of the table put down his pen, leaned back in his chair, lifted the sheets of notes he'd been making and studied them carefully. Andrew Salmon might be heading up the investigation, but he was by far the youngest man in the room.

'More coffee, anyone?' Without waiting for an answer, Ferguson, the overweight, slightly unkempt Head of Brussels Station, pushed himself to his feet. He moved over to the side table and picked up the glass jug sitting on the hotplate.

'Sir?'

The MI5 man gave a brief nod but did not look up from his notes.

Once all the cups had been refilled, Ferguson replaced the now empty jug, brought over a tray with the remaining croissants, and offered it around.

Montgomery-Jones waved it away. Ferguson and the two Belgian police officers each took one and the tray was placed within reach of Salmon who was still reading his notes.

Ferguson was finishing his second pain au chocolat when

Salmon looked up.

Salmon took out a handkerchief, removed his glasses and cleaned them. 'The important question is, was this a lone assassin or were the two incidents linked? Was the punch-up, the paint-bombing or both deliberately orchestrated to divert attention to allow the shooting and the escape of the gunman?'

'Possible, but unlikely.' Ferguson licked the last of the crumbs from his fingers. 'It would've meant a pretty big operation.'

'I concur,' agreed the Deputy Commissioner assigned to head up the police investigation. 'We arrested over seventy people in that incident alone, and from what we have discovered so far, they were made up of disparate groups with no apparent previous connections. A group of neo-Nazis, a few militant Trade Unionists from Liege, some Italian hotheads and various liberal idealists, but the majority were from two opposing groups of Belgians from either side of the Flemish French divide.'

'Who took the opportunity to beat the hell out of each other,' finished Ferguson with some relish.

'It is difficult to see a concerted common element,' Montgomery-Jones said quietly. 'However, it only takes two or three rabble-rousers to whip up a crowd especially when they are hyped up by strong convictions in the first place.'

Salmon nodded. 'We've seen that often enough in the London riots all too recently. Have we identified the original hecklers who started it all off?'

'The ringleaders appear to have melted away in the crowd as the police moved in, though from what we can make out on the camera footage, we think the chap who whipped out the banner is a German activist named Franz Müller.' Ferguson looked down at his notes. 'He's been arrested at several other such protests in Spain and France as well as his own country in the past couple of years, but apart from a hefty fine and a couple of cautions for incitement, he's never done anything likely to put him behind bars. From what we have from the BND [Bundesnachrichtendienst – German Federal Intelligence Service] he's not a likely candidate. He may be a bit of a loose cannon, enjoys causing trouble with a few of his like-minded cronies and is not above the odd punch-up, but involvement in any kind of assassination attempt is way out of his league. The BND are keeping a lookout for him if he returns to Germany, assuming we don't manage to track him down before he gets to the border.'

'Should we be doing more to find him now?' Salmon frowned. 'How about looking through CCTV records of just before the Demo began? Perhaps we can track him back to where he's staying.'

Ferguson gave a long sigh. 'How many man hours is that going to take. And to what end? If we do arrest him, what could we charge him with? Causing an affray? I doubt there's enough evidence to take him to court even if we do find him. It's as sure as hell that he's not going to volunteer any information about his associates. Shouldn't we be concentrating on Moorhouse's killer?'

Salmon's jaw tightened. Whether his anger was at Ferguson's challenge or because he couldn't refute the logic of it, only he knew. 'If it wasn't pre-arranged, that fracas was damn convenient for our gunman.'

'I agree one should always be suspicious of coincidences,' admitted Ferguson, 'but why hasn't any group come forward to claim responsibility? And the real distraction was what happened to Dimitriadis; and who could have predicted he would leave his seat? Does anyone know how he is by the way?'

'He was kept in hospital overnight. He was badly bruised and suffering from shock, but there were no broken bones and the last report I received was that he will be allowed back to his hotel sometime today,' said the Deputy Commissioner.

There was a pause before Salmon continued. 'Let's put that on one side for a moment. Do we assume that Moorhouse was specifically targeted or would any of the speakers have done? Was it someone with a grudge or a fanatical crackpot on some sort of personal crusade?'

'If Moorhouse wasn't the target, why didn't the shooter go for Dimitriadis? From where the gunman was standing, he'd have had a much better angle on the Greek. The man was walking towards him from the back of the stage. Moorhouse, on the other hand, was dashing from left to right across his line of fire.'

'Could Moorhouse have got in the way of the intended target?'

Ferguson shook his head. 'The lab boys have already looked at that possibility and there was no one behind. They're convinced Moorhouse was the intended victim.'

'That is also our assessment of the situation,' agreed the Deputy Commissioner.

'The gunman was certainly no amateur,' said Montgomery-Jones. 'He had no time to line up the perfect shot, yet the bullet went straight through the temple. Death was instantaneous.'

'Assuming he was a professional hit-man, it would suggest he was part of something bigger.' Salmon had the self-satisfied air of one whose theory has just been proved correct.

'Which is exactly why we haven't ruled out a link between the two events.' There was a touch of exasperation in Ferguson's voice.

'What do we have on the gunman?'

'So far, there is nothing on the media cameras or CCTV. All eyes were on the punch-up. We're still going through all the videos and pictures from the mobiles collected at the scene. Lots of Moorhouse hitting the deck, but nothing on the shooter. We have a few descriptions from people standing near, but as you would expect they are either extremely vague or conflicting.'

For the first time, the second Belgian spoke. He had been

the officer in charge of police security at the rally. 'The only thing that appears certain is that he was Caucasian, and he had something over his head. Some claim he was wearing a hoodie and others that he had a dark baseball cap pulled low over his forehead.'

'Wasn't it a warm day? Surely a man with a hood up would have stood out?' Salmon persisted.

The Belgian shrugged. 'Witnesses said he disappeared into the crowd as everyone panicked and started to run. We looked at the footage, but there were hundreds in caps and all sorts of hooded tops and jackets, besides he probably tossed it straight away. The whole Upper Town area was littered with all sorts of clothing and bags. No sign of any gun as yet so it looks as if he took that with him.'

'Or passed it on to some innocent looking old lady to put in her handbag,' Ferguson muttered sotto voce.

'Keep checking the footage,' Salmon snapped.

'You have to be joking.' Ferguson's chair rocked backwards. 'What hope do you have of identifying a single known individual in a crowd of 50,000 people stampeding through the city, let alone one who you have no idea what he looks like.'

The antagonism between the ambitious young man from Thames House keen to make his mark and the seasoned Head of Station who had worked his way up through the ranks was growing more and more heated by the minute.

'After nearly a whole day, we still have nothing concrete to go on?' Salmon glared at Ferguson. 'I had hoped you would have made more progress by now.'

'If that's all, sir; we need to be getting back to the incident room.' Ferguson jumped to his feet, jerked his jacket from the back of his chair, slung it over his shoulder and marched for the door. Without a word, the policemen rose to follow.

The door closed quietly enough, but the sounding of feet stamping down the stairs echoed throughout the top floor.

Breaking the hiatus that followed, Montgomery-Jones said

noncommittally. 'If we had a clear motive it would help. Perhaps something will come up in the enquiries into Moorhouse himself?'

Ignoring the comment, Salmon frowned. 'You've worked with Ferguson before. What do you think of him?'

'A few times. He is a good man. Very thorough.'

'Not just biding his time till retirement?'

'Certainly not. He may be old school, but I very much doubt Brussels is a "cushy" number.'

'There's no place for mavericks in the modern intelligence services.'

Montgomery-Jones smiled. 'He is certainly not that. He may have a particular way of working, but it would be a mistake to underestimate him. Or his team. They are very loyal. Plus, he has an excellent rapport with the police and the local authorities. When it comes to recruiting and running agents, he is one of the best and most experienced in the Service. He is a good man to have on your side.'

'Point taken.'

Montgomery-Jones put his papers together and got to his feet.

Still not ready to give in gracefully, Salmon suddenly snapped, 'Why did you spend so much time on the chap who was injured last night? I'd have thought your time would have been better spent here.'

Montgomery-Jones, already halfway to the door, turned and looked directly at the round-faced MI5 man. 'On my way to the train station to pick you up, I made a short diversion to the man's hotel in order to clarify one or two details. We received information of a report from one of the surgeons at the University Hospital who was suspicious about how one of his patients received his injuries. It was assumed at first that Robert Heppell was a casualty of the stampede after the riot. He had major head wounds, but they were inconsistent with a fall. The surgeon was of the opinion that they were caused by repeated blows from some type of heavy implement. That, and the total absence of any trampling injuries on the rest of his body, prompted him to report the details. Another possible murder attempt in the same vicinity in so short a time required investigation.'

'Surely that could have been handled by the police.

'Quite possibly. However, some interesting connections arose that I judged I was best placed to check upon, especially given that it involved only a short diversion.'

Salmon looked unconvinced, but he could hardly query the actions of a higher-ranking officer in the sister service especially one with Montgomery-Jones's reputation.

Chapter 9

It was no surprise that Robert Heppell was the sole topic of conversation as everyone gathered in the foyer to wait for the coach. Each new arrival was quickly told the news and even those of Fiona's party who were not members of the Swanley Association huddled in small excited groups.

Olive, the dowdy club secretary, was almost in tears telling all and sundry that it was all the fault of that dreadful woman. If it wasn't for her, dear Robert would never have gone to that stupid rally. Her words echoed the comments Hazel had made about Dee and Robert Heppell in reverse.

Once they had boarded the coach, Fiona made a brief statement that Robert was in hospital and that she would let them know as soon as there was any news. Information about Antwerp could wait until later.

Peggy was perched on a stone bench leaning heavily on her walking stick and staring down at her feet.

'Are you all right?'

The elderly woman looked up at Fiona and waved away her concern. 'I'm fine, dear. Just taking a breather while we wait for the others.'

Fiona settled herself next to the ample figure. 'We have been on our feet a long time.'

'But it was worth it.' Peggy gave a contented sigh. 'I hadn't realised there would be so much to see. Rubens must have been extremely wealthy to be able to afford such a huge house as this in the middle of the town.'

'It does include his studio and the art gallery where he exhibited not only his own work but that of other artists as well as his living apartments. Those rooms are quite small.'

'Well yes,' Peggy admitted, 'and I suppose he would need a pretty big studio for all those artists who completed his initial sketches. The art gallery was pretty impressive, especially the enormous apse at the end. It was just like some temple with all those marble busts and a great dome.'

Fiona laughed. 'It was modelled on the Pantheon in Rome.'

Through the archway on the far side of the courtyard, half hidden by one of the stone pillars supporting the portico, Philippa Western and Austin Pilkington could be seen in earnest conversation.

Peggy must have noticed Fiona was looking at the handsome couple.

'Austin is Bernard's nephew, you know.'

'I didn't realise.'

'To be strictly accurate he's Bernard's first wife's nephew. The son of Madeleine's older brother. Madeleine and Bernard couldn't have children, so Austin became a kind of surrogate son.'

'Have you known the family a long time?'

'Oh yes. Bernard Western grew up only a few miles from our house and I've known Austin since he was a boy. It was a big surprise to us all when Bernard married again, especially to a girl almost twenty years his junior. He met Philippa on a cruise round the Greek Islands about five years ago. She must have found it difficult when she first came with all Bernard's friends being so much older, but Austin spends a lot of time with them these days. He and Philippa play tennis together at the country club. Bernard loves his golf of course, but that's not her sort of sport.'

That explained why Fiona had noticed Philippa and Austin together so often. And why their close association never seemed to bother her husband.

'Though I'm not sure that the Association is really Philippa's thing. Bernard was one of the original members in the days when it was still called a Social Club.' She gave a hearty laugh. 'Most of us who have come on the trip are of course, which explains why we're getting so ancient. Not very exciting for her. She must find us all a boring load of old fogies.'

'But she and Gina Lithgow must be much the same age.'

'True, but. . .' There was a brief pause and Peggy seemed to pick her words carefully before she continued, 'Unfortunately, they don't have a great deal in common. Gina and Simon moved from Brentwood I think, somewhere in Essex anyway, when he took over *The King's Head* three or four years ago. I don't think she found it easy to fit in as an incomer. Simon's a different kettle of fish altogether and he's really thrown himself into the club since he joined. He offered to host our meetings at the pub. It didn't take much to persuade the committee to swap the draughty church hall for a cosy room with decent blackout for slideshows plus a bar on tap next door. Robert was very keen to adopt some younger blood into the Association and Simon's proved himself a willing workhorse. He's become Robert's right-hand man.'

'I enjoyed his talk on Rubens last night. It certainly added to this morning being able to picture the great man living and working in this very building.'

'It was good, wasn't it? I had no idea he was such an expert on Rubens and where did he get all those lovely pictures? It must have taken hours.'

'It's easy enough to download all sorts of stuff from the internet these days. It's amazing how much information you can find with just a few clicks of the computer keys.' Fiona whispered conspiratorially, 'As I can tell you from personal experience.'

'And here's me thinking your expertise came from years of study!'

They giggled like a pair of schoolgirls.

Fiona looked up when she caught snatches of conversation from the small cluster of people coming back through the arch from the gardens.

'. . . I wasn't standing for that. . .'

Dee's penetrating aggressive tone grated even at this distance. It seems however tactful Fiona had tried to be in not letting the rest of the party know that Dee had only narrowly avoided having to spend the night in the cells, Dee herself had no such qualms. She was happy to tell all and sundry how she had refused to buckle under the oppression to the right to free speech exerted by bullyboy police tactics. The woman appeared to be revelling in the experience. Had it occurred to her that her friend had been reduced to an emotional wreck for nine hours by her absence? And Hazel hadn't been the only one who had been anxious. Still, at least Dee Foley was one problem Fiona could now cross off her worry list.

She wondered if there was any news about Robert. She looked around for Barbara McArdle and spotted her with a small group of Swanley Association members talking on the far side of the courtyard. Better to wait until she could get the Rev.'s wife on her own. Besides, Fiona tried to reassure herself, if Janice had phoned, Barbara would have let her know straight away.

The last few stragglers were joining the group. Time to collect everyone together and head for the coach.

Lunch was in a small café in the pedestrianized market square and they were able to sit outside in the warm sunshine and watch the comings and goings.

Olive was looking decidedly unwell when they got back on board. Her face was drawn and her complexion even paler than usual. It was only a short drive to their next stop, but they had only gone a few streets when Olive came rushing forward.

'Can you stop the coach? I think I'm going to be sick.'

Winston hardly had time to find somewhere to pull out of the stream of traffic before Olive almost fell out of the door and vomited violently into the gutter.

Copious packs of Wet Wipes were handed forward and Fiona helped the elderly woman clean up. It was a busy area and it was evident that the coach would have to move on. There was nowhere suitable for Olive to sit and recover herself.

'I don't want any fuss. I'm fine now dear.'

Fiona was in a quandary. Although Olive now seemed considerably better, she was obviously in no fit state to continue for the rest of the afternoon.

As Olive stood by a litter bin wiping the last small splashes from her skirt, Fiona jumped back on the coach to get her a bottle of water.

'She insists that she doesn't want to go to hospital, but I can't send her back to the hotel on her own even in a taxi, and . . .'

'No problem, sweetheart,' Winston interrupted. 'If she don't mind getting back on the bus, it's only a couple of minutes to the cathedral. I can drop you and the others off, then run her back to the hotel. I'll see she gets back to her room safely. I'll be back in plenty o' time to pick you all up for the next stop.'

Olive readily agreed when Fiona put the proposal to her.

By the time they reached the drop off point, the colour was returning to Olive's cheeks, but that didn't stop Fiona worrying about her as the coach pulled away.

Ferguson put down the phone with a smile on his face. He picked up the notepad he'd been scribbling on during the call and walked over to Montgomery-Jones's desk.

'That was Berlin Station. They've come through with the info we asked for. I'm about to take it through to our Great Leader. Wanna come with me?'

There was a curt, 'Come in,' as he knocked on the door.

Salmon carried on tapping away on the keyboard as the two men entered. They both sat down and waited.

'Sorry about that, gentlemen. Just needed to write it down before it went out of my mind. What can I do for you?'

'You wanted background on Franz Müller, our banner-waving protester at the rally,' said Ferguson. 'Berlin Station are sending over all they have on him as we speak, but the gist of it is that he's a member of the international Blockupy movement against welfare cuts in government spending throughout the Eurozone. The word is that he was one of the organisers of the protest outside the European Central Bank in Frankfurt back in May 2013. It depends who you listen to – official sources say 1,000 people and the group themselves claim they had 3,000 supporters there. He was one of a small group of masked protesters who attempted to break the police cordon around the ECB offices. The protest managed to interrupt the business operations of the ECB for well over three hours until the police managed to clear the crowds in the surrounding streets with pepper spray.'

'But that doesn't make sense,' Salmon protested. 'Why was he trying to disrupt the rally? He should have been supporting it. Has he changed sides all of a sudden?'

'That was the puzzle from the start. We've checked the camera footage and at the start of the rally he and his cronies were definitely cheering on all the speakers. Applauding every point they made. It was only when Moorhouse got to his feet that they started heckling. We've been trying to decipher the wording on the banner, but it was never properly unfurled before all the chaos broke out. However, it looks as though they were anti-Moorhouse rather than the Anti-Austerity cause itself. We have managed to interpret some of the stuff they were chanting and let's just say the word traitor plus a few less savoury epithets featured prominently.'

'That does put a somewhat different complexion of things.

The next question is, did this group have anything to do with his assassination?' Montgomery-Jones looked thoughtful.

Salmon slammed his fist on the table. 'Well let's step up the search and find the man so we can bloody well ask him.'

It wasn't the succession of explosive sneezes, even though they made her jump; the thing that was rapidly driving Fiona to distraction was the constant noisy sniffs punctuated by long drawn out sighs.

Fiona glanced up into her mirror and it was clear that she was by no means the only one who was not looking forward to spending the next half hour cooped up in a coach with Aubrey Diamond intent on inflicting his misery, not to mention his germs, on everyone else. Gina Lithgow sitting across the aisle was giving him furtive murderous glances. They would be lucky to get back to the hotel without some sort of fracas.

It wasn't until they were getting off the coach that Fiona had a chance to speak to Barbara.

'Janice still hasn't phoned. Nicholas says because she may not be allowed to use a mobile in the hospital and she doesn't want to leave his bedside. He's probably right so I'm going over there to see what's happening. If he is still unconscious, I can at least sit and keep her company.'

'Why don't you wait until we've had a chance to check that there's no message at Reception. Janice might have asked one of the nurses to ring the hotel. If there's no news, give me time to check and see Olive is okay and then I'll order a taxi and we'll go together.'

Fiona's delaying tactics did nothing to reduce Barbara's determination. She was pacing up and down between the reception desk and the door when Fiona got back down again.

She did ask after Olive, but Fiona doubted the woman took in her reply. 'She seems much better now. She thinks it was probably the prawns in her salad. Either that or the mayonnaise had turned in this heat. She's planning on popping down to Terrace Café for something light a little later on and then having an early night.'

At least there was one thing she could be grateful for, Fiona thought as the taxi crawled its way through the traffic. Tomorrow's visit to Waterloo meant that there was no talk that evening and most members of the party had decided to sample the local restaurants for the evening meal which meant that she was spared any concern about leaving the rest of the group to fend for themselves.

'How's your French?' Barbara asked as they walked through the hospital doors.

Though by no means fluent, Fiona had had more opportunity to brush up on the language in the last few months, but the woman on the front enquiry desk had perfect English. First problem solved.

After a few taps on the keyboard she looked up from her screen. 'It will not be possible for you to visit Mr Heppell. Only family are admitted.'

'We do appreciate that, but can you tell us how he is?'

The receptionist shook her head. 'I do not have that information.'

'The thing is,' Fiona persisted, 'we are concerned about Mrs Heppell. She's been here for twenty-four hours. Is it possible to get a message to let her know we're here?'

The receptionist remained stony faced.

Barbara began to remonstrate but before she could intervene, Fiona heard her name being called. She turned to see Peter Montgomery-Jones walking towards her.

'I think I can tell you all you need to know.'

Barbara frowned but allowed Montgomery-Jones to steer her over to a quiet corner. 'There is a café area along here. Let us go and sit down and we can talk.'

Before Barbara had a chance to protest, Fiona said, 'I'm sure Mr Montgomery-Jones can help us.'

Only when they had sat down would he answer the stream of questions Barbara kept firing at him.

'I am sorry to tell you that Mr Heppell never recovered from his injuries.'

'You mean he's . . .' Barbara stopped, unwilling to say the word.

'He had to be taken back into theatre early this morning, but early this afternoon his condition rapidly deteriorated.'

'Then I must go to Janice. . .'

He put out a hand to stop her as Barbara jumped to her feet. 'She has her family with her. He was kept on life support until his two daughters were able to get here. The machines were turned off less than an hour ago.'

Barbara desperately blinked back her tears as she searched through her pockets for a tissue.

Montgomery-Jones took the immaculate white handkerchief from his top pocket and handed it to her. After a moment's hesitation, she took it and wiped her eyes.

'Allow me to fetch you both a cup of coffee.' Without waiting for a reply, he left them to recover from the news.

'I knew he was on the critical list but. . .' Barbara blew her nose and took a long deep breath. 'I can't pretend I ever liked the man and it was no secret I thought Janice would be better off without him, but I would never have wished him dead.'

She must have seen the look of surprise on Fiona's face and hurried on, 'I know I shouldn't say it, but he could be a very unpleasant man and in the last few years he's become a monster.'

'I can see he had a temper, but surely he didn't take it out on Janice?'

'No, no.' Barbara shook her head. 'Nothing like that. He was always ambitious – driven even – riding roughshod over anyone who got in his way. I know you think I'm prejudiced, but it wasn't because he took the chairmanship from Nicholas, it was the way he did it that I find so hard to forgive. He's changed the whole nature and purpose of the

Social Club as though all that we achieved before he came along counted for nothing. Plus, he manipulates people. He ferrets out their weaknesses and uses them for his own ends. You've only got to look at what he did to Noel.'

She stopped suddenly realising she had said more than she should to a virtual stranger. Fiona may have managed to curb her every instinct to probe further, but that didn't stop her wondering what kind of hold Robert might have over the kindly cleric and the charming, courteous club treasurer.

Barbara had recovered her composure by the time Montgomery-Jones returned. She took the tiny carton of cream from the tray and distractedly tore off the foil top.

'What happens now?' Barbara looked across the table at Montgomery-Jones. 'How is she going to get Robert's body back to Swanley?'

It was Fiona who answered. 'I'll let head office know and they will contact the Heppells' travel insurance provider and they'll see to all the necessary arrangements.'

'There will need to be an autopsy first,' Montgomery-Jones said quietly. 'I have a car outside. Allow me to run you both back to the hotel.'

In all the emotion-charged encounter at the hospital it wasn't until later that Fiona wondered why Montgomery-Jones had been there at all.

Day 4 Monday, Waterloo

Today we drive south to Waterloo and travel back in time 200 years as we explore the events of June 18th, 1815. After a lengthy battle, the Anglo-allied army under the command of the Duke of Wellington, aided by the late arrival of Gebhard von Blucher's Prussian army, defeated the Imperial French forces and brought an end to Napoleon's reign as Emperor.

Our first stop will be a short visit to the Church of St. Joseph, where Wellington is said to have prayed before going into battle, and see the plaques commemorating British and Dutch soldiers who fell in the battle.

Across the road is the Wellington Museum in the former Bodenghien coaching inn, which was chosen as the British Military headquarters and is where The Duke of Wellington, stayed on the nights of 17th and 18th June 1815.

When we arrive at the battlefield site there will be free time to explore the area and perhaps climb the 226 steps of the Butte du Lion built on the spot where the Prince of Orange, the future King of the Netherlands, was injured.

After lunch, we will tour the battlefield on board a four-wheel drive truck. Before we leave, there will be time to see the audio-visual show and the Panorama with its immense fresco complete with sound effects.

Super Sun Executive Travel

Chapter 10

There seemed to be only one topic at breakfast. The death of Tom Moorhouse was still front-page news in the British newspapers according to those who had downloaded the day's editions. The lack of progress by the Belgian authorities in identifying and apprehending his killer caused considerable critical comment. Fiona could hear the group talking at the next table.

'I agree. If this had happened in Britain there would have been arrests by now.'

Fiona wondered what they would say if they knew the British Security Services had been on hand from the start.

'And what about all those people injured as they tried to get away? Forty-three had to be taken to hospital.' Eleanor Prior's voice rose as she warmed to her subject. 'Some of them had to be kept in overnight their injuries were so bad. They should never have brought out the riot police. That's what caused the real panic. Did you see those pictures on the television last night?'

What would the response be when they learnt one of their own party was one of the fatal casualties? Time to go before she became embroiled in the conversation. Apart from anything else, if she was going to make a success of the day's guiding, she needed to read through her notes and study the photographs to ensure she recognised the various landmarks. For once, this was also new territory for the experienced Winston so she wouldn't have him to fall back on.

Ferguson had already unpicked a corner of the cling film and extracted a cinnamon whirl by the time Montgomery-Jones walked into the room. Without any hint of shame at being caught raiding the Danish pastries set for the later break, he tucked the loose edge back under the tray and turned to Montgomery-Jones.

'I'm surprised you're still here. I'd have thought you'd want to get back to London now his lordship's here to take charge.' Ferguson took a large bite of his pastry. 'Don't tell me you think Our Great Leader isn't up to the job?'

'I am sure Salmon is more than capable of heading up the enquiry. From what I hear, he has made quite an impression since he joined the service. He is one of the rising stars of Thames House.'

Ferguson gave a derisive snort. 'And does he like to make an impression? Any idiot can sit there and bark out orders.' Ferguson stuffed the last of the pastry into his mouth and chewed vigorously.

Montgomery-Jones walked over to the window and pushed it open, allowing a slight breeze into the stuffy office.

Ferguson swallowed and turned to Montgomery-Jones. 'Why have you decided to stay? I thought you were booked on last night's Eurostar. Isn't this an MI5 matter? Does it really concern you anymore?'

'Perhaps not, but it is a high-profile case,' replied Montgomery-Jones noncommittally.

Ferguson pulled a face. 'I grant you Moorhouse was something of a celebrity, but his death hardly has major consequences politically. It's hardly a threat to national security. Granted, he was a noisy pain-in-the-ass spouting his views all over the media, but he had little influence of any real consequence.'

'True, but there are some aspects of this whole affair that have piqued my interest, shall we say.'

'Oh?'

Any further discussion was halted as the diminutive Salmon bustled in carrying a stack of papers, which he proceeded to distribute on the table in front of each of the three chairs facing the large dropdown screen on the far wall.

'Right, gentlemen,' he said as the other two took their places, 'the purpose of today's meeting is to establish a list of probable candidates responsible for Moorhouse's death, be that individuals or groups. As we've said before, the number of people with a grievance is by no means small. The man managed to make enemies not only amongst those on the opposite side of the political spectrum, but amongst his ex-Union colleagues as well as this Block Occupy group he was involved with lately.'

'It's called Blockupy.'

'Whatever,' Salmon snapped, glaring at Ferguson for daring to correct him. 'We've already established that whoever actually pulled the trigger could only have been a professional marksman, so we can assume that we are most likely looking at a paid assassin. Such men don't come cheap, which means that the individual who ordered the hit not only had a strong motive but the wherewithal to lay out a great deal of money.'

'That must reduce our list somewhat,' said Ferguson.

'Exactly. However, it's a pretty big stretch of the imagination to think that the leaders of any British political party or the TUC [The Trades Union Congress] could be involved.'

'Which means we're back to square one?'

'As you know, researchers back at Thames House have been digging into Moorhouse's background which is why I've called this video conference so they can keep us updated.'

Salmon glanced at his watch, pulled the laptop towards him and started it up. A few moments later the head and shoulders of a fresh-faced man appeared on the screen. He looked to be in his early twenties, though he must have been a good few years older to have gained his current position in the service as a chief researcher.

'Good morning, Martin. Can we begin with introductions? On my right, Charles Ferguson, Station Head, Brussels, and on my left, Commander Montgomery-Jones, who's joined us from Vauxhall Cross [MI6 headquarters]. Martin Cumming, from Intelligence Analysis. Thank you for the information on Moorhouse you sent earlier. We all have copies, but obviously, we've not had time to read through them yet so if you'd like to take us through the salient points before we begin, it would be a help.'

'Certainly, sir, and good morning, gentlemen. I'll start with a potted biography of the man. Thomas James Moorhouse, born in 1958 in Rotherham; father a steelworker and a card-carrying member of the Communist Party. His mother worked in the canteen at the glass factory. Both parents now deceased. He was the youngest in the family with two much older sisters. His parents were ambitious for him and keen for him to go to grammar school. He managed to scrape good enough A levels to get onto an economics course at Bradford University, but dropped out at the end of his second year and joined his father in the steelworks. Several of his uncles worked in the mining industry and throughout the conflicts with the government in the mid '80s, he became a familiar figure on the picket lines and a full-time activist supporting the striking miners. This was followed by a variety of employment all documented in your notes on page 3.' Cumming paused as all three men shuffled their papers to look for the information.

'In '92 he became a fulltime union official and in 1998, after what was reputed to be a bitter feud, he was elected leader. His go-getting attitude and attempts to modernise the union earned him few friends among many of the older long-standing officials.'

'So how come he was elected?'

'Moorhouse was an inspiring speaker. He could whip up

the crowd like few others. He always managed to sway the masses. The rank and file members saw him as a crusading messiah capable of achieving great things for them. It was their vote that kept him where he was. To be fair, under his leadership, the Union did manage to achieve considerable concessions for the workers.

'But they didn't have to work alongside the man, eh?' Ferguson chuckled.

Salmon glared at Ferguson for daring to interrupt.

'Something like that,' Cumming agreed. 'In 2001 he was elected as MP for Rotherham, a seat held by Labour since 1933. He made quite an impression. For a while, he was thought to be the wunderkind of the party, destined for the front benches. He had all the right credentials for New Labour. He was young, personable and an erudite speaker. In the next reshuffle, he was made a Junior Minister in the Treasury. He was active on a great number of committees and was soon rubbing shoulders with the captains of industry with whom he gave every appearance of reaching considerable accord.'

'So what went wrong?'

'He toed the Party Line for some time, but his extreme left-wing roots eventually began to show through. He became disillusioned by the direction in which the Party was heading. He made several much-publicised attacks on government policies which he claimed penalised the poor and disadvantaged those who could least afford it. It may have earned him considerable support from the far left but as you can imagine, didn't make him too popular with the Blairites in the cabinet. Things came to a head when he gave a television interview where he was as vitriolic about the self-interest of his Party's leaders and their failure to fight for what he called true socialist values.'

'I remember that. Caused quite a stir,' said Ferguson.

'Moorhouse calmed down for a while after that and he kept a relatively low profile for a year or so. When the coalition came to power, he continued his attacks on the corruption of those in power. His frequent media protests about social injustice, the lack of affordable housing, a tax system that rewards corporate greed won him popular support and made him a household name. And it wasn't only those on the Government benches who were the subject of his vitriol. He also lambasted the Labour leadership and came under threat of the removal of the whip on numerous occasions.'

'Wasn't he involved in the Occupy London campaign back in 2012?' Salmon asked.

'Very much so. He's thought to have been instrumental in organising it. Although it failed to achieve its original aim to camp outside the London Stock Exchange, it did manage to set up a camp by St Paul's Cathedral. He was interviewed at the site demanding to know why all those who claimed to represent the working man were still sitting in the Commons Dining Room eating their subsidised five course lunches when they should be showing their solidarity with the very people they were elected to fight for.'

'I bet that went down a storm,' said Ferguson with a wry laugh.

'Especially when he gave an interview on morning TV a few weeks later, calling his own Party's leaders "a bunch of useless public school twats who had as much understanding of the real world as a monkey understanding the third law of thermodynamics." The final straw was probably what happened at the anti-fracking protest camp at Barton Moss.'

'Wasn't that where a flare was fired at a police helicopter as it tried to land?'

'It was. The police had a warrant to carry out a search of the site. Occupy London is a keen supporter of the Campaign against Climate Change and Moorhouse was there as one of the camp's main organisers. The protesters denied that they were responsible, and the media gave a great deal of coverage to Moorhouse arguing with the police officer in charge. As you can imagine, the whole thing became pretty acrimonious and as a result Moorhouse was finally expelled from the party. However, he still had the full support of his constituency members and it's interesting to speculate what would have happened at the next election had he lived. There was talk of him standing as a TUSC candidate.'

'What's that when it's at home?' asked Ferguson.

'The Trade Unionist and Socialist Coalition. As the name suggests, they're a mix of trade unionists, community campaigners and anti-cuts activists. They did well in the recent local elections up and down the country where they fielded candidates, increasing their share of the vote and in many cases only narrowly losing out to the labour candidate, but well ahead of the Tory and Lib Dem candidates. Though I'm not surprised that you haven't heard of them over in Belgium. They received very little coverage in the mainstream media. All the reports appeared to concentrate almost exclusively on the increase in UKIP's [United Kingdom Independence Party] vote.

'Can we move on?' Salmon made a show of shuffling the papers in front of him. 'What about these Press reports of him being seen talking with several members of this so-called alliance between the various Eurosceptic groups in the European Parliament a few days ago? By all accounts, they provoked quite a backlash from supporters of this new European Anti-Austerity Movement he's supposed to be such a prominent member of.'

'All our enquiries would seem to suggest that the story was blown up out of all proportion. Some UKIP MEPs [Members of the European Parliament] were dining with a couple of Danish Eurosceptic members in the same restaurant where Moorhouse had been eating and he was seen smiling and shaking hands with one of the women. Before joining UKIP, she'd been a labour councillor in Moorhouse's own constituency. They happened to bump into each other on the way out and it would have been strange if they hadn't acknowledged each other. Some paparazzi managed to get a photo of two of them looking more than friendly and though it stopped short of actually claiming Moorhouse was doing deals with the Eurosceptics, the resulting article implied as much.

'Despite all the explanations and denials of collusion, it certainly didn't endear him to his fellow activists or the rank and file members who claimed there was no smoke without fire. UKIP may like to pose as an anti-establishment party, but in reality, it is a party led by bankers and millionaires sitting well to the right of the Tory Party. The policies they are proposing will mean £77 billion of extra spending cuts on top of those the government is already imposing.'

'All in all, it sounds like we have a shipload of people lining up to dance on his grave even if they weren't responsible for bringing in someone to gun him down.'

'Can we dispense with the jokes and move on,' snapped Salmon.

'Certainly, sir. If you turn to page 5 in your notes, gentlemen.' There was a shuffling of pages. 'I would like to stress there is no particular order in the list you have there. It is not intended as an order of priority. Neither is it exhaustive by any means. Information is still coming in and being assessed.'

A picture of a swarthy grim-faced man with iron-grey hair and large angular spectacles appeared on the screen.

'Alex Bradshaw, who you see here, is the man Moorhouse ousted as Union leader. As I mentioned before,.Moorhouse had few friends amongst his fellow officers in the Union and his decision to stand for parliament posed significant problems for them. It left them having to face an extremely disgruntled workforce following the failure of the much-publicised three-day strike. The negotiations over pay and conditions broke down and Moorhouse refused to accept the offer on the table and threatened to call a strike. This led to an improved offer, but though there was considerable support backing Bradshaw's call to accept it, Moorhouse was adamant and called for the strike to go ahead. While all this was going on, the unexpected death of the standing MP in a motor accident led to a snap by-election. Moorhouse duly abandoned the Union to spend time canvassing. Without his support, the strike more or less fizzled out leaving Bradshaw, who'd taken over negotiations, having to make an embarrassing climb-down for the Union and accept poorer terms than originally offered. Bradshaw, who had to shoulder the blame, never forgave Moorhouse and just over a year ago, the two men met by chance in a local public house. Apparently, there was an altercation and they came to blows. The police were called and both men were arrested. Bradshaw ended up charged and convicted of causing an affray and sentenced to eight months in jail despite a strong feeling that it was Moorhouse who had provoked the whole affair. Bradshaw lost not only his freedom, but his reputation and his marriage.'

'Admittedly, he may have a motive of sorts, but he bears no resemblance to the description of the shooter. Does he have sufficient funds to hire a hit man?' Salmon asked.

'None that we can find,' came the quick reply. 'He may have done well financially during his time in the union, but his divorce settlement took a hefty chunk of that.'

The picture on the screen changed to a much younger man in his thirties.

'However, he does have a nephew, Reece Bradshaw, his deceased younger brother's son. Alex was very much a father figure when Reece was growing up and the two are very close. Alex has no children of his own. Reece Bradshaw was a sniper in the army. He came back from a tour of duty in Afghanistan suffering from some kind of mental disorder.'

'Has he been interviewed?' asked Salmon.

'Not yet, sir. We're still trying to get hold of him. He's supposedly somewhere in Scotland on a walking holiday, but he's wild camping so locating him is not going to be easy.'

'A deranged fanatic with a cause, plus all the required skills.'

Ferguson sat back in his chair with a smug look on his face. 'A definite possibility, I'd say.'

Salmon threw him a disapproving glance. 'Can we take a look at the other names on the list?'

Several more names were considered and ten minutes later, Salmon said, 'That certainly gives several promising lines of enquiry. Any other strong suspects?'

'As you can see on the last page, the list is a long one. There is an on-going feud between Moorhouse and Neville Truelove, the Tory MP for Richmond Park. Moorhouse's affair with Truelove's wife was front page news in the tabloids for weeks.'

'I seem to remember a picture of them coming out of some Soho nightclub. She was a stunning looking woman.'

'It was nearly ten years' ago now,' Cumming hurried on before Salmon could object to Ferguson's interruption. 'It was soon after Moorhouse had been made a Junior Treasury Minister and was making a name for himself. Which is why it hit the headlines, of course. Truelove was considerably older than his wife and was always considered a dull, timeserving MP who was rarely seen in The House. However, rather than diminishing Moorhouse in the public's eye, many thought all the more of him for being a Jack-the-Lad.'

'If every cuckolded husband took out a contract on his wife's lover, the country would be knee-deep in corpses. In any case, why would the man wait until now to take revenge?' Salmon reasoned.

'Truelove made a concerted effort to bring Moorhouse down after that. Apart from his cronies in parliament, he has friends in high places. Moorhouse found himself ostracised in a great many business circles and the Tory Press never missed an opportunity to find fault. Moorhouse didn't make it any easier for himself. Mrs Truelove was only the first in a whole string of such liaisons as far as Moorhouse was concerned. He appears to have developed quite a taste for attracting the wives of public figures. Admittedly no recent scandals have come to light, but it is a possible line of enquiry.'

'Given the high profile of this case and the media attention it's caused worldwide, I suppose we do have to consider every angle, however remote.' Salmon sighed. 'Let's schedule another report for the same time tomorrow. If anything significant crops up in the meantime, get back to me.'

'Of course, sir. Good morning, everyone.'

The screen went dead.

Chapter 11

Few people seemed particularly interested in the many large memorial plaques at the rear of the church dedicated to the British soldiers who lost their lives in the famous battle. They were far too busy huddled in small groups talking in hushed tones, no doubt sharing their reactions to Fiona's announcement on the coach on the way over. Robert Heppell had done little to endear himself to his newly acquainted fellow passengers in the couple of days he had known them, but the sudden death of one of their group had come as a shock.

Although word appeared to have spread amongst the Swanley Association members before they had boarded the coach, none had decided to abandon the day's outing. Perhaps they found solace in each other's company. As Fiona could have predicted, it was Olive, Robert's loyal club secretary and staunchest supporter, who took the news hardest. Barbara McArdle had taken it upon herself to ensure that the tearful woman was included and not left on her own.

After the initial shock, not all the club members appeared so visibly moved. Philippa and Austin were soon laughing and joking, Gina Lithgow had a self-satisfied gleam in her eye and Noel Appleby looked positively chipper and more spritely than she'd seen him all holiday.

Fiona decided to cut short their visit to the church and led them across the road to the small, somewhat cramped Wellington Museum where there was far more to distract everyone.

She took them straight to the room containing one of the most interesting curios in the small museum. In a small glass display case lay a wooden leg. 'The story goes that as they rode from the battle, the troops came under cannon fire. Lord Uxbridge turned to the Duke of Wellington and said, "By God, sir, I've lost my leg,". Wellington's reply was equally matter of fact, "By God, sir, so you have,".'

After a brief pause for the laughter to die down, she continued, 'By all accounts, Lord Uxbridge was quite a character. He was brought here to have the leg amputated; without any anaesthetic I might add. His only comment was, "The knives appear somewhat blunt". He was offered an annual pension of £1,200 in compensation for the loss of his leg, which he refused.'

To Fiona's relief, the atmosphere had lightened considerably. She allowed them all a few minutes to wander round looking at the rest of the exhibits.

'Shall we move on? Upstairs you'll find a series of plans that depict the course of the battle hour by hour. It is worth taking your time over those as you'll be able to appreciate what we'll be seeing when we make our tour of the battlefield this afternoon. Let's meet back down in the shop area in about half an hour at...' she glanced at her watch, 'quarter past.'

The group were absorbed in the unfolding story portrayed in the interactive displays and it was only when people began to drift back down to the lower floors, that Fiona was able to get close enough to each of the panels to read the information and appreciate them for herself. Gradually the noise subsided to gentle murmurings.

Fiona was busy following the advance of the red and blue coloured blocks representing each side in the battle when from across the room, came Eleanor Prior's penetrating whisper. 'I was sorry to hear about the death of your friend.'

'Robert? He wasn't exactly what I'd call a friend.' Gina

Lithgow tried to disassociate herself from the woman's obvious attempt to pry.

'He did seem a disagreeable sort of person,' Eleanor simpered.

'I meant; I didn't know him that well.'

If Eleanor sensed the rebuke in Gina's remark, she chose to ignore it.

'Is there any more news about how he died?'

'Not that I've heard.'

'Really? Surely your club members must have some idea?'

Whether it was Eleanor's implication that Gina must be out of the Association's inner circle or her own love of gossip, Gina decided to relent. 'The general view is that he was trampled in the stampede after that MP was shot.'

'Yes, but doesn't it seem strange that he should be at that rally in the first place?'

'Robert was very interested in politics. He rubbed shoulders with quite a few MPs. And he was going to stand as a candidate himself at the next election.'

'Really? Did he support this politician then?'

Gina snorted. 'Hardly! Robert was a staunch Tory. I doubt he had much truck with the likes of Moorhouse and all his Union buddies. But between you and me, Robert was a bit of a bully. Not a likable man…'

Gina's voice dropped and Fiona failed to catch the rest of the conspiratorial whisper.

Fiona decided it was time for her to go. Although she did not want to attract attention, it was going to be difficult to prevent the clatter of footsteps on the wooden floor as she made for the stairs. She could only hope that the two women were so engrossed in their conversation that they had no suspicions that their gossip had been overheard.

Fiona still wasn't sure what to make of Gina Lithgow. At first, she'd felt sorry for the woman because she appeared to be somewhat isolated and out of her depth with the rest of the Swanley Association people. With the exception of

Philippa, with whom she had little in common, she was much younger than the other members who had come on the trip. Lacking their education, she had none of her husband's social graces and hovered on the outskirts of the inner circle that she was so obviously desperate to be a part of. However, the more Fiona got to know the unprepossessing woman with her unflattering lopsided hairdo, the less she had taken to her. There was a marked spikiness to her personality, and she seemed to delight in making indiscreet spiteful comments such as the one she had just made about Robert.

There was plenty of time before lunch for everyone to have a look around the centre when they arrived at the battlefield site.

'There is an audio-visual show which tells you all about the battle itself and for those of you who are feeling are little more energetic, you might like to climb up to the top of the Lion Mound.'

'Up there! You have to be joking.' Jeffrey Prior gave her a look of mock horror and to judge by the number of groans, a good number of her passengers felt the same way.

'It really isn't as bad as it looks and there are steps all the way up,' Fiona assured them all with a beaming smile. 'The view from the top is well worth it. You can see the whole layout of the battlefield and there is a plan up there to help you work it all out.'

'I'm game. Anyone else?' said Austin. He was joined by Simon, Philippa, Dee and after a moment's hesitation, a reluctant-looking Hazel.

The highlight of the day would be the tour around the site in a four-wheel drive truck. Fiona left them all to their own devices and joined the lengthy queue to get their tickets for the battlefield tour.

When she emerged back outside, she decided to join one of the small groups sitting at one of the outside café tables drinking coffee.

'Dreadful news about poor Robert isn't it?' Despite her words, Fiona could detect no remorse in Gina Lithgow's voice. If anything, she looked and sounded quite pleased at the prospect.

'I still can't take it in,' Peggy said, her numerous chins wobbling as she shook her head. 'Poor Janice must be in pieces.'

'It must be a dreadful shock of course,' Gina leaned across the table and pulled the pot of sugar sachets towards her. 'But you have to admit, she'll be a lot better off.'

Peggy glared at her. 'What do you mean?'

'Well, let's face it.' Gina shrugged her shoulders. 'Robert can't have been an easy man to live with. I heard she took out a hefty life insurance on him. Plus, given the way he died, if she plays her cards right, she might even get a substantial compensation.'

If she read the stunned reaction on the faces of her two listeners, Gina didn't show it. She continued to pick through the sugar sachets to find a sweetener and then proceeded to tear off the top and empty it into her cup.

'Of course, it does mean that Simon will be the new chairman,' she continued as she stirred her coffee, a smug smile on her face. 'There's a committee meeting tonight, but it's only a formality. There isn't anyone else who could do it.'

'I'm sure he'll make a very good chairman.' The sarcasm in Peggy's voice appeared to go straight over Gina's head.

'I wonder if that means we'll get an invite to one of Philippa's famous dinner parties. I know Robert was always invited. I've always wanted to see inside their house. It looks so elegant from the outside. Probably not.' She gave a deep sigh. 'I don't suppose she considers me good enough for her posh friends.'

'I don't think you're missing a great deal. They're usually quite dull these days.'

'But I've heard she invites all these minor celebrities. Have you ever met any of them?' Gina was agog.

Peggy gave a deep sigh. 'They're not actors or singers. Not anyone you or I are likely to have heard of. The majority of them are captains of industry or business magnates plus the odd MP now and again. They're mostly friends of her father. He's the CEO or the Executive Director, whatever they call them, of some big insurance company in the City. Unless you find current economic trends and business legislation riveting, the evenings can be quite tedious. I'll admit the food is always fantastic, Philippa has this marvellous cook she brings in from Orpington. I keep trying to make up some excuse not to go, but it's difficult to say no. I know Philippa likes me there to make up the numbers, especially as there are usually so few women at the table. She says if I didn't go, she'd have no one to talk to and that she needs someone to inject a bit of sanity into the proceedings.'

'How disappointing. I thought her little soirees were supposed to be wonderful with all the great and the good of Swanley society attending.' It was all too obvious just how much Gina hankered to be included. As far as she was concerned, an invitation to one of the Western's dinner parties was something of a status symbol.

'I don't know about that,' Peggy snorted. 'They were great fun once upon a time, but as I say, the last one I went to was more of a business meeting than a social affair. Very dull. The men kept talking about business economics and the need for new policies all through the meal. It was a relief to escape into the other room for coffee and leave them all to it.'

'How quaint.' Gina's brittle laugh aroused a few glances from the neighbouring tables. 'I thought all that ladies leaving the men to their port and cigars went out with the ark. Besides, whoever bothers about even numbers at table these days?'

'It wasn't like that,' Peggy snapped. 'There were only three of us women out of the eight and it was only Robert and a couple of others who stayed behind. He wanted to talk politics with Jeremy Dyne and Sir Terence Mayhew. They're both very influential in the local Conservative Party. As I understand it, Sir Terence is a family friend of Philippa's parents and Robert persuaded her to invite them. Robert is . . . was keen to get himself nominated as the party candidate in the next election.'

'It's almost time for me to start collecting people up for lunch,' Fiona said, feeling the need to break the tension.

'Then if you'll excuse me, I must take myself off to the ladies.' Evidently glad of an excuse to leave, Peggy reached for her walking stick, heaved herself onto her feet and waddled away leaving Gina and Fiona to each other's company.

'Oh dear, I do hope I haven't upset her.' Gina did not look in the least contrite. 'Peggy is so protective of Philippa.'

'Does Mrs Western need protecting? She seems a strong personality to me.'

Gina gave a mirthless laugh. 'Peggy does fuss so. Philippa had a nasty accident a few weeks ago. She pranged her precious MG on the way home from her father's house in the country. Drove it straight into a tree. The car was a write-off.'

'My goodness. Was she hurt?'

'Broke a couple of ribs and got a few cuts and bruises on her right arm. Haven't you noticed she always wears a long-sleeved blouse to cover them up? They did keep her in hospital for a few days with concussion.'

'That sounds serious.'

Gina shrugged. 'I don't think it was really that bad. She was in a private ward of course, so they were in no hurry to push her out because they needed the bed. Her father is a millionaire, you know. Dotes on his dear daughter. Nothing but the best for our Philippa. Designer clothes and jewellery, you wouldn't believe. He bought her the sports car.'

'Very nice too.'

'Exactly. Though,' she leaned across the table towards Fiona and whispered, 'I heard the reason she smashed the car was because she and her father had had this flaming row. She stormed out of the house and was so upset that she wasn't concentrating on her driving.'

Gina was rapidly becoming as big a gossip as Eleanor.

People were beginning to gather. Time to join the others.

Ferguson tapped on the door of the small room at the end of the corridor by the staircase which Salmon had appropriated as his office and walked straight in.

'Good news,' he said before the Chief could object to him not waiting for a reply. 'Just been on the phone to Inspector Peeters. I put the word out round the local stations this morning, and apparently two of the banner-waving mob who were with our friend Müller were taken in for questioning before the rally broke up. They were interviewed individually and they both claimed that heckling Moorhouse was all Müller's idea. He was the one who orchestrated the whole little charade. Moorhouse was just another speaker as far as they were concerned. They knew nothing about him. Müller claimed he was a traitor to the cause and they just went along with it.'

'Did Müller explain why he thought Moorhouse was a traitor?'

'Apparently not. I spoke to the officer who interviewed them both, and in his opinion, they were bullyboys more interested in causing disruption than committed believers in the Blockupy cause so I suppose they didn't need a reason to target Moorhouse. Any excuse to cause mayhem.'

Salmon chewed on the end of his pencil, digesting the information. 'Did they know where Müller could have gone to ground?'

'According to them, the whole group were planning to go straight back after the rally finished to the hostel where they'd been staying. Someone has been sent to investigate the address.'

'Why wasn't it done at the time?'

Ferguson sighed. 'There were four officers trying to process over fifty people brought into that station alone. We're bloody lucky they bothered to take all the details. The poor devils were still at it in the early hours of the morning.'

'I suppose so,' Salmon conceded, 'but I want those two questioned again.'

'It's already in hand. As soon as they've been located, I'll speak to them myself.'

Without waiting for a reply, Ferguson left.

The gentle breeze had graduated to a chill wind and the dark clouds were scudding across the sky as Fiona emerged with the last of the stragglers from the Panorama, the large rotunda that housed a great wrap-around painting of the battle.

'That was so much better than I expected. I know you said it was a giant circular fresco and all that, but surrounding all the models, it felt like you were right there in middle of the action. A perfect end to a really great day. Thank you, Fiona.' Simon gave her a beaming smile.

'I'm glad you enjoyed it. As it wasn't part of the Association's original Fine Art itinerary, I wasn't sure if it would suit your members.'

He leaned down towards her as they walked towards the Visitor's Centre and said in a loud whisper, 'Between you and me, you can have too much of a good thing. All this academic approach can get a bit too precious. It's not supposed to be a degree course for heaven's sake, and it's nice to sit back and enjoy it.'

To judge by the nods and grins of those who had overheard, he was not alone.

'I think I liked the truck ride best. That was fun.' Charlotte Appleby pulled back the lock of hair sweeping across her face and tucked it behind her ear. 'I hadn't realised Waterloo was such a small town, but have you noticed there is nothing here at the battle site about Wellington? There's lots about

Napoleon, including a great big statue.'

'Perhaps someone should tell the French, he came second,' said Simon.

Fiona joined in the general laughter. She was just about to usher everyone back to the coach when her phone rang.

'Hello.'

'It's Peter. I promised to take you to dinner one evening. Can you be spared tonight?'

'Um.' As a mark of respect for Robert Heppell, the evening's talk had been cancelled and to judge from the comments she'd overheard throughout the day, the majority of the group had decided to take the opportunity to explore the nightlife of Brussels. There was nothing to keep her at the hotel. 'Yes, why not. That would be very pleasant. Thank you. Although…'

'Yes?'

'Did you have anywhere particular in mind?' She had limited her wardrobe to smart casual; nothing suitable to wear in some formal gourmet restaurant where he might be more used to dining.

'No. You tell me where you would like to eat.'

'How about somewhere in one of those streets just off the Grand Place with all the fruit and fish piled up in the stalls outside? I know it's crowded, and the good food guides dismiss the restaurants as touristy, but the displays are so colourful and the place has such a lively atmosphere, I think it might be fun.'

He laughed. 'Why not? I will pick you up at your hotel at seven-thirty. Would that be convenient?'

'I'll look forward to it.'

It was impossible not to feel a touch apprehensive as she slipped her mobile back into her bag. Had she done the right thing? Their previous encounters in Holland and in Germany had not always run smoothly, to put it mildly. At times, they'd been downright stormy, and she would willingly have thrown something at him, he had made her so angry. Nonetheless, it could not be denied that he was a strikingly good-looking man. He had a Mr Darcy quality. At times, he might appear remote and aloof, even condescending, but he possessed an attraction she found hard to explain. At least she'd be meeting him in more neutral territory. Much more in her comfort zone than his.

Chapter 12

'There's a call for you on line two, sir. A Dr. Dubois from the mortuary.'

He picked up the phone. 'Montgomery-Jones.'

'You asked me to inform you of the results of the autopsy of Robert Heppell. The cause of death was unquestionably the blow to the back of the head. It was delivered with considerable force by a heavy object. Not a hammer, something larger with an off-centre point. The corner of a brick maybe. I've sent particles taken from his hair for analysis. The results should be through tomorrow morning, but I am confident that they will confirm my findings.'

'Thank you for informing me so promptly. It is much appreciated.'

Montgomery-Jones put down the receiver, looking thoughtful. After a moment or two, he got up, walked over to the small inner office, and knocked on the door. Barely waiting for a reply, he pushed it open and went in.

Salmon looked up from his desk.

'I have just received information that may or may not be relevant to Moorhouse's assassination.'

It was a warm evening as they strolled through the Grand Place on their way to the restaurant.

'What with eating at the hotel and the lectures every evening, I've not had a chance to see the city centre all lit up at night. It's impressive in the daytime, but now, even with the crowds milling around it has an almost magical quality.'

'It does have a fairy tale quality to it.'

'Mr Montgomery-Jones! Don't tell me you're a romantic at heart?'

'Never let it be said!'

They walked down la petite rue des Bouchers and managed to find a table for two out on the pavement alongside a window box of small green shrubs which marked the boundary with the adjacent café. As he had left the choice of restaurant to her, she asked him to decide on the menu. Over a simple salad starter followed by moules marinière, they discovered a mutual interest in Mozart operas and more surprisingly, in choral music. Throughout the long years of her late husband, Bill's gradual decline during which she had become more and more tied to the house, her one evening a week at choir practice had been essential for keeping her sanity. Living in central London, Peter Montgomery-Jones had a wider choice and had chosen to join a baroque choir.

After she had scraped the last of the chocolate sauce from the edge of her plate, she sat back with a contented sigh.

'That was superb. My family claim that I make a mean chocolate torte, but I have to admit, this was excellent.'

'Coffee? Or would you prefer more wine?'

They drank their coffee, watching the world go by. Lights twinkled everywhere making the street almost as bright as in daylight.

'The whole meal was delicious, thank you, Peter. When do you return to London? I thought you were supposed to be going back after the weekend?'

'That was the original idea, but the events at the Anti-Austerity Rally have altered matters somewhat.'

'But didn't you say that someone else had been sent to head up the enquiry into Tom Moorhouse's assassination?'

'Indeed they have. However, there have been some unexpected developments which may or may not be connected with the case that I would like to follow up personally.'

'Do you mean because of Robert Heppell?'

His eyes widened and he said sharply, 'Why did you ask that?'

'Because he and Moorhouse knew each other.'

'What!' he said sharply, his cup hovered halfway to his lips.

'Moorhouse came to support a big Swanley Association campaign to save a special school. I'm not sure if it was Robert who actually invited him, but I understand they worked together on it. I assumed you knew. I thought that was why you were at the hospital.'

'No.' He shook his head, then hesitated for what seemed an age. 'I am breaching every protocol by mentioning it, so this is strictly between the two of us, however, there is something that I feel you should know.'

'That sounds ominous.'

'Heppell's death was not the result of an accident; his injuries were deliberately inflicted.'

'That's ridiculous.' Fiona put down her cup. 'Who on earth would want to kill Robert?'

'That is what we need to discover. The police will want to talk to you again and also to the rest of your passengers.'

Fiona's jaw tightened. 'I should have realised your invitation had an ulterior motive.'

'Emphatically not. I only received confirmation late this afternoon, long after I telephoned you.'

She glared at him. 'Confirmation possibly, but no doubt you were suspicious about his accident from the beginning.' His silence confirmed it. 'That's what this evening was all about. To soften me up with a nice meal in pleasant surroundings, then pump me with all sorts of questions to help with your investigation.'

'Fiona,' his voice had taken on that cool reasonableness that so frustrated her. 'I cannot deny I was already aware that Heppell's injuries may not have been accidental, but I do assure you that was not my motive for inviting you for dinner this evening. You were the one who brought Heppell's name into the conversation.'

'Am I going to find that the police are already making enquiries when I get back. No doubt the hotel management will be delighted at the prospect!'

Peter ignored her sarcasm. 'They are highly unlikely to send uniformed officers and they will be very discreet. Though I would imagine there is little chance you will see them until the results of all the forensic tests are available.'

'And what grounds can the police have to think one of my passengers was involved?'

'That is not what I am saying. First and foremost, they will want to build up a picture of Heppell and try to establish if he had enemies or if it was a random killing exactly as they would in any other murder investigation.'

'And no doubt, you will be involved?'

'I cannot interfere in a police case, but I admit, I do have an interest.'

'Which proves my point. You want me to be a spy in the camp.'

His jaw visibly tightened, and his voice took on the cold, detached official tone she knew of old and that never failed to arouse intense feelings of rebellion in her. 'I have *never* tried to involve you in any of my investigations. As I recall, I have tried very hard to ensure that you were not involved. I have urged you, countless times, to leave any investigations to those whose job it is to do so. You are the one who has always insisted on worming your way in, causing me all sorts of problems I might add. . .'

'If it were not for me, you would never have caught your smuggler or identified your terrorist,' she snapped.

'Your contribution has been invaluable, that I do not deny, but on the first occasion you very nearly got yourself shot and you also managed to put yourself in danger in Germany. Believe me, my main concern is for your safety.'

'Why am I here now if you don't intend to grill me about

what I've discovered about my passengers?'

He gave an exasperated shake of the head. 'My invitation was purely based on a wish to spend a pleasant evening dining together. Whether the police will want to talk to you, I cannot say. With the local force fully stretched dealing with the aftermath of Saturday's events, I imagine they will bring in a senior officer from an outside force to head up the investigation and it will be up to him to decide who to question.'

He picked up the bottle of wine, but when he went to top up her glass, she put her hand over the rim.

'No more for me. I have a busy day tomorrow.'

He splashed the rest of the wine into his own glass and upended the bottle in the ice bucket.

They sat in silence for a moment or two.

She was the one to break it. 'I wonder if Janice knows yet. The poor woman. As if things weren't bad enough already. Thank goodness she has her daughters with her.'

'I am sure she has been informed. The police always move quickly to ensure that the family do not learn what has happened from the media or any other source.'

'And to question her no doubt. Isn't the spouse usually the prime suspect?'

Gina's idle gossip about a recently purchased hefty life insurance sprang to Fiona's mind. Not that she had any intention of telling Peter Montgomery-Jones.

'You do know that Janice isn't staying with the rest of the party anymore?' she asked.

'I understand that all the rooms were booked in your hotel and she has moved to be with the rest of her family.'

'I suppose that's as good a reason as any, but if I were in her shoes, I don't think I would want to keep bumping into people coming up to give me their condolences the whole time.'

He gave a soft laugh. 'There is that of course.'

Day 5 Tuesday, Brussels

The Musées Royaux des Beaux-Arts house one of Belgium's premier art collections which includes 'The Assumption of the Virgin' by Pieter Paul Rubens, 'The Census at Bethlehem' by Pieter Brueghel the Younger and Hugo van der Goes' 'Madonna and Saint Anne'. After the guided tour, those who wish are welcome to remain to explore the vast collection still further or to join in a guided walk of the Royal Quarter.

The highlight of our afternoon tour will be a visit to the more intimate Horta Museum, home of the renowned Architect Victor Horta, father of Art Nouveau. His equal talent as an interior designer is magnificently reflected in the sweeping curves of its airy interior making full use of his trademark iron and glass elements.

Super Sun Executive Travel

Chapter 13

Fiona could hear the shouting even as she emerged from the Terrace Café after breakfast. She skirted round into the main body of the foyer and saw Bernard Western banging his fist on the desk. She couldn't hear exactly what he was saying to the stunned looking receptionist, but the normally mild, softly spoken man was clearly fuming.

Matters must be serious to rouse him to such a state. The redness infusing his cheeks was rapidly spreading to his balding pate. Any more of this and the man would have a heart attack.

'I cannot explain it, sir,' said the girl receiving the full blast of his fury.

'What appears to be the problem?'

'There's no "appear" about it!' Bernard turned on Fiona, eyes blazing. 'We hardly got a wink of sleep last night. Three times in the middle of the night that dammed phone woke us up. As soon as Philippa picked it up, the thing rang off. We tried leaving off the receiver but after five minutes, it made this dreadful noise. In the end, we had to drag Philippa's bed from the wall so I could crawl behind and pull the wire from its socket.'

'I'll send someone to check it straight away, sir,' said the woman behind the desk.

'You'll do no such thing,' Bernard snapped. 'My wife is still trying to get some sleep. As if that wasn't enough, poor Philippa was sick last night as well. Obviously, something she ate at dinner last night. I demand to speak to the manager right now.'

The receptionist hesitated only a second before picking up the phone.

'He'll be with you shortly, sir. If you'd like to take a seat . . .'

'I'm staying right here.' He gave another hefty thump on the desk bouncing the clutter sitting on it.

Fiona hovered, uncertainly. This was obviously not the time to ask if the couple would be joining the rest of the party for the day.

The manager appeared from a door behind the desk.

'This is the gentleman, sir.' The girl waved a hand in Bernard's direction and promptly disappeared to the far end of the desk.

The manager invited Bernard to his office leaving Fiona free to retreat back to her room.

The videoconference was in full swing. Salmon slapped his pen down on the desk and said portentously, 'Moorhouse ruffled a great many feathers in a vast number of places. We've spent a great deal of time looking at individuals who might have a strong personal motive for wanting him out of the way, but how are investigations into the political angle going?'

'As we established at the outset, the man has enemies everywhere, but it's proving difficult to unearth anything specific that might lead to actual murder,' Martin Cumming admitted. 'As we discussed at the very beginning of this enquiry, he wasn't flavour of the month with any of the parties or particular factions. One area we are looking into, however, is the hard-line group who are worried that the government may bow to rising pressure to increase taxes. The public support for the Anti-Austerity lobby's demand to raise the minimum wage, increase benefits for the low-paid and those on social security is growing steadily. Most of that is the result of the near hysteria Moorhouse managed to whip up during his frequent rants on the media. The hard-liners are worried that if the Government concede even halfway to those pressures, the only way they can pay for them is to increase taxes for the better paid. They have already pushed the boundaries to breaking point for middle-income earners and if they try to squeeze them any further, they are going to lose crucial votes in large swathes of the traditional Tory voters.'

'Does that group include the MP married to the woman with whom Moorhouse had an affair?' asked Montgomery-Jones.

Cumming nodded. 'Neville Truelove isn't what you might call one of the main lobbyists, but he has made his views pretty clear behind the scenes, so we are keeping an eye on him.'

'Good, good. Now can we move on?' said Salmon crossly.

Unperturbed, Cumming continued, 'It's difficult to see how any of the Old Guard could possibly be connected to Moorcroft's murder, but we have been looking into their associates. There are a considerable number of wealthy businessmen who might have a great deal to lose if the government introduce more stringent measures to examine their exact tax status. They are prepared to pay a high price to influence legislation in their favour. We have come up with a selection of names you might wish us to investigate further, which I will send you now if you wish, but I must emphasise all we have are vague hints and suggestions and nothing that might be considered in any way conclusive.'

'Is it worth the effort?' Ferguson was scathing. 'Removing Moorhouse is hardly going to make a significant difference. Moorhouse may have been adept at whipping up public opinion, but the calls to ease the burdens of the poorest in society are hardy going to melt away without him. Wouldn't your time be better spent investigating other avenues?'

'Agreed,' snapped Salmon. 'What other lines of enquiry are

you looking into? What about these Press reports of Moorhouse being seen talking with several of the Eurosceptic groups in the European Parliament last week? He had become the public face of the British Anti-Austerity Alliance. Any suggestion of him fraternising with the enemy so to speak must have upset several of their socialist elite. Many of them have been quite vocal about him ruining the group's reputation. As far as a good many of them are concerned, UKIP is only a hair's breadth away from the BNP [British National Party] and the other extreme Right-Wing factions. Although many of the rank and file who support the Alliance would dearly love to see curbs on the EU rights of East European workers to come in to take their jobs; the last thing the Alliance needs right now is to start haemorrhaging its more liberally minded paid-up members who are keen to protect the rights of all low-paid workers regardless of colour, creed or sexual orientation. Without the financial backing of wealthy supporters, the group needs every penny it can get. Is there any word that it's caused any rift between Moorhouse and any of the Anti-Austerity organisers?'

'I'm afraid not, sir. Most of those who rushed to disassociate themselves from Moorhouse when the photos first appeared seem to have been appeased when the full story came out.'

'You're saying we've got nothing,' Salmon snapped.

'We have ruled out several of the initial suspects, but our enquiries are ongoing, sir. We are still tracking all the electronic communications of each of our key suspects, but so far nothing useful has emerged.'

'Any luck running down the nephew of the ousted Union boss, the ex-army sniper?' asked Ferguson.

'Reece Bradshaw.'

'That's the one. Mentally unstable, with an axe to grind supposedly on some jolly jaunt communing with nature all on his tod. My money's still on him.' Ferguson lay back in his chair, hands behind his head.

Cumming tried to hide a smile. Whether it was at Ferguson's lack of decorum or at Salmon's obvious offended reaction to such unprofessionalism, it was impossible to tell.

'It would seem Bradshaw hasn't used his mobile since he left for Scotland. We know he used a credit card to buy a train ticket at Doncaster for Inverness six days ago, but it hasn't been used since.'

'But no proof he actually made the journey?'

'Not as yet.'

'Then keep pushing. The man can't simply disappear.' Salmon picked up his papers and shuffled through them.

'If we have to rule out the man's known enemies,' Montgomery-Jones's measured tones injected some calm into the increasingly fraught atmosphere. 'Perhaps we should take a look at his friends.'

'What the hell does that mean?' Salmon demanded.

'Simply that because Moorhouse was an MP, it does not follow that we are dealing with a political killing. In any case, it might be expedient to talk to those who knew him best. The information that we have so far is almost exclusively a matter of public record. Close family and friends might give us a very different picture.'

'His immediate family have been questioned, sir.'

'I am sure they have, Cumming. But we already know the man had friends in unexpected places. During his days in the Treasury he made very close ties with certain captains of industry to their mutual advantage. We know that Moorhouse eased the passage of certain measures that were likely to prove financially lucrative for his newfound friends. It may have been some time ago now, but he may have maintained contact.'

'I'll get someone onto it straight away, sir.'

'Good idea,' Salmon said quickly, trying to take back control. 'In fact, you can put a team onto it.'

As they waited for Cumming to make a note, Montgomery-

Jones said, 'Would you send over everything you have on Moorhouse's involvement in the Swanley Association's campaign to save a school and his links with Robert Heppell?'

'For goodness sake, Peter.' Salmon was exasperated. 'You're not still obsessed with the idea that there's some connection between the two deaths? Moorhouse's shooter is hardly likely to have stopped off and gone looking for a tourist when he's on the run.'

'I agree that it is highly unlikely that the same individual killed both men, however, with two murders within a mile of each other and within a short time, any possible link has to be thoroughly investigated.'

'I will get back to you, sir,' Cumming interrupted.

With that, the screen went dead. If Salmon had any intention of countermanding Montgomery-Jones's request, he had missed the opportunity.

Fiona was making a quick count as everyone collected in the foyer ready for the morning tour. Peggy emerged from the lift and came over.

'Just to let you know Felix asked me to say he won't be joining us first thing. He hopes to meet up with us later.'

'He's not ill, is he?'

Felix Navarre was one of the more reserved members of the Association and Fiona had not had more than the odd word with him. She could not recall if she had seen him at breakfast. As it was an informal meal, people tended to come and go and it was easy to miss those who came down later.

'Oh no, dear. He's fine. He's gone to talk to Janice. He didn't like to intrude on the family before.'

'Oh?'

Prompted by the puzzled frown on Fiona's face, Peggy explained, 'You won't know of course, Felix is Janice's lawyer. He won't have a copy of Robert's will with him obviously, although I fancy Janice and the family know what's in it anyway, but he will help her cope with all the other legal things that have to be done. He wasn't sure how long it will all take, but I've got my mobile with me and he's going to give me a ring when he's finished, so he'll know where to meet up with us again.'

'I see. Thank you for letting me know.'

It was not her place to tell the group the real cause of Robert's death and as far as she knew, no one else was aware of the situation. Would Janice choose to tell Felix? If so, perhaps she should brace herself for the fallout when he returned with the news that Robert had been murdered.

Fiona sighed. It looked like this might turn out to be another difficult day. They would get to know sometime; it was inevitable, but it would be so much better if they were informed officially by the police.

Fiona had arranged for one of the volunteer guides to give the group a tour of the highlights of the vast collection in the Musées Royaux des Beaux-Arts, which she decided was a good thing in more ways than one. It was always a relief not to have the pressure of spending a considerable amount of time reading up on and trying to remember significant facts about major exhibits, never mind locate them in the myriad of galleries, but in addition, today she felt decidedly under par.

She had spent a restless night. It wasn't just the shock of Robert's murder that kept her tossing until the small hours, but her sense of outrage. She felt used. Despite his denials, she was not convinced about Montgomery-Jones's motives the previous evening. She would take some convincing that the only reason he hadn't interrogated her there and then was because he realised there was absolutely no way she was going to let him.

It hadn't helped that he'd given her a lecture when they got back to the hotel. Told her to curb her natural instinct to meddle. To leave all the questioning to the police. He'd even had the cheek to point out that when she had tried to do a little sleuthing in the past, she had ended up putting her own life in danger. After what had happened in Holland, there may have been an element of truth in what he'd said, but though she'd ended up with a grazed cheek when her bag had been stolen on the trip to the Rhine Valley, the only reason he'd found her in tears was because the bag contained her favourite irreplaceable photograph of her dead husband, Bill.

Still, there was little point in letting the man spoil her day and pushing aside all thoughts of Montgomery-Jones, she tried to take in all the enthusiastic guide had to say.

Despite all her attempts, her thoughts kept drifting. In the end, she gave up trying. It still seemed hardly credible that one of the people around her might prove to be a murderer. It was impossible not to view them in a new light. Was it her imagination or did the majority of the Association members seem, if not exactly happier, she tried to think of an appropriate word, at least more relaxed. That was it. As though the absence of Robert Heppell had eased a tension that had pervaded the tour at the start. Philippa had lost the cool spikiness and become positively affable, the McArdles and Austin seemed considerably more at ease and Noel Appleby had come out of his shell altogether. As they moved from room to room, he was chattering away, laughing and joking with those around him in a way Fiona had never seen before. None of this indicated any guilt, but she could not help wondering what had produced such an effect.

The thought kept nagging at her as she followed the group, rounding up the stragglers as they moved from gallery to gallery. What kind of hold did Heppell have over so many of these people? What was it Barbara McArdle had said? Something about him manipulating people. "Ferreting out their weaknesses," that was the expression she'd used. Fiona remembered because it was such a striking thing to say. Was there something more to the relationship between Philippa and Austin that Robert had discovered and that he had threatened to tell Bernard? It was conceivable, but what possible hold could he have over the pleasant, affable Noel?

Perhaps she should not have been surprised that at the end of the tour, after they had thanked their guide and Fiona had discreetly handed over the sizable tip, the whole group followed her to the exit. After the fuss Robert had made on the first evening, she expected at least some of the group to opt out of the walk and take the opportunity to spend more time in the museum.

'Excuse me, sir.'

Montgomery-Jones looked up at the apprehensive young woman hovering in front of his desk. Emily was one of the junior members of the Brussels Station staff to whom the more routine duties were assigned. He gave her a reassuring smile.

'You asked me to look through the CCTV footage of the area to the west of Leopold Park after the shooting.'

'Indeed. Did you manage to find anyone resembling Heppell?'

'I'm afraid not, sir. Even with his distinctive beard, it's virtually impossible to recognise faces in the crowds running through the streets and the descriptions of the clothes he was wearing, cream short-sleeved shirt and dark blue slacks, match a large proportion of the men in his age group.'

'Not to worry. It was only a remote possibility. Thank you for trying, Emily.'

As the day wore on, Fiona's headache was getting steadily worse. Though still acutely aware of her lack of experience in the job, she kept reminding herself she was hardly a raw recruit. She no longer felt the sheer panic of having to gather up her party at a prearranged meeting place in a large city centre. With Winston's constant reassurance that it was her passengers' responsibility to ensure they were in the right place at the right time and not hers, she now took such things, if not exactly in her stride, with only a slight sense of trepidation.

Jeffrey and Eleanor Prior were the last to appear after the break for lunch. They had been waiting in the wrong place, but quickly realised their mistake when no one else arrived.

At the appointed time, there was no sign of the distinctive white coach with its yellow undulating wave down the side. Traffic in the busy centre was always unpredictable and it wouldn't come any quicker if she allowed herself to get agitated, Fiona told herself firmly.

She turned to find Felix Navarre, now back with the group, who was standing a few feet away talking with the Rev. McArdle and his wife.

'How is Janice? Is there anything we can do to help?' she asked him.

'As I was just saying to Barbara, she's getting plenty of support from her family and the authorities, plus your company's head office. Mind you, she is a strong lady and holding it together very well. She's coping far better than I expected.'

'Good,' Fiona said doubtfully. 'I'm sure she is. On the surface, anyway. There is a fair amount for her to do at present, and she needs to keep going for her family's sake. It's when she gets back home and it hits her fully, that she's going to need her friends around her.'

Felix turned and looked at her, a slight frown creasing his forehead.

'I lost my own husband not long ago,' she said by way of explanation and turned to see the coach pulling up alongside her. 'Even if you have had plenty of time to prepare yourself, the full impact of losing your life partner doesn't hit you for quite a while.'

Felix patted her arm. 'That is so true. My wife died a couple of years ago, so I do understand.'

She must be more tired than she realised. Normally, she made a point of not telling her passengers about her private life and wasn't sure why she'd done so now. Perhaps it was the relief that Felix appeared still unaware of Robert's murder and she was spared the resulting emotional turmoil amongst the party if he had brought back the news. Though how long it would be before they did get to hear and start panicking about murderers being on the loose was anyone's guess.

The Horta House exceeded Fiona's expectation. Several of the party lingered on the spectacular spiral stairway admiring the elegant iron balustrade or examining the detail in the matching curves painted on the walls. Others were wandering from room to room on the top floor. Fiona was about to enter one of the smaller bedrooms at the back of the house when she heard someone talking inside.

'They say she only married him for his money. He had some high-powered job in the city, made a packet on the investment markets apparently. Worth a fortune,' Eleanor Prior's stage whisper was easily recognisable.

'Oh?' There was no enthusiasm for more detail in the voice of her listener.

'Well it can't have been for his looks, now can it?' Eleanor gave an unpleasant laugh. 'Mind you, I'd say, having to live with that overbearing monster all those years, the woman deserves every penny she gets. She's well shot of him.'

It wasn't Philippa and Bernard Western they were talking about, but the Heppells. Fiona was still hovering, wondering whether to creep quietly away or walk in when Liz Kennedy emerged. Catching sight of Fiona, she gave a weak grin, clearly embarrassed at being overheard in a conversation that she had not engineered and had clearly found uncomfortable.

If the rumour was true, it might give Janice a motive for murder, but how much of what she'd said had Eleanor made up or possibly misinterpreted from some throwaway remark by one of the Association members?

Chapter 14

Salmon opened the door of the general office and looked around, a disgruntled look on his round moon face.

'Anyone seen Ferguson?'

Montgomery-Jones looked up from his desk. 'I believe he has gone to the hostel to interview the warden about Müller and his two associates.'

'Tell him I want to see him as soon as he gets in.'

Without waiting for a reply, Salmon was gone.

'Yes, Mein Fuhrer!' came a soft voice from the corner.

Montgomery-Jones turned and raised an eyebrow at the young woman standing at the photocopier.

Emily shrugged her shoulders. 'Well, he didn't even have the good manners to say please.'

It seemed that Ferguson was not the only one tested by Salmon's leadership style.

Some twenty minutes later came the sound of heavy footsteps climbing the stairs. The door was pushed open and Ferguson stood pulling down the knot in his tie and undoing the top button of his shirt.

'Those stairs will be the death of me.'

'His Lordship's looking for you,' Emily informed him.

'For pity's sake! Let me take my coat off first.' He pulled out his chair, shrugged out of his suit jacket to reveal large dark patches beneath the armpits, hung it over the back and sat down. 'He can wait five minutes while I get my breath back. Boy, it's hot out there!'

Emily was already halfway to the door on her way back down to the main office on the second floor when he said, 'You wouldn't be a darling and get me a cup of coffee would you, Em?'

'What did your last slave die of?'

He gave her his most engaging helpless schoolboy smile. 'Pretty please.'

She gave a tinkling laugh. 'Okay boss, but just don't let Mr Salmon catch you or I'll be in trouble too for not passing on the message. Would you like one too, sir?'

'Please, Emily. That would be very kind,' said Montgomery-Jones.

As Emily disappeared into the small kitchen, Ferguson flopped back in the chair and stretched out his legs. He slowly shook his head and raised his eyes heavenwards in mock exasperation. 'That man! I'd hardly had time to walk through the door this morning when he was chasing me up to hear if I'd heard any more about the whereabouts of Müller's two associates. I told him yesterday I'd let him know as soon as.'

'I take it the police have not yet managed to track them down again?' asked Montgomery-Jones.

'Nope, seems they collected their stuff from the hostel straight after they were released and disappeared off into the night. The German police are checking up on their home addresses, or at least the ones they provided at the time, so it's a waiting game. Seems the rest of Müller's mob had already cleared the decks and hightailed back to Germany. All except Müller himself. According to the warden, he's not been seen since they all left for the rally on Saturday morning. All his stuff is still at the hostel. I texted our great leader as soon as the info came through so why he had his knickers in such a twist this morning is anyone's guess.'

'We have no way of knowing whether Müller himself has decided to return home without stopping to collect his belongings or decided to hole up somewhere close to the city?'

'That's about the size of it. I checked through his belongings. Just a couple of spare shirts, a toothbrush, and a rucksack. Nothing worth putting himself at risk going back for. The warden wasn't able to tell me any more than the police reported back to me last night.'

'A wasted journey, then.'

'I did manage to get a much better description of each of them. Not that the warden could tell me much. Didn't cause any trouble when they were there, but then they didn't have much time anyway. They arrived late the night before and left for the rally first thing after breakfast. I spoke to a couple of English backpackers staying there at the same time, but they couldn't add anything much. Said the group were pleasant enough to the others staying in the place, but they kept pretty much to themselves. Apparently, most of group couldn't speak English anyway, and neither girl spoke German.'

'I'm looking forward to a nice sit-down and a cup of tea,' Peggy confided to Fiona, leaning heavily on her walking stick as they walked into the hotel foyer. 'It was another lovely day, I enjoyed it immensely, but all day on my feet is not good for my old pins.'

Fiona smiled. 'It's surprising just how tired you can get wandering around inside looking at things, isn't it? That's why I always recommend comfortable shoes. It can be quite hard on the back as well in museums when you keep having to lean over to read the inscriptions, though thankfully we didn't have to do much of that today.'

As the last of her passengers disappeared towards the lift, Fiona noticed a tall, balding man in a jacket and tie, clearly not a hotel guest, get up from the banquette and walk towards her.

'Mrs Mason?'

'I am.'

He held out a hand. 'Inspector Dumont of the General

Directorate Judicial Police. May I have a word?'

She knew someone would want to talk to her as soon possible. She did her best to give him a warm smile. 'Of course.'

Whether he sensed her reluctance, or he was considerate by nature, he said quickly. 'Not now. I appreciate you have only just returned. Shall we say fifteen minutes?'

'That would be great.'

She was back down in under ten minutes. He led her to the same room where the two uniformed officers had interviewed her a few days before. So much had happened in the intervening two days, it seemed a long time ago. There was another plain-clothes man already seated at the table. Fiona smiled to see that one of them had thoughtfully ordered a tray of tea. The signs were that this was not going to be a harsh grilling, but as she was all too well aware, looks could be deceiving.

'I appreciate that you have already made a statement earlier in the week, but we still need to uncover as much detail as possible.'

The Inspector gave no hint of how Heppell had met his death. Once again, she went through who was missing from the morning tour, her best approximation of the time they left the Hotel de Ville and she had last seen Robert Heppell and who had been with him. He also wanted to know what she had done from that point onwards and if she could remember seeing any of the group later in the day and where exactly they had been and when.

The whole process took some time, but having been forewarned by Montgomery-Jones, she had given some thought to the matter beforehand and was able to give him a lucid account.

'Thank you very much, Mrs Mason. That is very helpful,' the Inspector said as he slipped his notebook into a document case.

'I presume you will want to talk to other members of the

Swanley Association?' she asked as she stood up.

He glanced at his watch. 'It is getting near your dinner time. Perhaps it would be better to do so after everyone has eaten.'

'I'm not sure if you are aware, but there is a talk immediately after dinner and I imagine most of them would like to attend if that is possible. We could see if any of them have changed early and are having a drink in the bar before dinner, if that would be any help?'

'That would be most kind.'

Fiona was not aware of any heightened tension over dinner and though she did not speak directly to either Simon or Bernard, both of whom she knew had been interviewed earlier, it seemed that everyone was still unaware of Robert's murder. Either they had not been told or the police had asked them not to pass on the information.

Word had spread, however, that the police were asking questions.

'I don't understand why they're making such a fuss now,' muttered Jeffrey Prior. 'It's not as if it's going to change anything, is it? The poor man's dead. None of us were there, so what's the point.'

'Perhaps it's something to do with insurance,' Joan Cahill suggested. 'These companies want all sorts of police reports before they hand over a penny.'

Time to change the subject. Fiona poured herself another glass of water and said, 'Did any of you go to see the façade of the Musical Instruments Museum at lunch time? The one with the "Old England" sign I mentioned that was worth a look if you were interested in Art Deco architecture.'

'Is that the one in the old department store? The one with the iron work and huge windows?' Liz Kennedy seemed just as eager to talk about something more agreeable. 'We didn't go inside as there wasn't time, but the outside was fantastic. Malcolm took several photos, didn't you, darling?'

Fiona was one of the last to leave the room after the talk. Felix was still busy dismantling the laptop from the hotel's projection system and packing it away.

'I'm not sure I knew much about Hans Memling, other than his name, of course,' she said as she helped roll up the extension leads.

'Shall I let you into a secret, neither did I before this talk. A couple of hours reading Wikipedia and downloading a few images into PowerPoint one evening and you can pretend you're an expert.'

'Felix,' she said in mock horror. 'I'm shocked!'

They both laughed.

'I suppose I'd better go and see what these policemen want. There's at least four officers out there, but apparently, the inspector wants to talk to me specifically. Are they interviewing everyone? Do you know what it's all about?'

'He spoke to me when we first got back to the hotel. He wanted to know when I'd last seen Robert.' She deftly avoided a direct answer to his question.

'All a bit rum, don't you think?' He picked up the laptop case. 'I'll just pop this up to my room and I'll join you in a tick.'

When Fiona walked into the lounge bar, she was surprised to see Montgomery-Jones sitting in a corner with a group of half a dozen Association members. She felt her jaw tighten. He'd admitted he had an interest in the case, but he'd given no indication he was involved in the questioning.

'Can I get you a drink, Fiona?' Bernard Western was at the bar.

She went to join him and perched herself on one of the high stools. Not the easiest of tasks for someone who stood only five-foot-three in her stockinged feet. As they chattered about the day's events she couldn't help glancing over his shoulder at Montgomery-Jones who was in her direct line of vision. He didn't exactly look in interviewing mode. He certainly wasn't dressed for the part. It was disconcerting to see him without the habitual three-piece suit. He wasn't even wearing a tie. And he was lounging, the only possible word she could use to describe it. He was leaning back, one arm against the back of the long settee, laughing and joking with everyone. If she hadn't known he was in Brussels, she would have thought he had a double. This was Montgomery-Jones as she had never seen him. Even the previous evening, when he'd been dressed in more casual clothes, he hadn't behaved with such a laid-back nonchalance.

'I can't get over how light and airy it all seemed. The whole house soared to that magnificent glass cupola; don't you think?'

'Sorry, Bernard. I was miles away there. Yes, it was glorious, wasn't it?'

'It was the effect of that central staircase. It dominated the place.'

'Absolutely.'

'Such a pity we had to cancel the talk on Art Deco on Monday evening. I'd have loved to know. . .'

As Bernard continued to wax lyrical about the magic of the Horta House, all Fiona's attention was fixed on Montgomery-Jones. Now the woman was flirting with him. She watched Philippa lean towards him as she sat a few feet away on the settee, looking up at him through those long seductive lashes of hers. She propped herself on an elbow and gently stroked the gold bangles up and down her forearm. And he was lapping it up! Loving every minute. It was a good thing that Bernard had his back to them.

Fiona wanted to scream.

'. . . all right, Fiona?' Bernard was looking at her, expectantly.

'I'm sorry, Bernard. What did you say?'

'I asked how you were feeling. You've gone very pale.'

'To be honest, I do feel a little light-headed. If you'll forgive me, I think I'll take myself off to bed.'

'Are you sure you'll be okay? Would you like me to see you

to your room?'

'I'll be fine, Bernard. I'd rather not make a fuss.'

She slid off the stool and made her way out towards the lifts.

Day 6 Wednesday, Bruges

The historic centre of Bruges is a UNESCO World Heritage Site and with its grandiose gothic architecture, is one of the most perfectly preserved medieval towns in Europe.

Our guided walk will take in the beautifully restored Gothic Stadhuis (town hall); the 13th century Market with its medieval gabled houses; the Holy Blood Basilica; the stunning 83 metre octagonal tower; the13th century Belfry with its carillon of 47 bells and the pretty Begijnhof and the romantic, tree-lined lake of Minneswater. The Gruuthuse Museum is housed in a large 15th-century mansion, once the home of a rich merchant and has an exceptional collection of Old Flemish paintings and impressive range of tapestries and furnishings from the 13th to the 19th centuries.

After a late lunch, join us for a picturesque boat ride along the Reien Canal. In the free time that follows, you may choose to look at the Flemish masterpieces housed in the Groeninge Museum or the Memling Museum in the small chapel of St John's Hospital, which houses six of the greatest works by Hans Memling. Alternatively, you can visit a traditional chocolate maker or the Lace Centre in the northeast of the town.

Super Sun Executive Travel

Chapter 15

For once Salmon was late arriving for the morning meeting.

'Where is our lord and master? He was the one who demanded a breakfast meeting. If he was going to haul us in an hour earlier than usual, the least he could do was be on time.'

Ferguson had already poured himself a cup of coffee and helped himself to two large bacon rolls.

Montgomery-Jones looked at his watch. 'It is only three minutes past seven. He was still on the telephone when I came past his office.'

'Any more info come through on friend Müller and his associates?'

'Not that I have heard. That could well be what Salmon is trying to find out right now.' Montgomery-Jones placed a glass of orange juice and a cup of coffee by his papers on the table and walked over to the windows and opened both sets. 'It is getting warm in here already. I think we are going to need the electric fan.'

The sound of footsteps rapidly ascending the wooden staircase was followed by heavy breathing as Salmon stood in the doorway getting his breath back.

'Sorry to keep you waiting, gentlemen.'

'Allow me to pour you a coffee.'

Salmon threw Montgomery-Jones a grateful nod, made his way over to the table, put down the laptop he had tucked under his arm and sank onto the chair. He waited until

Montgomery-Jones had placed the coffee cup in front of him.

'I've just been speaking to Berlin. There's been nothing from them since they sent the initial report on Monday.' His jaw tightened. 'They say they're still keeping a lookout for Müller, but so far he's not been seen since he left to join the rally at the end of last week.'

Ferguson glanced at Montgomery-Jones and raised his eyes heavenwards as Salmon busied himself setting up the laptop ready for the video conference with London. Cumming was already waiting when the connection was made.

'Our investigations have thrown up a new line of enquiry. Last November, Moorhouse was involved in some investment scandal involving some East European farming scheme. I won't go through the details, but they are in your notes. He invested a great deal of his own money into the project whilst it was still in its infancy and persuaded several people to do the same. The expectation was that the whole thing would take off once the scheme was awarded EU funding. At the time, the bid looked certain to go ahead, but at the last minute the whole thing was turned down. The problem was Moorhouse got wind of what was happening and withdrew his investment just days before the collapse.'

'Presumably, he failed to inform his fellow investors.'

'A great many of them certainly. Several of those he had personally recruited lost a great deal of money. We are still in the process of making enquiries about four of them.' A composite picture of four photographs came up on the screen. 'Sidney Hamilton, top left, a retired city banker now living in Doncaster; Edmund Pearce, top right, who runs a national logistics business with headquarters in Sheffield; Finley Simons, bottom left, who owns a chain of golf clubs and fitness clubs mostly in the South Yorkshire area and finally Oliver Rushton from Rotherham, owner of a long-established family-run bakery chain.'

'Hamilton and Rushton are clearly too old and the wrong

build to fit the description of the actual shooter. I suppose an ex-city banker might have the wherewithal to hire a hit man although it would have to be a huge concern for a family bakery chain to have provided sufficient funds for Rushton to raise that much cash. What do we know about the other two?' Salmon said.

'This is where it gets interesting. They are both members of the same shooting club. Simons doesn't own it, but he does have shares in the company. He claims to have spent most of last Saturday on the golf course with a friend whom we haven't yet been able to talk to; he left for a holiday in the Seychelles the next day. We have confirmed that Simons had dinner with a lady friend that evening, but he could have easily driven back from Brussels in time to keep that arrangement. Pearce is very much a hands-on man and claims when one of his men called in sick first thing on Saturday morning, he decided to drive the lorry himself. The delivery definitely took place and there is paperwork to back up his story, but Pearce is a slippery character. South Yorkshire police suspect him of using illegal immigrants as drivers and he could easily have arranged for one of them to have done the job, providing Pearce with an alibi. He didn't lose the most money on the East European investment, that was Hamilton, but he was the one who could least afford it.'

'I suppose it would be too much to hope that our cuckolded MP was an investor?' asked Ferguson.

Cumming smiled. 'Truelove. Actually, he was. Only a modest one admittedly. However, he was one of those who managed to pull out before the crash. Somewhat late in the day admittedly and he certainly didn't make a killing, but he didn't lose his original investment either. Not much of a motive there, I'm afraid.'

The meeting went on for another few minutes before Salmon called it to a close.

As usual, Winston was already halfway through breakfast by

the time Fiona arrived in the almost deserted Terrace Café soon after seven o'clock.

'You look rough this morning, sweetheart. You going down with that chap's cold?'

'I didn't sleep too well, that's all.' That was putting it mildly. After a second restless night, she'd woken on the alarm with a dull headache. This obsession with Peter Montgomery-Jones was not good for her mental state and it wasn't doing her physical health much good either. 'I'll be fine once I've had a cup of tea and woken up properly.'

'Don't suppose this early start helps much either.' He poured out a cup of tea for her as she slipped onto the chair next to him.

'You can say that again, but there is so much to cram into this morning, the earlier we can get to Bruges the better.'

'On the bright side, leaving this early does mean we should be out of the city before the rush hour gets underway. That ring road gets pretty busy at the best of times. There's roadworks on the A10 west of Ghent, but no reports of any major problems this morning, so fingers crossed, everything should run to schedule.'

'Winston, before you go,' Fiona glanced round to ensure no one else was in earshot. 'I think I should tell you some rather disturbing news. You know the passenger who died the other day.'

'Trampled in the stampede, weren't he?'

'That's just it. I was told last night that it wasn't an accident. Mr Heppell was murdered.'

As she had anticipated, the wonderfully unflappable West Indian took it in his stride. He must be getting used to this habit she seemed to be developing of having her passengers meet violent ends.

'Have they caught the man what done it?'

'That's just it, no. And what's more, they don't seem to have any idea who might be responsible. That's why I wanted you to know. But I don't intend to inform the rest of the party.'

'No point in causing more upset,' he agreed.

'I expect they'll find out eventually one way or another.'

'You think one of them did it?'

'I have no idea. Mr Montgomery-Jones and the local police assured me they don't think any of us are in any danger, so whether that means they have a suspect already in custody, your guess is as good as mine.'

'He wasn't exactly Mr Popularity, was he? Surprised me the rest of that Swanley lot agreed to come on holiday with him in the first place.' He piled his dirty plates together, screwed up his paper serviette and dropped it on top. 'Don't you worry, I expect your fella will have it all sorted in no time, but in the meantime, I'll keep my ears open and my mouth shut.' He put his giant hand over hers and gave it a gentle reassuring squeeze. 'Though you know you can chat things over if you want to, sweetheart. I is always here for you.'

He gave a broad smile and got to his feet.

'Thank you, Winston. I'll see you later.'

Fiona sat sipping her tea. She had thought long and hard about telling Winston but now she was glad she had. It was surprising how comforting it was to feel she wasn't the only one who knew the truth. Despite her comment to Winston, it didn't seem logical that Robert Heppell should have met his end at the hands of some stranger. Surely the most logical suspect was one of their party? If she was going to have to spend her next few days mixing with these people, one of whom might just be a murderer, having Winston by her side made all the difference. From her first day as a tour manager, the bear-like Winston had been her rock. Unlike many other of the tour managers, Fiona was not fussy about where she was sent, but her one stipulation was that she should be teamed up with the dependable West Indian driver.

She collected her breakfast from the buffet and had just sat down again when she saw Felix.

'Come and join me,' she invited.

After a few pleasantries, the topic got round to Janice. 'It's good that Janice has so many close friends around her.'

He frowned. 'I'm more of an acquaintance really. Though as their solicitor, I've known her and Robert for some time. Janice is the one who persuaded me to join the Association after my wife passed away. She was very kind to me. Very caring at what was a difficult time, but other than at club meetings we don't really socialise.'

'I see, but it must be a great help to Janice you being over here to help sort out all the legal bits and pieces.'

'Yes,' he said doubtfully. 'The trouble is I don't have access to all the paperwork, that's all back in the office. But I can save her the trouble of hassling them to find out the details rather than her having to keep phoning I suppose.'

'Because my husband Bill was ill for such a long time, we'd sorted out the financial arrangements long before he died, but I have a friend whose husband died suddenly. She had dreadful problems because everything was in their joint names and all their accounts were automatically frozen.' This job was not good for her moral welfare! She was beginning to, if not exactly lie, twist the truth somewhat.

'I'm only the Heppell's solicitor, not their accountant of course, but as I understand it, Janice has a fair amount in her own name including that beautiful house of theirs. She inherited her father's family business.' He frowned. 'I'm being very indiscreet.'

Fiona smiled. 'I won't tell a soul.'

He gave her a conspiratorial grin. 'The only reason I know is because I queried it when Robert made no mention of their house when we discussed the bequests when drawing up his will.'

It was tempting to probe further and ask if he knew anything about a life insurance policy, but that would be a question too far. She had already made the man uncomfortable; anymore, and he would become suspicious. It was enough that Janice could be crossed off the suspect list.

Fiona felt surprisingly relieved. There may not have been much time for her to get to know the woman, but from their few conversations, Fiona had rather taken to Janice's no nonsense, down-to-earth approach to life.

Strange though that there should be two quite separate rumours. It was possible that Gina's mean sideswipe about a hefty life insurance had been prompted by the girl's sense of grievance towards her husband's new associates who she felt looked down on her, rather than having any basis in fact. However, that didn't explain what Fiona had overheard the next day about Janice marrying Robert for his money. Eleanor Prior had only just met the Heppells, possibly hadn't spoken to either of them, so would she know anything about their financial affairs? Was someone deliberately trying to muddy the waters and cast suspicion? Someone who knew Robert had been murdered.

Apart from Aubrey Diamond coughing and spluttering behind her all the way to Bruges – the man seemed determined to pass his cold onto everyone in the group – the journey went relatively smoothly. Winston dropped them off at the corner of the central square and Fiona gathered her party to begin the walking tour.

'This beautiful wedding-cake building is one of the oldest Town Halls in Belgium. It was built in the late 14th and early 15th centuries. . .'

It had taken some time for everyone to finish taking copious photos of the fairy tale building with its intricately carved white façade and move on. Fiona glanced anxiously at her watch as she waited for the stragglers to emerge from the tiny Basilica of the Holy Blood tucked into the corner of the Burg by the Town Hall.

Peggy came to join her.

'Where did you get to last night? Your friend was so disappointed he missed you. He'd come specially to see you.

He was waiting in the lounge. We said you wouldn't be long and persuaded him to join us in the meantime.'

'I went up early.'

'He's such a lovely man, isn't he? And so good-looking! I could fancy him myself,' Peggy chortled.

Fiona forced a laugh and hoisted her guide pole.

'Time to move on everyone,' she announced. 'Now if you'd like to follow me through Blind Donkey Alley, we'll go and take a look at the fish market.'

Ferguson kicked the door of the kitchenette closed with his foot and walked over to Montgomery-Jones's desk.

'You still at it?'

Not only was Montgomery-Jones sitting at the computer in his shirtsleeves, his jacket on the back of the chair, he had his elbows on the desk, chin cradled in his hands, intently studying the screen.

'I've brought you a coffee.' Ferguson put two steaming mugs on the desk and pulled up another chair. 'You've been staring at that film footage all morning.'

'Thank you.' Montgomery-Jones smiled. He rolled back his chair and stretched up his arms to relieve the tension.

'Found anything interesting?'

'I have been trying to work out the wording on the banner our friend Müller was attempting to wave.'

'And?'

'Müller and his associates may have been German, but as far as I can tell the message is in English. The only letter visible of the first word is the final "e", but given the fact that the heckling did not start until five minutes into Moorhouse's speech and that the writing is in English and the length fits, I think we can safely assume that it must be Moorhouse's name.'

'Sounds about right. Pity the police didn't think to ask Müller's two cronies what it said. But what about the rest?' Ferguson leaned closer, staring at the footage. 'With Müller waving the damn thing around all the time, I can't make out anything else. The chap supposed to be holding the pole at the other side doesn't lift it up before the shots ring out and the camera swings away.'

'I wasted a good half hour trying to translate it into German, but making an educated guess, going over each small section of film over and over again, all I can piece together is "Moorhouse is a traitor to the cause." There is more, but that part of the banner is never raised high enough to be legible.'

'Given that is pretty much the sentiment of what many of them were chanting, I'd go along with that. In fact, I'm prepared to put money on it.'

At lunchtime, Fiona noticed Olive sitting alone at one of the outside tables and felt a pang of guilt. Robert's death had clearly affected the intense woman very deeply. The lack of any real signs of sorrow at his passing amongst his so-called friends had left her without anyone with whom she could share her grief, and this appeared to have isolated Olive even more.

'May I join you?'

Olive looked up as though jerked back from faraway thoughts. 'Please do.'

'I hope you're over that nasty bug you had the other day. No more problems.'

For a moment, Olive looked bemused then she said, 'Oh yes, quite recovered, thank you.'

Olive sat stirring her coffee absent-mindedly. This was going to be hard work.

'Are you enjoying your day?'

Fiona hadn't expected her to wax lyrical about the jewelled splendour of the silver tabernacle housing the Basilica's sacred phial supposedly containing drops of blood washed from Christ's body, or about the famous terracotta bust of Charles V in the Gruutuse Museum, but Olive's withdrawal into her own little world was a definite cause for concern.

'I keep thinking about poor Robert,' she finally admitted. 'Why were those police asking all those questions last night?'

'I expect they are trying to find out exactly what happened.'

'But why did they want to know where we were that afternoon? It's not as if any of us were with him at the time.'

Fiona shook her head. 'I can't answer you, I'm afraid. I would imagine they are trying to find who was the last person to see Robert and when that might have been. I think accident reports have to be as detailed as possible these days.'

'I suppose so.' Olive took out a handkerchief and blew her nose loudly. 'He was such a wonderful person. He revolutionised the Association; made it what it is today. It's true that lots of the older members weren't too happy when he took over, but before him, it was little more than a meeting place for a group of lonely old people and half a dozen single mums. Now, thanks to Robert, it's grown into the social and cultural heart of the whole of the area. We have members in Hextable, Crockenhill, Wilmington, Dartford, Eynsford and even as far as Sidcup. We raise a lot of money for some really prestigious projects. Robert had all these important contacts whom he persuaded to contribute, and he was always finding new ones. Networking they call it. Robert was so good at that.'

'I'm sure he'll be missed by everyone.'

Olive's face crumpled. She looked as though she was about to burst into tears. Suddenly, she clenched her fists and said, 'None of the others seem to care.'

'They are probably just keeping their feelings hidden so as not to spoil the holiday for anyone else.'

'Some of them maybe, but you haven't heard the nasty things they've been saying. They would never have made remarks like that if Robert were still alive.'

'What sort of things?'

'Horrid things. How he always got his own way and rode roughshod over people. It's so obvious they're jealous because they're not capable of coming up with good ideas. Even his so-called friends seem happy now he's gone. Look at Noel. He's chairman of the local Conservative Party and he was the one supposed to be sponsoring Robert as the party candidate at the election, but he's turned into the life and soul of the party these last two days. Anyone would think he's glad Robert's dead!'

'I'm sure that's not true.'

'And he's not the only one!' Now Olive was in full flow, nothing was going to hold back the outpouring of resentment that had been building up since the news had broken. 'That Philippa Western has never had a good word to say for Robert. Snooty miss! Thinks she's above the likes of us just because her father's about to be knighted for services to industry. *He* may be some bigwig in the City and hobnob with all these highly influential people in business and in government, but she's no better than she ought to be.'

It looked as though her suspicions about the relationship between Philippa and Austin were well founded, Fiona decided.

'I could tell you tales about what that young lady got up to in her student days that would make your hair curl. Her father had to use every bit of his influence, and a great deal of money, to hush up the scandal.'

Olive suddenly realised that she had allowed herself to get carried away and said a great deal more than she had meant to. She turned away, bent down to pick up her handbag resting by the leg of her chair and made a great show of rummaging inside. Eventually she pulled out a handkerchief and loudly blew her nose.

Fiona looked at her watch. 'It's probably time we thought about moving. We don't want to be late for the canal cruise.'

Olive was still sniffing and wiping the tears from her eyes as they walked back into the restaurant to find the toilets.

Fiona put a hand on her arm. 'I do understand how upset you must feel but do try to put it all behind you for an hour or two. Robert wouldn't want you to feel miserable all the time, now would he? He'd want you to enjoy the cruise. Most people think that it's the highlight of the day if not the whole tour.'

It wasn't exactly a lie, even if the words had come from some guidebook she'd been reading.

Chapter 16

Peggy was the last to leave the coach and Fiona helped her down the steps.

'Thank you, dear. It's been a lovely day. I think Bruges is my favourite European city. It's so unspoilt and small enough for me to be able to walk round and see all its treasures. I've visited it many times before, but never on a market day, so that was lovely.'

'Let me help you with those bags. I presume all these boxes of chocolate and biscuits are for friends back home. You'll never get through these on your own.'

Peggy laughed. 'They are, but they look so good I'm not sure I couldn't polish them all off myself.'

Fiona pushed open the glass door and they went into the foyer of their hotel.

'Are you sure you don't want me to help you carry these up to your room?'

'I'll be fine, dear. You get on. You must have lots to do.'

As soon as Peggy had gone, Fiona felt someone take her by the elbow and gently but firmly steer her away from the crowds to a quiet corner.

'Have you been avoiding me?'

'Peter! You made me jump. I didn't see you there.'

'Where did you disappear to last evening?'

'I was tired, so I went straight up to my room after the talk.'

He shook his head. 'Only after you saw me.'

Damn. He'd noticed her in the lounge after all.

'Are you still annoyed with me? I had hoped you might have forgiven me by now. Will you come and have some tea with me now or are you going to find an excuse?'

'I'll come on condition you don't start interrogating me as though I was some criminal.'

'I never interrogate you.' He gave her a pained look.

There were few people in the café, and they were able to find a quiet table out on the terrace.

'I do not understand what I did to make you so angry. I assure you the reason I invited you to dinner was purely for the pleasure of your company. The only reason I mentioned Robert Heppell at all was that I thought you would accuse me of not telling you when you did discover that he had been murdered.' He gave her a boyish smile that he must have known she would find irresistible. 'I could not have won either way.'

'Perhaps.' There was no point in maintaining the affronted resistance. Especially as she knew, that for all his arrogance and highhandedness, he did have a point. However, she wasn't quite ready to be mollified. 'What I do object to is the way you assume I will automatically fall in with your plans. I refuse to let you intimidate me or cajole me into feeding you information I may have picked up about my passengers.'

'Fiona,' he shook his head in exasperation. 'From the moment I first met you in that hotel in The Hague, I realised that no one could ever intimidate you. The way you made me wait before you would provide me with a passenger list was evidence of that. I soon learnt that it was impossible to persuade you to do anything you did not wish to do. Nonetheless, I do value your keen observation and insight and your assessment of people, which is why, I freely admit, I find them so valuable in my investigations. I fully appreciate that your prime motive for getting involved at all is your compulsion to protect your passengers. One you take far beyond the call of duty, I might add. However, admit it, you enjoy sleuthing. Your curiosity knows no bounds.'

Fiona burst out laughing. 'Peter Montgomery-Jones! That was some speech. If coercion won't work, try flattery!'

'I meant it!' He said indignantly. 'If you recall, I did not invite you into my earlier investigations; you wormed your way in.'

'I suppose so,' she conceded. 'Okay. You win.'

She poured herself a second cup of tea. 'Before I agree to answer any of your questions, let me ask you one. By your own admission, Robert's death is a matter for the local police, hardly the British Secret Service, so why are you interested in the case?'

He took a moment or two to answer. 'Because I believe there may be a connection between his murder and the assassination of Tom Moorhouse.'

'Does that mean I no longer need worry that I have a murderer amongst my passengers?'

'Certainly not! For a start, I appear to be the only one on the team who seems to feel that two murders within a mile of each other in a very short time frame is a co-incidence that is worthy of more than passing investigation. So far, I have come up with nothing and I accept that it is far more logical to assume that the panic caused by the riot provided one of Heppell's enemies with a perfect opportunity to kill him. The evidence that we have suggests that it was an opportunistic rather than a planned killing and as such makes any link with Moorhouse's death even more tenuous.'

'I assume that long and tedious explanation means no.' She grinned.

'Mrs Mason, are you making fun of me?'

'Have I ever told you, you can be a trifle pompous at times?'

'Frequently. It is one from a long list of your descriptions of me that includes patronising, pretentious, arrogant, egotistical and overbearing.'

She laughed, feeling the colour rising to her cheeks. For someone with a reputation for super-human tolerance in the face of provocation, quite why it took so little for her to fly into a petulant temper with Peter Montgomery-Jones, she had never been able to fathom. Best to make a joke of it. 'And that's just your good side.'

'That aside, I doubt that any of Heppell's fellow passengers are likely to confide any murderous intent they may harbour or any suspicions concerning their friends to the police. You, on the other hand, have a natural empathy with people that allows them to talk freely in front of you. It is possible that in an unguarded moment, one of them may let slip some comment that might remotely provide a possible motive. People love to gossip.'

'If you are looking for a list of people who will not shed a tear at his passing it could be a long one. Robert Heppell seems to have been a master craftsman at upsetting everyone he came in contact with. Including me. Though whether he might have provoked one of them into a sudden desire to stick a knife in his back is another matter entirely.'

Montgomery-Jones leant forward, elbows on the table and steepled his fingers, looking serious. 'Then perhaps it is a good thing that I can provide you with an alibi. As I recall we were together drinking coffee in the Grand Place when the shooting took place. Heppell's body was discovered less than thirty minutes later. Even if you had managed to find a taxi, there is no way you could have reached the murder scene in under half an hour.'

Fiona burst out laughing.

He smiled and sat back drinking his tea.

'I can't pretend I haven't given it some thought,' Fiona admitted. 'It would be unnatural not to. For what it's worth, and I may be on the wrong tack completely, but it would not surprise me if our Mr Heppell turned out to be a blackmailer.'

Montgomery-Jones's expression rarely showed emotion, but his eyebrows rose, followed by a deep frown. 'Are you certain? He was a man of some substance I will admit, and he did have a well-paid job in the City before taking early retirement, but the bulk of the Heppell estate comes from his wife's inheritance.'

'Yes, so I've heard,' Fiona nodded, 'but that's not what I meant. I'm not suggesting it was anything to do with extorting money from people. I think he ferreted out information and used it to manipulate people into doing things to advance his own plans. By all accounts, he was very ambitious, there was something decidedly Machiavellian about him. But before you start asking me any questions, all I have to substantiate my hunch are vague impressions with no evidence to back them up. Let me give it more thought and if I do come up with anything more definite, I'll let you know.'

'Interesting.' Montgomery-Jones looked thoughtful. 'That could be useful.'

Fiona looked at her watch. 'Heavens, is that the time. I must dash or I'll be late for dinner.'

As she turned to look back at him when she reached the door, she could see him still sitting there lost in contemplation.

The Baudouin Restaurant adopted a policy of open dining. Apart from the vegetarians Patrick and Joan Cahill, and Glenda Diamond on a gluten free diet, who all sat in the same places each evening for the convenience of their waiters, the rest of the party tended to fill in the tables as they came into the dining room.

This evening Fiona noticed a subtle change. Now they were more than halfway through their holiday, loose friendships had developed. The quiet, unassuming Cahills had gravitated towards Liz and Malcolm Kennedy whilst the Priors appeared to have more in common with the Diamonds. Over the last couple of days, Fiona had noticed that whereas the Cahills and Kellys liked to take in as many sights as possible during their free time, the other four liked nothing better than an excuse to find a café to sit and natter, though in fairness to Glenda Diamond, her weight problems meant that she couldn't walk far.

There had always been a more obvious grouping between the Association members. The younger and newer ones appeared to have formed their own little clique, leaving the older members to their own devices.

Olive's comments about Noel Appleby at lunchtime had confirmed Fiona's observations. It was not by chance that she joined a table where he was sitting with his wife, Charlotte, together with Felix Navarre, the Rev. McArdle and his wife, and Olive whom Barbara McArdle was doing her best to look after.

'What did you do after the cruise this afternoon?' Fiona asked Charlotte.

Charlotte glanced at her husband before answering. 'We had a look at the market, then went back to the Begijnhof and had a stroll round that big lake area and ended up at a lovely old gate into the city.'

Noel grinned. 'We decided to play hooky and not do the culture thing. You can only look at so many Flemish Old Masters.'

'Don't say that in front of Fiona,' laughed Barbara. 'I expect we've got another museum full of them tomorrow in Ghent.'

'Actually no. Tomorrow is mainly a walking tour. A gentle stroll alongside the river with its impressive old guild houses and on through the town to the castle. But I do have one painting for you, Van Eyck's "Adoration of the Mystic Lamb" which is in one of the side chapels in the cathedral. Though I suppose it's not so much a painting as a huge altarpiece made up of a dozen or so separate panels. But I promise you will be impressed. You will have an audio guide to explain what you're looking at and I expect we'll get a preview at the lecture tonight. Isn't Van Eyck the subject of tonight's talk? I've no idea who's giving it though.'

'It's Bernard, if I remember rightly.' Nicholas pushed his

glasses higher up his nose and turned to his wife. 'Isn't it, dear?'

Barbara nodded. 'And if we are going to be doing a lot of walking tomorrow, you must remember to take your stick.'

Montgomery-Jones returned to the Station Headquarters soon after 8 o'clock. It was already getting dark outside but like in any other murder room, work continued round the clock and lights blazed throughout their small area of the building. Leaving the night staff to their duties on the second floor, he mounted the stairs up to the smaller office dubbed the incident room where he had been given a desk. Despite the hour, he was not surprised to see the Station Chief was still there talking on the phone.

Ferguson's face broke into a beaming smile as he put down the receiver.

'Developments?' queried Montgomery-Jones.

'You could say that. One of my agents has managed to track down Franz Müller. Seems he was holed up in Brussels after all. He's being held at the local nick. I'm just off to interview him. Care to join me?'

As they walked down the stairs, Montgomery-Jones asked, 'Is Salmon aware that Müller has been detained?'

'Not yet, I've only just heard myself.' When Montgomery-Jones raised an eyebrow, Ferguson sighed. 'Tell you what; you drive while I give him a ring.'

Chapter 17

Franz Müller's command of English was by no means fluent, but as both Ferguson and Montgomery-Jones spoke excellent German there was no need for an interpreter.

The man who sat across the small table in the interview room was built like a heavyweight boxer. He had a round bulldog face with a large squashed nose that looked as though it had been broken sometime in the past. His short neck disappeared into massive bulging shoulders. He glared at his interrogators with all the pent-up aggression of a pugilist sizing up his opponent before a fight.

'You aint got no right to arrest me.'

'As far as I'm aware,' said Ferguson, 'you have not yet been charged. At the moment, you are simply helping us with our enquiries.'

Müller clenched his fists and his bulging biceps stretched the seams on the sleeves of his cheap cotton T-shirt almost to bursting point. 'I was at that rally to make a legitimate protest.'

'Rubbish. You were there to cause trouble. You don't believe in any cause. You couldn't care less about the Anti-Austerity Movement. You and your mates saw it as an opportunity for a good old punch up.'

Müller slammed his fists on the table and leaned forward with a pugnacious thrust of his chin. 'That's not true! We're committed members of the Blockupy movement.'

'Rubbish! You just like intimidating people. You don't even

know what the group stands for.'

'Blockupy opposes the European austerity regime and the rule of the EU-Troika. We are campaigning for the Europeanisation of our fight for real democracy. Our aim is to persuade all low-paid workers and the unemployed to join together in days of collective action and resistance against our respective governments' failure to respond to our needs. It is their politics of crisis that impoverish our lives and the lives of millions of people around the world. All men have the right to be free of hunger and lead decent lives.'

Ferguson slowly clapped his hands in mock applause. 'Great rhetoric! Straight out of the manifesto. You don't even know what half of those big words mean.'

'I had a perfect right to protest. What happened at that rally was nothing to do with me. I did nothing wrong.'

'Everyone was quietly listening to what was being said on the platform until you and your group of thugs started heckling Moorhouse. And you were the ringleader. The one who unfurled the banner and started waving it around causing mayhem.'

'Yeah maybe.' Müller lurched forward, half out of his seat. 'But I didn't shoot nobody!'

'Was it simply coincidence that your little disturbance diverted attention at the critical moment that Moorhouse was shot?'

'That was nothing to do with me,' Müller repeated thrusting out his chin.

'You have to admit; it does look a little suspicious that you just happened to be calling the man a traitor, moments before he died. Is that why you melted into the crowd before anyone had a chance to speak to you and hid yourself in a backstreet hidey-hole?'

'Who said I was hiding?'

'Then why jump out of a back window when the police came to talk to you? That smacks of guilt to me, doesn't it to you?' Ferguson turned to Montgomery-Jones.

'I can think of no other reason why Herr Müller might not wish to speak to us.'

Müller sat back, arms folded across his chest, jaw clenched; his attempt at sullen resistance belied by the wariness in his eyes.

'You have no right to keep me here. It's against my human rights,' he blustered.

Ferguson smiled and leaned back in his chair. 'I think you'll find we have every right to question you, sunshine. This is a matter of British National Security. A Member of Parliament has been assassinated and your little demonstration could be part of a terrorist plot. Under the Terrorism Act of 2006, we can hold you for questioning for 90 days.'

The small piggy eyes widened momentarily, and his voice came out as a strangulated shriek. 'But I keep telling you, that shooting was nothing to do with me.'

Ferguson changed tack. 'What can you tell us about Tom Moorhouse?'

'I don't know squat.'

'Come on now, you called him a traitor. I thought you two were supposed to be on the same side?'

There was a rapid tapping sound of Müller's heel on the wooden floor as he jiggled his knee up and down, but he said nothing.

'All I'm asking is what did the man do to upset you and your fellow demonstrators? Why would you disrupt his speech supporting the very same views that you claim to hold so dear? I confess I didn't actually hear his speech, but isn't that what Moorhouse was campaigning for too?'

'Moorhouse was a traitor to the cause.'

'So you keep saying. But how so?'

Müller folded his arms and glared at them.

Suddenly Ferguson leaned across the table pointing his finger inches from the man's nose. 'You can't tell us because you don't know, do you?'

Ferguson sat back and smiled. When next he spoke, his

voice had lost its adversarial tone. 'Why make the banner?'

The powerful shoulders shrugged.

'Are you saying you don't know?'

'It weren't my idea. I just went along with it.'

'That's not what your friends told us. According to them, you were the one who claimed Moorhouse was a traitor and the whole charade with the banner was your idea.'

Müller stuttered, 'No but. . . I was told. . .'

Realising he had fallen into Ferguson's trap, Müller sat back in his chair. The thrust of his chin and the clenched jaw indicated that all they would get from now on was sullen silence.

'Told what? And more importantly, by whom?'

The steady tick-tick of the wall clock was the only sound in the room.

For the first time, Montgomery-Jones spoke to the accused man. 'If you were not involved in the actual conspiracy to assassinate Moorhouse, did someone pay you to stage a fracas of some sort?'

Müller's face was a picture of conflicting emotions, but he said nothing, neither denying nor confirming what Montgomery-Jones had suggested.

Ferguson smiled and waited patiently. After five minutes, he turned to Montgomery-Jones. 'He doesn't seem to want to tell us. No matter. What he's already said is more than enough to charge him with complicity in the murder of a British citizen so we can leave it at that. I'll get the custody sergeant to put him in the cells.'

He got to his feet without looking at the man still seated at the table. The abject terror in the man's face no longer fitted with his reputed militant rabble-rouser image.

Ferguson turned to Montgomery-Jones, and in a complete change of style, said casually, 'Fancy a cup of tea, old boy?'

The two men strolled to the door. The moment it clanged shut, the languid air they had adopted disappeared.

'You definitely hit a nerve there. What on earth made you

think he might have been paid?' Ferguson asked as they walked along the corridor.

'Call it sudden intuition.'

'He didn't deny it, and it certainly does make sense, but whoever it was, he's not going to tell us in a hurry. Let's leave him to stew for half an hour while we look into his bank accounts and then try again.' Ferguson sighed. 'If that doesn't work, we'll have to let him go. All we can prove is that he heckled a speaker and raised a banner. Nothing he did could be construed as an act of violence against any individual so, as it stands, we don't have enough to hold him, let alone charge him. He's probably well aware that all he has to do is sit tight and say nothing, but it's worth a try.'

Montgomery-Jones looked thoughtful as he pushed open the door into the police station rest room. 'It may be that he does have to be released, but could our Belgian colleagues find sufficient grounds to retain his passport? A query about national security perhaps?'

'Would that stop him hightailing it back to Germany?'

'Possibly not, but it might just give us a few more hours to make further enquiries.'

Montgomery-Jones glanced around and gave a slight frown. 'I expected Salmon to be here by now or, at the very least, to have answered the message you left.'

Ferguson took out his mobile. 'Oh dear,' he said, sounding anything but, 'I seem to have switched it off, but he has left me a text.'

'What does it say?'

'"Hold the interview until I get there." Perhaps we should wait until he arrives before we have another chat with friend Müller.' There was a definite twinkle in the Station Chief's eye.

They walked over to the drinks making area by the sink in the corner. As the two men busied themselves finding clean cups, teabags and milk, Ferguson said, 'You know who Salmon reminds me of?' He didn't wait for an answer.

'Harry Potter. Short, chubby and with that same moon face and glasses.'

'The man is good at his job. He is no schoolboy.'

'Grant you that.' Ferguson scooped two heaped spoonfuls of sugar into his mug. 'It's just a pity he has to be so damned officious about it.'

It was late by the time Fiona eventually crawled into bed. She had stayed up far longer than usual talking with members of the Swanley Association in the lounge after the presentation. Not that she had been able to concentrate much on Bernard's talk. Bernard Western was by far the least stimulating of the speakers so far. He was obviously nervous and though he clearly knew his subject well, probably far better than the previous speakers had known theirs, his mumbled presentation was peppered with copious ums and aahs. By the time he was halfway through his explanation of the imagery in the various panels of Van Eyck's "The Adoration of the Lamb", she was thoroughly confused. Though to be fair, it was probably as much her fault as his. With everything she had on her mind, she found it difficult to give his talk all her attention.

It was all very well Montgomery-Jones telling her not to put herself in danger by asking questions, but it was difficult to think of any questions she could ask that might help learning anything useful in any case. She could hardly go up to Noel Appleby and blurt straight out, 'What hold did Robert have over you and what did he want in return.' He was the club treasurer. Could it be something related to that?

She liked Noel. Always charming and polite. It was impossible to think of him of all people being discovered cooking the books. Though he could not be ruled out. His wife had been alone when Fiona bumped into her in the historic shopping arcade. He may have said he was returning to the hotel, but that hardly constituted an alibi for the time of Robert's murder.

Perhaps she should find out more about these people. She had built up a good rapport with Peggy. She trusted the woman's judgement and sound good sense, but although Peggy seemed happy enough to express her views openly to Fiona, the woman was loyal to her friends and her confidences would only go so far. By far the most indiscreet of the members was Gina Lithgow, but her judgement was highly suspect and in Fiona's opinion, the woman was nursing too many deep-seated grudges to be a reliable source of information.

As Fiona put out the light and settled herself beneath the covers, she let her thoughts wander over previous conversations, trying to piece together information about each of the likely candidates. Noel could not be crossed off the list, but what about Nicholas McArdle? There was certainly no love lost between Barbara and Robert Heppell and that antipathy seemed to stem from Robert's treatment of her husband. What was it that she had said when they were in the hospital? Something about it was not that he took the chairmanship of the club away from Nicholas but the way he did it. Had Robert forced him somehow?

Fiona curled into a ball and pulled the duvet higher over her shoulders. Perhaps she was trying to make something of nothing. It was very difficult to think of the ever-patient, mild-mannered cleric whose thoughts always seemed to be elsewhere, having the energy for harbouring any violent emotion, let alone be capable of planning to kill someone. Could the same be said for his wife? Might her indignation on her husband's behalf be enough to drive her to revenge? She was genuinely distressed about Janice. However much she believed her friend was better off without Robert, would she be prepared to put her through this ordeal?

There was another candidate. Fiona had witnessed a conversation between Robert and Philippa Western on that first evening that strongly suggested some tension between them. Had he been threatening her? The behaviour between

Philippa and Austin Pilkington suggested a relationship that extended far beyond the bounds of mere friendship. Had Robert proof of their affair that he would take to Bernard if she did not fall in line? But what could she possibly offer him in return for his silence? Could it have something to do with these famous dinner parties? According to Peggy, whereas they had once been rather elegant social affairs, since Robert Heppell had become a regular guest they had changed in character. Prominent men of industry, politics and influence were now invited, and their presence had turned what had once been pleasant evenings amongst friends into business affairs. Perhaps she could find out more about what went on on those occasions without arousing suspicion.

She was just drifting off to sleep when a sudden thought jerked her wide awake again. What about Dee Foley? It was all very well trying to find a motive amongst those who knew Robert Heppell well, but the one person he had really fallen foul of in recent days was the vehement, confrontational lesbian. They may have known each other for little more than twenty-four hours, but if ever two people looked like coming to blows, it was those two. They didn't seem capable of being in the same room together for ten minutes before they were engaged in a slanging match. If they had come across each other by chance at the rally, it was doubtful that either of them would walk away without engaging in some kind of skirmish. Could she have struck him in a fit of rage? A physical response to some provocative slur. Not a pre-meditated killing at all.

Montgomery-Jones had said it had been an opportunistic killing, but it might help if she knew exactly how the man had died. Perhaps he might be persuaded to tell her.

Chapter 18

Once Salmon had been briefed on the outcomes of the interview with Müller, he was happy enough to let Ferguson take the lead when they went to speak to the German activist for a second time. Not prepared to hand over the reins completely, Salmon insisted that he accompany Ferguson, leaving Montgomery-Jones to watch the proceedings from the observation window.

Ferguson took time to settle himself comfortably in his seat. He straightened up the brown manila folder that he'd put down on the table and arranged the ballpoint pen in perfect alignment. Eventually, he looked up and asked conversationally, 'Herr Müller, now you've had some time to think, what have you got to say to us?'

Müller's eyes were wary, and he stared suspiciously at Salmon.

'Don't mind my friend here,' Ferguson said cheerily, 'he's just come along to help us sort out this mess you've managed to get yourself into. Now where did we get to? Oh yes. You were about to tell us who told you Moorhouse was a traitor.'

Müller clamped his jaw shut.

'Was it the same person who paid you to stage your little charade that set the ball rolling?'

'I ain't saying nothing.' Müller folded his arms across his chest, the resolute set of his features was belied by the tell-tale drumming of his heel.

Ferguson laughed. 'But you just did, Herr Müller.'

Müller scowled.

'Did you think we wouldn't bother to check your bank records?'

Ferguson let the silence hang for some time. When he got no response, he opened the folder tipping it so that Müller couldn't see what he was looking at. Eventually he looked up and said, 'These make very interesting reading.'

To his credit, Salmon showed not a flicker of surprise though he was well aware that, although a request for the records had been made to the German authorities, it would be some time before the results would come through. Ferguson was staring at a printout of the Station's budget figures for the previous month.

Müller chewed his lip. 'I won that money betting on the horses.'

'Really? Can you prove that?' Ferguson slipped a pack of blank paper out of his file, laid it on the table and picked up his pen. 'Give me the details. Tell me the names of the horses you put money on and the bookie you used?'

'I don't remember.'

'Come now. You don't really expect us to believe that, do you? Do you often gamble on the gee-gees?'

Müller shook his head.

'What made you decide to put this bet on?'

'Had a hot tip, didn't I.'

'But you don't remember the name of the horse or where it was running?' Ferguson gave him a pained look and slowly shook his head from side to side. 'How much did you stake?'

'Fifty euros.'

'That's an awful lot of money for a man who doesn't play the horses. Who gave you this tip?'

'A friend.'

'Name?'

'Can't remember.'

Ferguson threw up his hands and tutted in disbelief.

'Someone I met a few times in the pub, weren't it? Didn't

166

catch his name,' Müller said quickly.

'Quite a bundle to lay out on the say-so of a virtual stranger.'

The heel tapping began again in earnest.

'Said he knew the jockey and it were a dead cert.'

'Favourite, was it?'

'Yeah. No!' he corrected himself quickly. 'An outsider.'

'Good odds?'

'Yeah.'

'Must have been pretty astronomical to give you that much of a pay-out! Or did you put it on an accumulator?'

'Must've done.'

'Who gave you the tips on the other horses.'

'I just stuck a pin in the paper.'

'Where did you place your bet? At the racecourse or with your local bookie?'

The rapid batting of his eyelids and the contortions in his face indicated that Müller was trying to weigh up the consequences of either answer.

'Did it online, didn't I?' he said eventually.

'Then you'll be able to prove that when we investigate your computer history, won't you?'

'No!' The words came out as a rush. 'I didn't do it at home. I went to one of them internet café places.'

'Bullshit! When was all this little charade supposed to have taken place?' Ferguson slapped his hand on the table. 'Come on Franz, you can't have forgotten that already. How long ago was it? A week ago, two weeks?'

'Three.'

Ferguson put down his pen, slipped the paper back into the folder and picked it up tapping the bottom edges on the table to straighten the sheets inside.

'Let me level with you, Franz. You are in serious trouble here. A man has been assassinated. Not just any old Tom, Dick or Harry, but a serving Member of the British Parliament and in front of an international audience. It's high profile. World news. Your little demo provided just enough distraction for the gunman to do the job and make his getaway. There's enough evidence to link the two together in a conspiracy. And without the shooter, we are going to have to have someone to throw to the wolves if only to prove to the British public and the World at large that the British Authorities will not allow such an outrage to go unpunished. You could end up spending the rest of your natural life in some high security prison.'

'You can't prove I had anything to do with no conspiracy!'

'Oh, we're getting there, Franzie boy, believe you me. I told you before, we suspect there could well be a terrorist element to all this, so we can hold you for 90 days while we take our time to tie up all the loose ends.'

Ferguson sat back and folded his arms, letting the seconds tick away. Eventually, he leaned forward, and his voice took on a more conciliatory tone. 'The reason I asked my colleague to sit in with me for this interview is that he is in a position to offer you a deal. You tell us who paid you the money to stage your demonstration, all you know about him and his plans, and in exchange, my colleague here will be able to ensure that any charges against you regarding what happened at the rally are dropped.'

Müller blinked rapidly calculating the odds.

'Far be it from me to rush you, Franz, but we may not have a lot of time.'

Müller swallowed. 'Okay, okay. I was paid. But I don't know who it was, so don't ask. I had this phone call, didn't I? He didn't give a name. Said he'd arrange for the cash to be delivered to the hotel where I was staying.' Now he saw his worst nightmare beginning to fade away, he was becoming more confident and his voice stronger. 'Don't ask me how he got my mobile number or knew where I was staying 'cause I dunno. He said I had to take the sim card outa my phone, put it in an envelope and leave it at the front desk. I was to tell the clerk someone would collect it in exchange for a package with my name on it.'

'Where was this hotel?' asked Ferguson.

'Strasburg. I were on a demo, weren't I? Against them French Front National lot. Bloody fascists!' Now he'd decided to reveal all, Müller was back in his stride.

'This voice,' said Ferguson. 'What did it sound like? Young, old? Did he speak in French or German? What about an accent?'

Müller shrugged his massive shoulders and screwed up his face. 'Youngish, I guess, but it were muffled so I couldn't really tell. He spoke in German, but not like a native. Could've been French I suppose.'

Ferguson took the writing pad from his folder and tore off a couple of sheets of paper and put them in front of Müller, then placed his pen on top.

'I'd like you to write down everything you can remember. I want as much detail about that conversation as you can recall. The exact words or phrases if possible. When the call was made, when the money was delivered, every detail that comes to mind. I need the name of the hotel, how long you stayed there and a timetable of what you did for the whole time you were in France. Remember, the more you give us, the easier we're going to find it to grant you immunity from any charges.'

Müller picked up the pen and began to write.

There was no one else in the off-duty room when the three men walked in. Ferguson headed for the kitchen area in the corner.

'Either of you two fancy a cuppa?'

'You were sailing pretty close to the wind back there. What was all that about holding him for 90 days? There hasn't been as much as a whisper about any terrorist threat.'

'But he didn't know that, did he?'

'What if the man had called your bluff? We have got nothing on him.' Salmon accused him.

'True.' Ferguson laughed and continued to sort out mugs and teabags. 'But it worked though, didn't it? Would you rather I'd let him go?'

Salmon pulled out a chair from under the table and sat down. 'Luckily for you.'

'I prefer to call it good judgement.' He carried the three mugs to the table and carefully set down the two he held in one hand, only narrowly avoiding spilling their contents onto the Formica-topped table as they tipped alarmingly. 'I've been in the game long enough to recognise an overgrown bully when I see one. All bull and bluster, stand up to them and they crumble straight away.' For once, even Salmon couldn't destroy the Brussels Station Chief's good humour.

Salmon stared at him over the top of his glasses. 'If you can believe what the man says.'

'Granted,' Ferguson said, still grinning ear to ear, 'but we'd be idiots not to follow it up.'

Salmon nodded and grudgingly admitted, 'True. I'll contact Thames House and get them onto it straightaway.'

He picked up one of the mugs and took a sip and immediately pulled a face. 'This stuff is barely drinkable!'

Ferguson laughed. 'What did you expect? Good old British Yorkshire tea? You're in a Belgian Police Station and they prefer coffee.'

Salmon put down his mug. 'Is there any evidence any of our suspects have been in France lately? We checked that none of them were in Belgium or in any of the neighbouring countries at the weekend unless they came in under the radar, but I didn't ask for GCHQ [Government Communications Headquarters] to track down where they were three weeks ago.'

Ferguson shook his head. 'It's highly unlikely that he delivered the money himself. If he had the savvy to demand the sim card so that his call couldn't be traced back, he'd hardly risk being seen. He'd have used a messenger. That phone call could have been made from anywhere.'

'I realise that,' Salmon snapped. 'But to avoid involving more people than absolutely necessary he may have been in the area to sort out the money. We need someone to speak to the desk clerk of Müller's hotel in Strasbourg and get as much information about the delivery boy as possible.'

'I'll go,' Ferguson said quickly. 'Best if one of us goes and it's only a four-hour journey from here. I can be there first thing in the morning and if all goes well, I could be back here again early to mid-afternoon. It I take a driver; I can even get some shuteye on the journey down.'

'Fine.' Salmon turned to Peter Montgomery-Jones. 'You've not said a word. What's your take on all this?'

'I was wondering if we have not been too premature in assuming that Müller's caller was one of our suspects. He spoke in German with a French accent.'

'Is that relevant? True, it might possibly rule out those who don't speak German, but would Müller be able to distinguish a French accent from any other? Isn't it more likely he was mistaken? We've heard nothing to suggest that Moorhouse ever made an enemy of someone in France.'

'If Müller claims his caller had a French accent, I am inclined to believe him. He may not be an educated man, but he is well travelled and has obviously spent some time in France over the years. If you are asking my opinion, I believe there is a distinct possibility that the caller was much more likely to be the gunman himself. Choosing to assassinate a man in a public place in front of crowds of people is an extremely risky undertaking. Firstly, he had to get Moorhouse out from behind the bulletproof screens and secondly, if he was going to pull out a firearm and make his getaway without being apprehended, he required some sort of diversion.'

There was a moment or two of silence while the other two men considered Montgomery-Jones's assertion.

'So, our assassin is likely to be a Frenchman?'

'Or possibly Walloon, Swiss or from Luxemburg. Even

Canadian. The reports we have so far suggest our killer was Caucasian, so it is less likely that he is Algerian or from any other of the African countries where French is an official language.'

Salmon smiled. 'I'll get Cumming to provide us with a list of all known French speaking guns for hire.' He got to his feet. 'Well, gentlemen. At last, I believe we may be getting somewhere. Well done, both of you.'

As the door closed behind him, Ferguson turned to Montgomery-Jones with an exaggerated mock wide-eyed stare. 'Did I hear right? Did that man just give us a compliment?'

Day 7 Thursday, Ghent

Ghent was the second largest city in Medieval Europe, and it became a major industrial centre in the 18th and 19th centuries. Its past glory is reflected in its outstanding architecture. The town can justly claim to have more listed buildings than the rest of Belgium put together.

Our walking tour begins along the Graslei, one of Ghent's most picturesque streets, to see the rows of elegant, perfectly preserved 12th century guild houses overlooking the River Leie. Other highlights of our tour include the Romanesque High Gothic Cathedral of St Bravo, named after a local saint and its priceless 15th century altarpiece "The Adoration of the Lamb" painted by Jan Van Eyck; the 14th century belfry and adjacent Cloth Hall; the awesome 12th century Castle of Gravensteen with its square-cut towers and imposing gatehouse from where the counts of Flanders wielded their power; and the church of St Nicholas, Belgium's finest example of the austere Scheldt gothic style.

Super Sun Executive Travel

Chapter 19

The Graslei was looking at its best as they strolled along its cobbled street. The step-gabled roofs of towering guild houses pointed up into a cloudless, vivid blue sky with their sandstone façades perfectly reflected in the still, turquoise waters of the River Leie. The pace of life seemed less frenetic than in Bruges and Brussels, and the lack of milling crowds allowed each of the party to amble at their own pace in the warm sunshine.

This was how tour guiding should be, Fiona thought as she waited for the last of the photographers to catch up at the first stopping point.

'These beautiful old houses are a testament to the incredible blossoming of Ghent's economy during the Middle Ages. Every house on the Graslei has its own history but this one, the Staple House, with its arched windows and doorways is the oldest and dates from the twelfth century. It's where the city's grain was stored for hundreds of years until a fire destroyed the interior. A little further on, we'll come to the Corn Measurer's House. You'll easily recognise it because it has a clock tower behind it. Take your time if you would like to stop for photos and you can catch us up at the house next to that which is the Guild House of the Free Boatmen.'

It was a good opportunity as everyone dawdled for Fiona to check on Olive. At least she seemed a great deal more relaxed than the previous day when Fiona had last spoken to her. She still seemed to be isolating herself from the rest of her friends in the Swanley Association.

'Are you not a photographer, Olive?'

Olive pulled a mobile phone-sized camera from her pocket. 'I've taken a few but I prefer to buy postcards. My efforts never seem to do justice to these beautiful old buildings.'

Fiona laughed. 'I know what you mean. I always manage to get telephone lines across the middle of the picture or the arm of a giant crane spoiling the skyline.'

'This is nice here though. No ugly scaffolding or traffic to spoil it.'

'Would you like me to take one of you? Then you can prove you've been here.'

Olive's face broke into a rare smile. 'Yes please. That would be lovely.'

'How about across the river with the houses in the background?'

'I can show that to my nephew when I get back,' she said as Fiona handed back the camera. 'I expect he'll visit soon.'

'Does he live far from you?'

'Only in Dartford. But you know these young people. They lead such busy lives, but he is very good to me. He and his wife always pop over around Christmas and take me out for my birthday.'

'That's nice.' Olive appeared to live a very lonely life. Perhaps that was why she was so enamoured of Robert. Being secretary of the Swanley Association gave her status as well as an activity to fill her days.

'Do you have any other family?'

'My sister died a while back. I do have a brother out in Australia, but we've lost touch really.'

'That's a shame.'

Olive frowned and a pinched look came over her face. Perhaps she sensed Fiona was feeling sorry for her. She turned away sharply and stared at the small group of fellow passengers coming to join them. 'Oh, I don't know,' she muttered. 'At least I don't have a relation to be ashamed of.'

The contemptuous sneer in the woman's voice startled Fiona. What could have prompted such a heartfelt, bitter remark? Who had she been referring to? Closest to them were Nicholas and Barbara McArdle but only a few steps behind came Charlotte and Noel Appleby. As far as Fiona knew, Olive had no reason to dislike the gentle clergyman or his more forthright wife, but Noel's lack of mourning at the loss of a supposedly close friend, especially one whom Olive idolised, had certainly earned her animosity. There was also Charlotte's coolness at the mention of her son at their meeting outside the lace shop a few days before which added to Fiona's suspicions. What had Appleby Junior done that had earned Olive's contempt?

Fiona told herself not to jump to conclusions. The rest of the party were approaching, and Olive might have been referring to any one of them. She sighed; perhaps she was reading far too much into a casual throwaway remark in any case. That was the trouble with amateur sleuthing. It was impossible not to see clues in the most innocent of situations and unlike the police, she was in no position to ask questions. Even if she was correct in her assumption, it did not mean that it had anything to do with Robert's death. In fact, it was difficult to see how it was relevant at all.

Lunch was booked in one of the many cafés that lined the Kornmark. Fiona ushered the group to the tables reserved for them. Feeling that she had been neglecting those in her party who were not members of the Swanley Association, she decided it was high time she sat with some of them. As she glanced around the small tables under their bright umbrellas overlooking the busy square, she spotted a couple of spare seats with the Priors and Diamonds. Her resolution only went so far. Eleanor's love of the sensational, her ability to make a melodrama out of seemingly innocent incidents, was more than Fiona could cope with. Luckily, there were still spare seats next to Liz and Malcolm Kennedy.

She had only just sat down when she noticed Hazel standing in the café doorway looking around, a lost expression on her face.

'There's seats here, hen. Come and join us?' Liz beckoned her. 'It's pretty busy, isn't it?'

Somewhat reluctantly, Hazel came over and hovered behind an empty chair. 'I was waiting for Dee. There's quite a queue in the Ladies.'

'There always is,' Liz said with feeling. 'Malcolm claims it's because we women get chatting in there and forget the time.'

'Rubbish,' laughed Fiona. 'We may exchange the odd friendly word as we stand in the queue, but the sooner we can get out of there the better.'

The light banter had little effect on Hazel. She took off her cardigan and draped it over the back of the chair, then dithered looking back at the café entrance.

'Why don't you sit down, hen?'

'I'll just go and see where she is.'

'No need,' said Fiona. 'Here she comes.'

Dee emerged from the doorway with Philippa. They stood together talking and laughing. Hazel pursed her lips and she hurried over to the couple.

Liz shook her head slowly from side to side. 'That girl seems to go to pieces if Philippa comes anywhere near Dee. Did you see them at Waterloo the other day?'

'No. What happened?'

'Hazel was so rude to the poor woman. It was embarrassing. All Philippa did was smile and make some innocent remark when Dee stumbled walking up the slope. Hazel accused her of making fun of Dee which wasn't the case at all.'

Although it was impossible to hear what the three were saying, it appeared that Philippa appeared to bear no grudges about the earlier incident and was inviting them both to sit at her table. Hazel shook her head vigorously and pulled Dee away, a scowl on her normally pretty face.

'I thought Bruges was beautiful, but I think I like Ghent even more,' Liz said to cover the tension once the two joined them and had sat down. 'I love the effect of these wonderful old houses. Each one is so different, but they all blend together.'

'The best thing about it is that there's no traffic. You can wander about the whole city centre without fear of being knocked down which is great when you're taking photos,' said Malcolm. He was one of the keenest photographers to judge by the size of his camera and the number of changeable lenses in his camera case.

'That must help to keep these buildings so clean,' added Dee. Relaxed and at ease, she was positively affable.

'The waitress is coming to take our orders so perhaps we should take a look at the menu,' Fiona suggested.

'Everything seems to come with chips,' Hazel protested.

'They are something of a Belgian speciality. They're double fried to make them extra crispy,' said Fiona.

'Then I'm definitely not having any.'

The others laughed, not unkindly, at the expression of horror on Hazel's face.

'You are on holiday, hen,' said Liz. 'And with your wee slim figure, you've no need to worry anyway.'

'Just forgo the salad cream,' teased Dee. 'Have you seen the crowds in Brussels at the chip stands buying cartons of chips with great dollops of mayonnaise on top to eat in the street? They're more popular than ice creams stalls.'

At least Fiona had one thing she could be grateful for. After her brush with the law, Dee Foley had become something of a model passenger. Over the last few days, Dee and Hazel had kept pretty much to themselves. They were perfectly polite and pleasant to everyone and never caused Fiona problems by being late or argumentative. Dee Foley was obviously trying very hard, because in Fiona's estimation,

Robert Heppell may have brought out the worst side of her character, but Dee was not someone for whom the give and take of social interaction came naturally.

Was all this an act to cover up her crime? The woman was certainly headstrong and had a quick temper. It wasn't difficult to imagine Robert Heppell provoking some sort of confrontation that quickly got out of hand causing her to lash out. Fiona shook her head. She really must stop letting her imagination run away with her! The woman was hardly a killer! A far more logical explanation for her more circumspect behaviour was the realisation that she had only narrowly escaped a serious charge. Just be grateful, Fiona told herself, that you no longer have the worry of Dee upsetting the other passengers.

The routine early morning video conference had been postponed until Ferguson's return from Strasburg. Thames House and GCHQ were no doubt grateful for the extra time it provided to pursue their various lines of enquiry. Work at both establishments might well continue round the clock, but any enquiries involving personal interviews to supplement the electronic intelligence were impractical in the early hours of the morning when the vast majority of the public at large might be expected to be in their beds.

Ferguson had phoned to report that though he had managed to speak to the manager of the small budget hotel Müller had used in Strasbourg, it had taken a couple of hours to track down the girl who had been at the front desk when the package was delivered.

A little after three o'clock, Montgomery-Jones tapped on the door to Salmon's office.

'Ferguson has telephoned to say that he is approaching Leuven and should be here in half an hour or so.'

'Good.' Salmon sat back in his chair. 'I'll get through to Thames House. We might as well link up as soon as he gets here so Cumming can be in on the debrief. Save Ferguson having to go through everything a second time. Would you arrange for someone to organise some coffee?'

'Certainly. I doubt Ferguson has had much chance to eat since he left here. I expect he would also be grateful for a sandwich.'

Salmon gave a curt nod and picked up the phone.

Ferguson was in full flow. 'The receptionist said she didn't take much notice as she was dealing with a couple of guests. All she can remember is that the man was dressed in black leathers and kept his helmet on. At the time, she assumed he was a dispatch rider from some delivery company. He asked for the envelope she'd been told to give him. She saw him open it and take out something very small, but she had no idea what it was as she was busy sorting out the couple's bill. When she turned back to the messenger, he was already heading for the door. There was a brown paper package left on the desk with Müller's name printed in felt tip pen on it.'

'She didn't see his face?'

'Not really. He had the visor up, but all she could see were his eyes. And no. She can't remember what colour they were. She thinks he was medium to tall and average build.'

'Which means she has no real idea.' Salmon was not a happy man.

'Probably. But she did remember his hands. They were very pale with long, thin fingers, quite delicate for a man.'

'A woman, do you think?'

'I asked her that, but she didn't think so. He didn't say much, just asked for the envelope, and his voice was husky and a bit muffled because he was still wearing his helmet, but he definitely spoke in French. I tried to get her to remember if he sounded like a local. On reflection, she didn't think so, possibly from the south, Provence or Languedoc, but he only said a few words, so it was difficult to tell. There was nothing about his accent that made her think that French was his second language and she claims that in her job, she's got to be pretty good at judging people's nationalities.'

Salmon looked sceptical.

Montgomery-Jones said, 'It is a talent that many receptionists in towns with a large number of foreign tourists appear to develop.'

'If you say so,' Salmon conceded. 'Not one of our suspects then. Could he be our shooter do you think? It is pretty vague, but none of it conflicts with the description we have from eyewitnesses at the rally.'

'Agreed,' said Montgomery-Jones.

'So,' Salmon turned to the screen, 'Do we have anything on any known French guns for hire.'

Cumming was busy tapping away at his keyboard. 'Two, plus a Belgian from Liege. The first is Charles Fournier, not his real name but an alias it's believed he used on a false passport on a flight to Turkey, known to have connections to Milieu, the underground group that operates in the French metropolitan areas and is well known for being involved in high level organised crime.'

The image on the large screen changed from Cumming to his laptop and the picture of a swarthy, square-faced man with stubble hair appeared.

'That doesn't look much like our man,' said Ferguson.

'True,' Salmon said quickly, 'but let's not rule him out. The descriptions we have are vague and conflicting. These men are nothing if not adept at disguising themselves.'

'And we should consider that the most likely scenario is that the gunman, whoever he might be, would most likely send a messenger. It would be the safest option as far as he is concerned,' Montgomery-Jones pointed out.

'True,' snapped Salmon. 'What else do we know about this one?'

'Very little. The closest anyone has ever come to him is when a rival Milieu boss was gunned down on the streets of Marseilles.'

The face of a second man replaced the first.

'This is Andre Leroux. Ex Foreign Legion. Went off the radar in the late 1990s. Not known to be associated with any particular criminal fraternity but believed to have been involved in shootings in various parts of North Africa, the near East as well as several European countries. The Belgian is another mystery man. Goes by the codename of Jean the Gun and we have no pictures. All we do know is that he has worked for a Mafia mob based in the Crimea on numerous occasions.'

'The picture of Leroux is the closest match, but that's not a lot to go on.'

'Naturally, I'm sending over everything we have on all of them, not that there's much more you are going to find of any use, although one thing is worth pointing out, Leroux was left-handed. I don't remember seeing anything about which hand the gunman used in the descriptions we had from you.'

The three men in the room looked at one another shaking their heads. 'Neither do we. We'll follow up that angle,' Salmon said.

'The request for any information about the possible current whereabouts of all three men has been sent through to Interpol, sir. The moment I hear anything, I'll be in touch.'

'Thank you, Cumming. Good work.'

The link was broken, and the three men packed their things together. Ferguson put his hands on the table, stretching his arms and back, then gave a great yawn.

'Have you had any sleep at all?' There was a hint of concern in Salmon's enquiry.

'I dozed a bit in the car.'

'Then go home and get to bed.'

Ferguson looked at him in surprise.

Salmon's face twitched. 'You're no use to anyone in that state.' He turned sharply and hurried through the door and down the stairs.

'My, my,' said Ferguson with a chuckle. 'Anyone would

think he was embarrassed revealing his softer side.'

Chapter 20

The journey back from Ghent had been uneventful with surprisingly little traffic and they had arrived back much earlier than expected. Fiona helped Glenda Diamond down the steep coach steps and held her arm as the decidedly over-weight woman struggled to ease her stiffened legs to follow the rest of the party into the hotel.

'Spending all week on my feet is beginning to take its toll. A nice quiet evening for me, I think.'

'There is another talk this evening if you're interested,' Fiona suggested. 'I believe it's about Bruegel. I quite like his pictures of country scenes with those wonderful characters going about their everyday lives.'

Glenda wrinkled her nose. 'Not really our thing, and besides, Aubrey still has a bit of a cough. Can't have you disturbing everyone else can we, darling?'

Fiona's usual routine was to file the day's notes and fill in Super Sun forms straightaway. As she knew from experience, it was all too easy to forget the details if she left it for more than a day or two. Did anyone at Head Office actually bother to read all these endless bits of paper? Did it really matter if they arrived at the designated coffee and comfort location at 11.05am or 11.15 or if it happened to be raining at the time? Still, it was odds on that the one time there was some sort of problem or complaint would be when she had failed to complete the paperwork accurately.

Fiona opened the drawer and tugged at the folder. It came

out with a jerk and the whole sheaf of papers tumbled to the floor.

'Damn and blast!'

She scooped them together and laid them on the bed.

Time for a break. She would go down, find a comfortable chair in a quiet corner of the lounge, and order a pot of tea. That lot could be sorted out later. There was plenty of time before she needed to get ready for dinner. She might even take a book to read. The novel she'd brought with her, a light undemanding Richard and Judy Summer recommendation, was proving to be quite entertaining.

When she reached the lounge, it was evident that several other people shared the same idea. All of the small clusters of chairs alongside the windows, where she herself would have preferred to sit, were taken, but she managed to find a table alongside the wall tucked in by the side of the bar.

The waiter was kept busy and trying to catch his eye plus the chatter and various comings and goings around her made it difficult to concentrate on her book. She had to re-read the page several times before she found herself able to lose herself in the story.

'Good book?'

She looked up at the towering figure now standing over her. 'Peter!'

'May I sit down?' She waved him to the seat beside her.

'You're becoming quite a frequent visitor to the hotel. What brings you here?'

'To see you, naturally.' He smiled. 'I apologise for not telephoning earlier in the day, but I was busy with the investigation and was not sure when I would be free. I came on the off chance. The receptionist said that your coach had returned, I tried ringing, but when there was no answer, I thought I would try in here.'

'I'm sorry. I must have left my mobile in my room.'

'It is a little early, but may I get you a drink?'

'I've ordered a pot of tea. I'm sure they can bring another

cup. As you are still wearing a suit, do I take it that this is a business rather than a social call?'

'It is, I am afraid.' His voice dropped, but there was little chance of anyone overhearing. The nearest people were a couple of tables away and with their backs to the wall, no one could approach without their notice. 'Have you had any more thoughts about Heppell and his blackmailing exploits?'

'Nothing I have any evidence for. Only vague impressions and various rumours flying around, some of which I already know are wildly wide of the mark.'

'Such as?'

She told him the gossip about Janice benefiting from her husband's life insurance policy and Felix Navarre's assertion that she was a wealthy woman in her own right.

'Indeed, she is. As his wife, she was naturally the first to be investigated.'

Fiona pulled a face. 'It's a sad reflection on our society that the person most devastated by the loss of a loved one in such appalling circumstances is the first one to come under suspicion.'

'I do not need to tell you that most murders are committed by a partner or close relative. Very few are committed by strangers.'

'But surely. . .?' Fiona stopped.

'In Heppell's case, I think there can be little doubt that he was killed by someone he knew.'

'Which I presume,' Fiona said after a long pause, 'means that it was almost certainly one of my passengers?'

'It is a definite possibility and one we cannot overlook. However, . . .'

'Please spare me the lecture about taking care and not asking questions,' she interrupted with some asperity. 'That's exactly why I can only give you wild conjectures. I have no way of confirming them.'

'I do appreciate that.' He smiled and asked conspiratorially, 'What have you heard?'

She told him about Noel Appleby's son. 'Robert behaved abominably to Noel. You would have thought he would be grateful for all the support Noel was giving to his political campaign. I can only assume that Robert had some sort of hold. . .'

'Peter!' A voice rang out from the doorway. Philippa swept across the room, hand outstretched, bringing Fiona's story to an abrupt halt. 'How lovely to see you again.'

Montgomery-Jones was on his feet and they greeted one another like long lost friends, even air-kissing each other's cheeks, much to Fiona's surprise.

It was almost as though Fiona wasn't there. After a couple of minutes of inconsequential chat, Philippa gave him a coquettish smile. 'I mustn't keep you.'

For a moment, Fiona wondered if Peter would ask her to join them. Instead he said, 'Lovely to see you again, dear lady.' His gaze followed her as she sashayed to the bar giving him a last lingering look.

This was a side of Peter Montgomery-Jones Fiona had never seen before.

'A good-looking woman our Mrs Western,' he said as he sat back down in the armchair. 'What do you make of her?'

'You seem appear to know her a great deal better than I.'

'Her father is Henry Ensley.' Montgomery-Jones was still looking at Philippa as he asked, 'Has anyone mentioned him at all?'

'Only in passing. A prominent man in the City, so I understand. Exerts a great deal of influence in high places.'

'Indeed, he does.' Montgomery-Jones looked thoughtful. 'It would be interesting to know if he has any connection with Heppell.'

'Why don't you ask Philippa?'

She hadn't meant to sound so tart, but he was too busy to notice, watching Philippa as she perched herself on a high stool at the bar showing off her shapely long legs to advantage. There was no doubt that the tall, sleek woman was strikingly handsome, but it was a surprise that Peter Montgomery-Jones of all people should be seduced by her brittle charm.

'I didn't realise you two knew each other.' Had it sounded as much of an accusation to his ears as it had to hers?

He turned back to look at Fiona and said, 'We only met for the first time the other evening.'

'Really?'

Before she could ask any more questions, he parried with one of his own. 'And what else have you learnt about her?'

'According to Olive Scudamore, Philippa led a very wild youth.'

'Didn't we all,' he laughed indulgently.

I certainly didn't, she thought with a touch of rancour. He must think me a very dull woman. For goodness's sake, woman, she told herself. Anyone would think you were jealous. Best to make a joke of it.

'Mr Montgomery-Jones! I'm shocked.'

'Probably best forgotten. More tea?'

He leaned forward and picked up the teapot.

Some ten minutes later, Fiona noticed Dee join Philippa at the bar. Once drinks had been ordered, the two went over to a table in the corner.

Montgomery-Jones followed her gaze. 'Is that the woman who managed to get herself arrested?'

'Dee Foley. Yes, it is.'

Fiona frowned.

'Is something wrong?'

'Not at all,' Fiona assured him. 'It just seems a strange pairing. I wouldn't have thought those two had much in common.'

'Oh?'

'Philippa rarely spends any time with the women in the group. She's very much a man's woman and Dee claims to despise the privileged classes.'

Montgomery-Jones gave a low chuckle. 'All this sleuthing

is having a bad effect on you, Mrs Mason. You are beginning to read intrigue and conspiracy into perfectly innocent events. This is probably nothing more than two people happening to meet in the bar and striking up a conversation because there is no one else there that they know.'

'You're right. I'm turning into a suspicious old biddy.'

'You were telling me about the Rev. McArdle and his wife?' He was back to his old self as though the encounter with Philippa had never happened.

'You've met Barbara, and Nicholas is a dear. Robert ousted him out of the chairmanship of the social club, but quite how he managed to do it, I have no idea. It doesn't help that because of Robert, the club has morphed into the Swanley Association with a very different character. Nicholas doesn't seem to harbour any resentment and although I can't quite say the same for his wife, I find it impossible to think of either of them as suspects for Robert's murder. Or, for that matter, guilty of anything that might give Robert any excuse to blackmail them.'

Their conversation was brought to an abrupt halt by a disturbance at the corner table. A red-faced Hazel Tonkin was standing over Dee, clenching and unclenching her fists. Dee appeared to be mildly amused by her friend's evident distress.

The fraught exchange grew louder.

'How could you do this to me?'

Dee put a hand on Hazel's arm. 'Calm down, sweetie. You're making an exhibition of yourself.'

Hazel brushed it away and turned to Philippa. 'You're nothing but a cheap tart for all your expensive clothes and flashy jewellery. You think you can just bat those false eyelashes of yours and people will come running.'

'Hazel!' Dee was on her feet, an ominous frown on her face, but Philippa appeared to find the situation highly amusing and began to laugh, which did nothing to improve the situation.

Hazel stamped her foot, then with one of her half sob half sigh cries, she turned and rushed from the room. Dee watched the retreating figure, a stunned look on her face.

'Let her go,' Philippa said. 'She's probably best alone until she calms down.'

Dee shook her head and stomped off after her friend.

The drama had caught the attention of everyone in the room and after a few seconds of embarrassed silence, the low chatter resumed.

Montgomery-Jones raised an eyebrow. 'I do appreciate that Miss Tonkin is a highly-strung young lady, but that furore does seem somewhat extreme.'

'Hazel has always been a trifle clingy, but ever since Dee was arrested, she's become so possessive it's frightening. Dee only has to smile at someone else and Hazel starts sulking. Though I have to say, she's never reacted quite this badly before.' Fiona sighed. 'I wonder how long it will take before news of that little charade will spread through the hotel. No doubt, it will be the major talking point during this evening's meal at the Super Sun tables.'

'I have to say, Fiona,' Peter said with a twinkle in his eye, 'There never seems to be a dull moment on one of your tours.'

'Tell me about it.' She glanced at her watch. 'And talking of dinner, I must go and get changed if I'm going to be ready on time. Was there anything else you wanted to know before I leave?'

'Nothing that will not keep. Perhaps we can discuss it over dinner tomorrow evening if you will allow me to take you out again?' He must have seen the surprise in her expression because he smiled and added, 'It would give you a chance to escape for a few hours.'

'That certainly sounds tempting.'

They walked together into the foyer. She was already having second thoughts by the time they reached the front door. 'Perhaps I ought to take a rain check. Will you give me a ring?'

'Take care.' He bent and gave her a parting kiss on the cheek. He was gone before she had a chance to react.

Chapter 21

Her encounter with Montgomery-Jones meant that she was later returning to her room than she had intended.

'Damn!' The mess of papers on her bed greeted her as she walked in the door. She had forgotten all about them.

She was tempted to shuffle them together and stuff them in a drawer until later so that she could lay out the clothes she was going to change into after her shower, but they would only sit on her conscience. Best to try and put them in some sort of order now.

At this stage of the tour, there was no need for her to be down in time to greet people at the door as everyone knew which tables were reserved for Super Sun guests. Nonetheless, she liked to be there to check there were no problems. This evening, by the time she arrived, most of them were already in the restaurant and the tables were filling up fast.

'Do come and join us, Fiona.'

She could hardly ignore Eleanor Prior. Reluctantly she slipped into the seat next to Jeffrey. At least she would have him as a shield between her and his wife's non-stop chatter.

Dee and Hazel were the last to arrive and once they passed by, Eleanor leaned forward and said in a conspiratorial stage whisper to the rest of the table's occupants, 'Did you hear about that girl's hysterics in the lounge earlier?'

Before Fiona could think of something to say to stop her, Eleanor was in full flow.

'The silly woman's behaviour just isn't natural,' said Glenda, lips pursed in disapproval. 'If Dee as much as talks to anyone else, Hazel starts looking daggers.'

'Anyone would think she'd found them in the clinch the way Hazel was acting,' agreed Eleanor with relish.

'I think it's just because the poor girl is a wee bit insecure.' Liz Kennedy was doing her best, but it was time to change the subject.

'Did you enjoy today, Jeffrey?' Fiona turned to the man sitting next to her.

'Me?' Jeffrey Prior looked a little startled. 'Er. Yes, very nice thank you, Fiona.' He'd obviously been in his own little world. He was evidently used to switching off once his wife went into gossip mode.

It was as the soup dishes were being cleared away that Glenda asked, 'Are the police going to be asking us any more questions, do you know, Fiona?'

'I've no idea.'

'I wondered when I saw you with that man in the lounge earlier. The one in the three-piece suit who came to ask questions after all that trouble at the rally. He seemed to be giving poor Hazel a right grilling at the beginning of the week. She was in tears.'

'She was upset because Dee had been arrested. He was just trying to help,' Fiona protested.

'He was here a second time when we all thought Robert was missing. He was asking you a lot of questions, Fiona.' Eleanor looked at her suspiciously. 'Is he a policeman?'

'Mr Montgomery-Jones is a friend. More of an acquaintance really. Because we both happened to be in Brussels at the same time, he came to have a chat, that's all. It wasn't official.' Perhaps she should have a word with Peter. It might help to avoid any more difficult questions if they met some place where they were less likely to be seen in future.

'I don't understand why the police wanted to talk to all of

us anyway,' grumbled Aubrey Diamond. 'It wasn't as if any of us were there when that chap was killed. We'd only just met the man for heaven's sake! Anyone would think he'd been murdered the way they kept asking questions about where we were and who we saw that day.'

'Well, me and you are in the clear,' said his wife smugly. 'That was the morning we stayed here in the hotel because of your rotten cold.'

'And me and Jeffrey were nowhere near that demo either. After we came out of the Town Hall, we went for a coffee and then we had a look round the shops. As I told that policeman on Tuesday, I've got a receipt for the chocolates we bought in that glass arcade place and for the lunch we had in that street behind the Main Square with all them restaurants.'

'That's right,' piped up her husband. 'And it can't have been Gina and Simon Lithgow either because we saw them in the restaurant opposite.'

Liz Kennedy gave a little laugh. 'Malcolm and I went to the museum and we spoke to that nice Rev. Nicholas and his wife and I'm sure they'll vouch for us if we all need to provide alibis.'

Fiona could hardly tell them that it was no game, but in all likelihood, none of these people had ever been on the suspect list. They were all virtual strangers as far as the Swanley Association Chairman was concerned. What possible motive could any of them have? Still, it was good to know that the Lithgows could also be crossed of the list. Not that either of them had ever been a serious contender. Robert's death might mean that there was a good chance Simon would inherit the chairmanship, but that was hardly a motive. It was a relief to know that Nicholas and Barbara McArdle were definitely in the clear. Fiona had grown rather fond of the elderly couple.

Peter Montgomery-Jones must have access to the results of the police interviews, so he must know where everyone was. Why hadn't he told her? She might not be part of the investigation, but he had enlisted her help. The least he could do was let her know which of her passengers she need no longer suspect. Surely, such information was hardly a breach of confidentiality likely to jeopardise the investigation.

'. . . and Gina told me if it hadn't been for his father, he would have gone to prison . . .'

Fiona's attention was suddenly brought back to the present. Eleanor Prior and Glenda Diamond were in a tight huddle. With Jeffrey Prior sitting between Fiona and the two women, it wasn't easy to catch what was being said.

'A thoroughly bad lot apparently. A gambler. Lost everything. His wife took the kiddie and went to live with her mum. Apparently, he owed money to some loan shark so, in desperation, he stole all this money. Thousands of pounds from his father's account and then, if you please, he. . .' Eleanor leaned closer to Glenda and whispered the rest, her hand in front of her mouth.

'No! The club funds?' Glenda's eyes were wide with excitement.

'True. It was all hushed up, of course. The police were never involved and even the committee members don't know about it. But you must keep it to yourself. I promised Gina I wouldn't tell a soul.'

Fiona had noticed Gina and Eleanor chatting together on a couple of occasions since that day she'd overheard the two of them in the Wellington Museum. Perhaps it was inevitable that the two great gossips in the group should gravitate towards one another. Nursing a sense of grievance at being made to feel inferior to her fellow Association members, perhaps it was inevitable that Gina would relish the opportunity to get her own back when she found a sympathetic ear. It didn't take a detective to work out who they were talking about, especially as Noel Appleby was the Association's treasurer, but how far could the story be believed? Both Gina and Eleanor were sensationalists, not above embellishing a story for a bit of dramatic appeal. With both of them adding their two pennyworth, just how much real substance was there to Eleanor's lurid account? If it were true, how had Gina, of all people, got to hear about it in the first place?

One thing could not be denied. If Robert had known that Noel's son had managed to get his hands on funds belonging to the Swanley Association, it certainly gave him ammunition to blackmail the affable club treasurer. In return for keeping the whole affair secret, Noel must have agreed to further Robert's political ambitions. As President of the local Conservative Club, he would have a great deal of influence and any nomination he made for the next parliamentary candidate would be likely to be accepted. Presumably, it also explained why he had no choice but to accept Robert's continued put downs even in public. Robert no doubt despised Noel's weakness for letting him humiliate him in front of his friends. The man had been a callous bully.

Fiona felt so angry that, for a brief moment, it flashed through her mind that it was no bad thing that Robert Heppell was no longer around.

Fiona found herself sitting next to Olive as they waited for the evening presentation to begin.

'Robert was due to give this talk, you know,' Olive said, lips pursed in disapproval.

'Then we must be grateful that Noel volunteered to take it on at such short notice. It would have been a shame to have to miss another one.'

'Robert did all the work. He did the research and found the slides and put it all together. His presentation and all the notes were on the laptop so anyone could do it.' Olive pulled out a handkerchief and dabbed at her eyes.

Fiona put a hand on her arm. 'I'm sure Noel will do it justice. It will be a kind of tribute to Robert to show just how much he contributed to making this such a successful holiday for everyone, don't you think?'

'Yes, I suppose so.' She managed a weak smile. 'He was such a wonderful person. I do miss our little chats. He used to take me into his confidence a great deal, you know.'

'Really?'

'Oh yes. He would often sound me out about new ideas he had for the Association. He used to say he valued my opinion,' she added with a touch of pride. 'Sometimes he'd ask me to gauge the general feeling about some of the more controversial measures he was thinking of introducing. Suss out those who might put a spoke in the wheel if you know what I mean. Keep an ear out for anyone who might oppose him. Forearmed is forewarned, he used to say.'

The poor woman was obviously besotted with the man, Fiona thought. And how like him to use her devotion to put a spy in the camp. No doubt she would pass on every snippet she managed to pick up.

And not just about future Association matters, either. What better way to pick up any indiscretion or weakness that might prove useful to him at some future date?

Fiona was standing by the bar when she heard the soft jangle of bracelets behind her and a soft husky voice said, 'Interesting man that friend of yours who was here earlier. Quite a charmer, isn't he.'

She turned and smiled at Philippa. 'Peter? I suppose he is.' This could be dangerous territory. 'But he's more of an acquaintance than a friend.' Best to say as little as possible.

'We were talking the other evening. It seems we have friends in common. I went to school with Lord Martingdale's daughter and it turns out Peter is a second cousin or something to Sir Rupert and he knows Marissa quite well. They ride to hounds together.'

Don't rise to the bait, Fiona told herself. If this was the woman's attempt to put her down, to show her she didn't move in the same circles, it was best not to let Philippa know that she was succeeding. 'It can be a surprisingly small world.'

'Can't it just?' Philippa gave a brittle laugh. 'Would you believe he also knows Daddy?'

'Really?'

'Oh yes! Daddy works in the City, but he acts as an adviser on various finance and business committees, so he mixes with a great many people in government. He tells some very interesting stories about some of these politicians. According to him, they may talk the talk, but when it comes down to it, they haven't a clue. Frightening really.'

'Did he know the MP who was shot the other day here in Brussels?'

'Moorhouse?' For a brief moment, Philippa appeared disconcerted, but she covered it quickly and continued offhandedly, 'I seem to remember years ago they were both on one of those quango things looking at maximising business opportunities abroad or some such. But once Tommy had blotted his copybook and became such a rabble-rouser, I can't see Daddy having much to do with him.'

'How did your father get to know Peter?'

'They probably touched base at one of those big City functions were everyone goes to network. I went with Daddy to a few of those great banquet affairs after Mummy died when he needed a partner. Very boring and the food was terrible! Tough meat in congealed sauces with lukewarm vegetables, soggy from sitting on hot plates for half an hour while they attempted to serve a hundred and fifty people all at once.'

'Definitely not the case when you host your social events,' Fiona said giving her most charming smile. 'I hear the food at your dinner parties is always delectable.'

'Oh?' Philippa looked at her suspiciously.

'Peggy tells me your soirees are the talk of the town.'

Philippa gave a self-deprecating laugh. 'Dear Peggy. Actually, she hasn't been for a while. Daddy brought a few of his business friends the last few times and they talked business all evening. In fact, . . .'

'Can I get you two lovely ladies a drink?'

Austin pushed between them and put an arm around each of their shoulders.

Damn. Just when she might have learnt something of value.

Day 8 Friday, Brussels

This morning we return to The Upper Town of Brussels. Our first visit will be to the magnificent cathedral of Sts. Michael and Gudule which is the national church of Belgium. It is the finest surviving example of Brabant Gothic architecture. Inside, we will see the Grenzig organ, the Baroque pulpit depicting the expulsion of Adam and Eve from the Garden of Eden and the statues of St. Michael the Archangel killing the dragon, symbolic of his protection of the city, and of St. Gudule, a 7th-century saint much venerated in the city.

Larger than St Peter's Basilica in Rome, it would be difficult to miss the mighty Palais de Justice, one of the grandest of King Leopold II's ambitious projects. Built towards the end of the 19th-century, this Neo-Classical building was designed by Joseph Poelaert who took for inspiration the temples of the great Egyptian Pharaohs. The Palais de Justice still houses the Brussel's law courts.

We will return to the Place du Grand Sabon. Here you can admire the 18th-century fountain and Art Nouveau facades of the elegant town houses which surround the square or perhaps explore some of the treasures in one of the antique shops before lunch in one of the many popular cafés.

After lunch, we will visit one of Brussels' famous chocolatiers where we will be given a demonstration on preparing chocolate and be able to sample some of the delicious handmade chocolates.

Our final visit will be to a lace workshop to admire Brussels' world-famous lace, watch the women demonstrating this age-old local craft and learn about bobbin lace.

Super Sun Executive Travel

Chapter 22

Fiona was halfway through breakfast when Simon Lithgow came up and slid onto the chair beside her.

'Sorry to catch you while you're still eating.'

'Not a problem. Nothing wrong I hope?'

'No, no.' His face broke into a boyish grin. 'We were wondering about putting on a slide show for everyone as a sort of celebration finale of the holiday. Between us we've got some great photos and we thought it might be nice to round it all off with pictures of us all having a great time. It's been a pretty tragic trip one way and another, certainly had its moments, so we thought it might be good to end it all off on a happier note.'

'I think that's a splendid idea.'

'Everyone will probably be busy packing tomorrow evening, so we were thinking about doing it tonight, if that's all right with you?'

'That sounds sensible. Although I will need to check with the hotel to see if we can use the room again this evening. I think they have already put the tables back and arranged it as a conference room, but I'm sure that won't be a problem. I'll let you know before we leave this morning and then you can tell everyone when we get on the coach.'

'Fantastic!'

Fiona was not allowed to enjoy the feel-good factor for long. As she cleared away her breakfast things and turned to leave the café, she almost bumped into Jeffrey Prior and Aubrey Diamond standing in the aisle engrossed in conversation.

'Sorry, Fiona. Didn't see you there.'

'No problem.'

'Humph,' Aubrey snorted. 'If only!'

'Something wrong?' Fiona asked. 'Where are Eleanor and Glenda? Are they not coming to breakfast?'

'They're both upstairs. Eleanor was really poorly in the night. Rushing to the loo every five minutes she was. She's taken some tablets and she's okay now, but she won't be coming with us this morning. If she feels up to it, she might join us after lunch. I came down to have breakfast with Aubrey and Glenda and it seems she was ill as well.'

'That's right. She weren't as bad as Eleanor, but she's just going to have a cup of tea in the room.'

'Oh dear.'

'We was just wondering if it was something they ate last night. They both had them pastry things with fruit and cream, which neither of us had. But you did too, didn't you, Fiona? You didn't have no problems though, did you?'

'No but then I didn't have any cream on my tart.' She looked around the room and spotted Liz and Malcolm Kennedy. 'I think Malcolm had cream on his though. He looks hearty enough, but you could go and ask.'

Jeffrey gave a sniff. 'I still think it was the salted nuts we had with our drinks in the bar after. Eleanor loves nuts. She polished off the lot. I'm always telling her, you don't know how long those little dishes have been hanging around. I bet they just top 'em up rather than throwing out all the stale ones at the bottom.'

'If there is nothing more I can do for you, I must be getting on. Do tell your wives I hope they'll be better soon.'

The morning's video conference was in full swing. For once, Salmon was not being his usual blustering self. He seemed more subdued than usual. It was almost a week now since

Moorhouse's assassination. Despite the initial breakthrough after the interview with Müller, the investigation was grinding on painfully slowly and the team appeared to be making little headway. There was still no further progress in the attempt to identify who had ordered the assassination. If Salmon had hopes of making a name for himself by a swift closing of the case, they were rapidly being dashed.

Cumming's news that a publican in Fort Augustus, at the half-way point on the Great Glen Way from Inverness to Fort William, had identified Reece Bradshaw as an overnight guest on the day after Moorhouse's shooting had dampened even Ferguson's usual ebullience.

'Seems it had been sheeting it down with rain all day, so Bradshaw needed somewhere to dry out.' Cumming informed them.

'And what of the other suspects?' asked Salmon.

'The majority of the names of potential individuals who might have taken matters into their own hands, have now been thoroughly investigated and ruled out including,' Cumming looked down at his notes. 'Alan Bradshaw, Edmund Pearce, Oliver Rushton, Stefan Bobienski and Adrian Thomas. We're still waiting on details concerning Sidney Hamilton, Tony Harding and Afzal Khalid.'

'Which means that if we're talking about a contract killer, it's going to be a damn sight harder to make a link with whoever employed him when the list of suspects gets longer by the day.' Ferguson was losing heart now he had lost his prime suspect. 'I presume our techno-spymasters haven't turned up anything useful?'

'Not as yet.'

Montgomery-Jones looked up from his papers. 'What about Moorhouse's fellow investors in the failed East European Agriculture venture? Are these all the names?'

'Yes, sir. And I cross-referenced them with any of his known business contacts from his days in the Treasury as you requested, sir. That list may not be exhaustive, but there are four matches – Humphrey Egmont, Sir Charles Morris, Henry Ensley and Jonathan Hanley.'

Montgomery-Jones smiled. 'Interesting.'

'You seriously think one of them had something to do with Moorhouse's killing?' Salmon asked. 'They all got out in time and made a killing so what possible grievance could they have? Even if they were implicated in the misappropriation of EU funds in this investment scandal, Moorhouse was hardly likely to spill the beans. That would involve him having to admit his own involvement and end up like them with a hefty prison sentence.'

'True, but few of the other suspects investigated so far possess sufficient resources to pay for a contract killer. The bank accounts and financial records of those that have, show no substantial withdrawals in the last three months. Each of these four is a man of considerable means and no doubt they all have small fortunes hidden away in overseas accounts.'

'I take your point.' Salmon conceded. 'Now we have to look for a possible motive. Any ideas, gentlemen?'

It took some time to sort out the details with the hotel for their evening slideshow. First Fiona had to track down the appropriate member of staff to check that the room was available, then another to arrange for the room to be set up and yet a third person to negotiate the extra cost for the company. Thankfully, she was well within the budget that Super Sun allowed for any additional expenses that might arise. No chance of a last-minute study of her guiding notes for the day's activities. She barely made it to the foyer before they were due to set off.

It wasn't until they stopped for midmorning coffee that she remembered Peter Montgomery-Jones's invitation to dinner. She waited until everyone had finished and was preoccupied gathering their belongings in preparation for the return to the coach before she found a quiet corner where she could use her mobile.

'It's Fiona. I really am sorry about this, but I'm afraid I'm going to have to cry off our arrangement for tonight.'

Once she had explained he said, 'That is disappointing. Is there any chance of you being able to get away at lunchtime?'

She had so much to tell him. It wouldn't be easy, but today, to maximise everyone's free time, the programme had been arranged to allow clients to make their own eating arrangements. With luck, she would not be missed.

'I could manage an hour or so. We are going to be in the Sablon area. The group will be eating in various cafés in the square, but I'd rather we weren't seen together if you don't mind. It would avoid awkward questions and I don't want any of the passengers to think I'm shirking my responsibilities taking time out.'

'There is a café on the Rue des Minimes just off the north-east corner of the square. How about I meet you there?'

'Fine. Around twelve-thirty?'

'Take care.'

She slipped her phone back into the inner pocket of her tote bag and turned to walk to the designated meeting point. Philippa stood watching her intently from the far side of the café terrace. Had the woman been listening in to her call? Surely not. She was too far away to hear anything. She gave Philippa the best smile she could muster and walked towards her. 'Are you ready to go?'

Philippa returned her smile and nodded. 'Remind me, what's next on our agenda?'

'The Palais de Justice. I'm sure you'll enjoy it. It's a spectacular building.'

'I'm sure. Tell me, will you be seeing that good-looking friend of yours again?'

'You mean Peter?' She was on dangerous ground. 'He is very busy. I think he's in meetings for the next few days.'

'I didn't realise he was actually working over here. I thought he was on holiday.'

'He said something about having to attend some sort of

conference or other and combining it with a bit of a break.' Fiona said quickly. 'As I said he's more of an acquaintance than a friend.'

'Eleanor Prior seems to think he's a policeman. Is he involved in investigating Robert's murder?'

'Trust Eleanor!' Fiona raised her eyes heavenwards in mock exasperation. 'That woman has a very vivid imagination. To be honest I'm not exactly sure what Peter does.' At least that was only half a lie. 'He works in some government office, I believe. A Civil Servant of some kind, I guess.'

Philippa didn't seem convinced. 'He was asking a lot of questions that evening he was sitting with us in the lounge.'

'That's natural, isn't it? Everyone's been talking about the Moorhouse shooting and if someone happened to mention a Super Sun passenger was one of the victims in the riot that followed, it would be bound to arouse anyone's curiosity, don't you think?'

'Did he ask you about Robert?' Philippa asked suspiciously.

'Of course, we talked about what happened to him, but only in passing. Why? Is it important?'

'No, no. I just wondered that's all.' Philippa turned away and went over to speak to Austin. They exchanged a few words before she moved to stand next to her husband.

Did she imagine it, Fiona wondered, or was Austin Pilkington glaring at her? His expression was certainly serious and somehow, she didn't think it was simply the sun shining into her eyes that caused his slight frown.

Peter Montgomery-Jones was already waiting by the time Fiona arrived at the café.

'I thought we'd sit inside as you seemed not to want to be seen with me.' There was a playful twinkle in his eye, and she noticed that, rather than wearing his usual three-piece suit, he was dressed like any other tourist. She wondered if he had had to return to his hotel to change.

She gave an apologetic smile. 'I've already had to fend off questions. A couple of my guests seem to think you were with the police. I could hardly tell them you work for Her Majesty's Secret Service, now can I?'

'Why would they think I was a policeman?'

'Eleanor Prior saw you questioning Hazel about Dee. I did try and disabuse her of the idea, but to no avail it would seem. Philippa also mentioned it this morning. When I denied it, she started pumping me to find out what you do for a living and what you're doing in Brussels at all.'

'Really?'

'That's the reason I think it might be best if we're not seen together in future.' She gave him a mischievous grin. 'We can't have people thinking I'm a spy in the camp passing on any secrets to the enemy.'

'Tell me about this Eleanor Prior. Is she a member of Swanley Association?'

Fiona shook her head. 'No, but not much misses our Eleanor. She is the group gossip. She revels in the merest hint of scandal. In fact, she was the one who spread the word about Noel Appleby's son embezzling the Association funds. How accurate that might be is another matter. A case of Chinese whispers you could say, heavily embellished as the story has been passed on.'

'If there is any truth in the story, it would certainly have given Heppell a hold over Appleby senior,' Montgomery-Jones agreed.

'It's a reasonable assumption that Eleanor got the story from Gina, but what's been puzzling me is how Gina Lithgow got to hear about it. I was thinking about it in bed last night and the only explanation I can come up with is that although Noel is attempting to pay back the money his son took, there's probably still a big hole in the accounts. Presumably, Robert found out because, as Chairman of the Association, he was the second signatory on the club cheques and knowing him, demanded to see the accounts. Perhaps, once Simon became chairman, Noel decided to take him on one side and explain the situation and ask for his discretion. It would have come out eventually anyway. Knowing Gina Lithgow, I can imagine her listening in to their exchange somehow. I can't see Simon passing it on even to her because he must know his wife wouldn't be able to resist telling all and sundry.'

Montgomery-Jones gave a wry smile. 'It all sounds very plausible.'

Fiona picked up her baguette and wished that, like Montgomery-Jones, she had ordered the soup. Trying to munch on the end of the nine-inch roll without the tuna mayonnaise filling oozing out everywhere was going to be no mean feat. Even cutting it in half would be a messy affair. So much for being dignified and ladylike!

Once she'd finished her mouthful, she said, 'Another thing I learnt from Eleanor, and this I have no reason to doubt, was the whereabouts of several of the group at the time of Robert's murder. I appreciate the police will have statements from everyone in the party, but I presume it helps to have them confirmed?'

'Indeed.'

It was difficult trying to talk and concentrate on attempting to make as little mess as possible, so she waited until they had finished eating.

'I was talking last night to Philippa.' His forehead creased in a suspicious frown. 'Don't worry, she approached me, and I didn't pry.

'She happened to mention that you know her father.'

'Know *of* him,' he corrected.

'She seems to think the two of you are on friendly terms.'

'There is every likelihood that our paths have crossed at some function or other, but I confess I cannot recall being introduced.' He gave a deprecating laugh. 'However, I may have let her think that it was rather more than that.'

'And you wonder why I call you devious? Anyway, the

subject got round to the dinner parties that she hosts in her own home. It seems that her father has been to a couple in recent months, bringing various business colleagues with him. I think it is probably safe to assume he and Robert must have met.'

'That is very useful. Thank you.'

'I don't know if it's of any relevance, but she also mentioned that her father and Tom Moorhouse served on the same committee some time ago.'

'I did suspect that that might be the case.'

He sat back with an uncharacteristically broad smile that he seemed incapable of suppressing even if he did try to cover it up by hiding behind his cup as he drank the last of his coffee. She had never seen him so elated. As he replaced it on the saucer, he looked up. 'Did you learn anything else from the estimable Mrs Western? Did she ever meet Moorhouse?'

'She didn't say, but she did call him Tommy.'

'Interesting.'

Should she tell him about the argument Philippa had had with Robert on the first day when they'd arrived at the hotel?

Montgomery-Jones smiled. 'Do I take it from your expression that you do not have a high opinion of the lady?'

'What I think is irrelevant,' she said quickly. 'What I mean is I don't know her well enough to form an opinion.'

She was saved further embarrassment by a waitress who came to take away their empty plates. Fiona glanced at her watch.

'Heavens, is that the time? I need to go. Thank you for lunch.'

She jumped to her feet and left him sitting at the table, deep in thought.

Chapter 23

Several people were already waiting by the time Fiona reached the rendezvous point in front of Notre Dame du Sablon including Dee, but no Hazel. Fiona had noticed the tension between the two women earlier when they were outside The Palais de Justice. Obviously, the fallout from their very public spat in the hotel lounge the previous evening was still far from resolved. Although they had sat together for the short coach journey to the cathedral, they had kept a noticeable distance from each other all morning as the group had toured around.

'Hazel not with you?' Eleanor Prior asked.

She had only just re-joined the group after her morning's recovery at the hotel and here she was, stirring up trouble again.

'She's just coming. There's quite a queue in the ladies' loo!' Dee attempted a smile, then turned away and came across to speak to Fiona. 'Where are we off to next? It's the chocolate shop, isn't it?'

Dee's question was probably only a ruse to avoid Eleanor's probing, but Fiona was only too happy to keep up the charade.

'It's a little more than just a shop. First of all, there's a presentation and then we'll go and see a demonstration of how pralines are made. You can even give it a go yourself if you fancy.'

'What I want to know is if we get any free samples.'

'Oh, I should think there just might be one or two,' Fiona said with a laugh, 'And if you all play your cards right, I think we might all get a hot chocolate drink.'

'Scrumptious!'

They were both still laughing when Fiona noticed Hazel crossing the square towards them, looking far from happy. She was certainly not at the top of that young lady's Christmas card list, Fiona realised.

Dee had obviously caught her friend's glare and said under her breath, 'Oh for goodness' sake!' Nonetheless, she put on a bright smile and went over to slip her arm through Hazel's.

'Why didn't you wait for me?' Hazel accused.

'It was far too crowded in there, sweetie. Besides, you knew where I was.'

There was an expectant air in the small office as they waited for the video link with Thames House. Cumming had telephoned to say that his team had discovered information linking Henry Ensley and the MP Neville Truelove and Salmon had requested a video conference so that Montgomery-Jones and Ferguson could be involved in the discussions.

Ferguson settled in his chair cradling a mug of coffee that he had brought in with him. Salmon glared but said nothing and turned back to his laptop.

'Good morning, gentlemen.' Cumming's smiling face appeared on the screen.

It took only ten minutes for Cumming to provide a short résumé of both men's careers and recent activities.

'Not only did the affair end Truelove's marriage, he was made to look a complete buffoon. Truelove was lampooned in the press.'

Cumming's face disappeared from the screen to be replaced by a copy of a newspaper cartoon. Truelove was depicted as an obese old man, with a large bulbous nose, lying sprawled in a chair fast asleep in front of the fire, a bottle of whisky and an overturned tumbler on a small table beside him. Behind him, a slim young woman, a finger held to her lips, was creeping towards a figure who bore a remarkable resemblance to Moorhouse, peeping around the door.

'Truelove may not have had ambitions for a seat in the cabinet, but any hopes of being anything other than a lowly backbencher were well and truly scuppered,' Cumming continued. 'Truelove never forgave Moorhouse. Nor has he let his hatred simmer in silence. Far from retreating to lick his wounds, he has never missed an opportunity to get back at Moorhouse. We know he hired a private detective to find anything that he could use against Moorhouse. Reports began to appear in the press about financial irregularities in certain contentious government funded projects which appeared to implicate Moorhouse. They fell just short of libellous, quoting so-called well-placed but unidentified sources, which in all likelihood, were Truelove himself. It would seem that the stories had little foundation in fact, but by then the damage was done. Moorhouse's rise was on the wane.'

'And how does Henry Ensley fit into all this?' Salmon asked.

'Ensley rose to become one of the youngest CEOs of a major investment company ever appointed.' Cumming outlined the man's considerable achievements, his moves to head up increasingly more prestigious companies and the various finance quango and government-appointed committees on which he was asked to sit. 'As a Junior Treasury Minister, Moorhouse sat on several of the same committees as Ensley and by all accounts, the two men struck up, if not a friendship, at least a close working relationship. Ensley is a frequent visitor to the House and he and Moorhouse were frequently seen there together, right up until last year when Moorhouse decided to spend virtually all his time campaigning for Blockupy and the Anti-Austerity Alliance. In his Treasury days, they partnered each other on the golf course and Moorhouse was an occasional weekend guest at Ensley's place in the country.'

'What about more recently? Are you saying they fell out with each other?'

'There's no evidence of that. The fact that they were both heavily involved in the recent European Agriculture debacle would suggest not. Whether it was Ensley who warned Moorhouse to get out or the other way round, we don't know.'

'We now have confirmation that there are strong connections between Truelove and Moorhouse and Ensley and Moorhouse that go much deeper than mere acquaintance.' Salmon pushed back his chair and walked over to the whiteboard. He picked up a marker pen and wrote MOORHOUSE at the top of the board. Halfway down, he printed the other two names to form a triangle.

'Truelove has a strong motive to wish Moorhouse dead.' He drew a red arrow between the two names. 'And if nothing else, a close working relationship between Ensley and our victim.' He linked both names with a blue line.

'Okay, so what's this connection between Truelove and Ensley you want to tell us about?' Ferguson asked turning back to look at the screen.

'Both men live within a few miles of one another in Richmond,' said Cumming. 'They have known one another for over thirty years and move in the same social circles.'

'We can assume both men are close friends.' Salmon turned back to the board and picking up the blue marker again, drew a line between the bottom two names.

'Friends possibly, but they have their differences. Truelove comes from the old landowning classes, by no means destitute, but the old family estate is now long gone. A dyed-in-the-wool Tory. Ensley on the other hand, is something of a self-made man. Middle-class hard-working parents, ex-grammar schoolboy with a real business flair. He's not a political animal. Happy to rub shoulders with anyone if it suits his business interests.'

'Whether motivated by friendship or mutual interest, we can assume that the two are happy to support one another, if only to be in a position to call in a favour in return in the future,' said Ferguson.

'We have discovered that it was Truelove who nominated Ensley for a CBE,' Cumming pointed out.

Montgomery-Jones smiled. 'I wondered if that was the case. That knighthood means a great deal to Ensley. He has achieved everything else he ever wanted in life and a Queen's Honour is the one thing that has eluded him. Given what we now know, it would appear a strong possibility that it was Ensley who suggested to Truelove that he sell his stake in the East European Agricultural Project before it finally collapsed.'

'What are we saying here?' asked Salmon excitedly. 'That in return for Truelove's help, he would be prepared to get rid of Moorhouse?

Montgomery-Jones shook his head. 'Ensley is no saint, far from it. Even if it cannot be proven, it is no secret that he has made a small fortune from insider trading and a string of Russian Mafia type contacts. Whether it takes a ruthless man to get to the top or a man is made ruthless by his position of power is debatable. Nonetheless, the point I am trying to make is that I find it difficult to believe that Ensley, friend or not, would allow himself to be persuaded by Truelove to be involved in any kind of attempt on Moorhouse's life, even in return for something he holds so dear. However much he might sympathise with Truelove, his own dealings with Moorhouse, at least as far as we know, have always been to their mutual advantage. He has made a great deal of money out of their joint schemes. Far from wanting Moorhouse out of the way, Ensley had much to gain from any future business ventures they might be engaged in.'

'Are you saying all this,' Salmon waved his hand at the board, 'is meaningless?' You were the one who asked for links to be investigated in the first place. We would never have wasted our time over it if it hadn't been at your insistence.'

'Not at all,' Montgomery-Jones said calmly. 'The answer is there somewhere. I am convinced of it.'

He stood up and walked over to the whiteboard. 'There is a fourth name that I believe we should add to this mix. Robert Heppell was murdered at around the same time as Moorhouse only a short distance away. Not by a gunshot, but by a blow to the back of the head, probably with a brick. We now know that Heppell had met all three men. We've already established his working with Moorhouse, and it seems that Heppell also engineered meetings with Ensley and Truelove through Ensley's daughter over whom he exerted some kind of hold.'

'How does that help us?' asked Salmon.

'We know Ensley is desperate for a knighthood and any hint of scandal would ruin his chances. It is not impossible that Heppell discovered something to Ensley's disadvantage. I can think of no other reason why Ensley would persuade Truelove to support Heppell's parliamentary ambitions.'

'Sir.' Everyone in the room turned to the screen. 'Sorry to interrupt, but you were asking yesterday about Ensley's daughter?'

'Did you discover anything of interest?' Montgomery-Jones returned to his chair.

'Philippa Western was something of a rebel at university. In her first year at Imperial College she gained a reputation for frequenting nightclubs and wild parties like a good many students of her age. She managed to get herself arrested and her father had to bail her out on more than one occasion. She seemed determined to kick over the traces and joined a high-end escort agency. In all probability, it was to get her father's attention because she certainly didn't need the money. He may have given his family very little of his time and attention, like a great many men in his position, but he bought her a flat in Sloane Square and provided her with a very generous allowance. Her father hit the roof when he discovered that several of her clients included some of his own colleagues. The whole thing only came to light when he was trying to lobby some MP over a very expensive dinner. The MP had had far too much to drink and started bragging about his previous night's liaison with a prostitute. When he mentioned the girl had a birthmark on her right buttock, Ensley realised the man was talking about his daughter.'

Ferguson gave a whistle then sat back in his chair, hands behind his head. 'If Heppell got hold of that little story, Ensley would have bent over backwards to keep the whole thing under wraps. If it had come out, he would have had to kiss goodbye to any dreams of a knighthood.'

'Much as I hate to spoil the celebrations, gentlemen,' All eyes turned to Salmon who was leaning back against the wall by the whiteboard, arms folded across his chest. He pushed himself upright and strode back to the table. 'May I remind you, our remit is to uncover the person behind the assassination of Tom Moorhouse. We may have established that Ensley had good reason to want this Heppell character silenced before he could make trouble, but how does a motive for the death of an insignificant local councillor actually assist our investigation? I suppose it would be too much to hope for that the MP concerned was Moorhouse?'

'I'm afraid we don't have a name, sir.' Cumming looked suitably penitent. 'But it can't have been Moorhouse because he wasn't on the relevant committee. It was one of three men, two Conservatives and one Liberal Democrat.'

'Pity.' Salmon's voice was scathing. 'In which case, gentlemen, can we get back to the case in hand.'

'Have you tried the drinking chocolate? It's absolutely delicious. I must go and buy a packet before we all get back on the coach.'

As Peggy hurried over to the shop area, Fiona turned back

to the counter and picked up the small cardboard cup she'd been given. She took a small sip then put it down. Much as she loved chocolate, this was much too sweet even for her.

Everyone appeared to have enjoyed the chocolate workshop and most of the party got back onto the coach laden with carrier bags after the visit to the shop. As she settled down in her seat and they began to move off, she felt decidedly queasy. Definitely too many praline samples at one sitting!

Their next stop was at the Lace Centre and although there were the odd mutterings from some of the men, even they appeared to be fascinated to watch the skill of the traditional lace makers and the speed with which they twirled the bobbins and added pins to their pillows as the patterns developed. Although the rest of the afternoon passed without incident, the tension of the last few days had begun to take its toll. The sight of their hotel as Winston turned the final corner had never been so welcome.

For once, Fiona took the lift up to her room on the fifth floor. She decided to fill in the day's paperwork sitting propped up with pillows on her bed, but once it was done, she lay back and closed her eyes. It took some effort to rouse herself from her comfortable position, but she told herself firmly, duty called. It would be as well to check that the room had been set out for the evening lecture before she went into dinner. Although on reflection, it might be a good idea to find out how long the evening's entertainment would take.

There was no sign of Simon in the café, so Fiona made her way to the lounge bar. A few of the tables were occupied by groups of her passengers, but still no Simon. However, she spotted Gina sitting with Peggy at the far end enjoying the last of the summer sun still streaming through the window.

'I was looking for Simon. Is he still in your room?'

Gina pulled a face. 'Sorry. No idea where he is. He deserted me as soon as we got back to the hotel. Austin collared him the moment we got off the coach to talk about photos.

They're probably holed up somewhere with Bernard and Noel, busy looking through today's shots to add to tonight's slideshow. They could be anywhere.'

'No matter.'

'Why don't you join us? You look as though you could do with a nice cuppa.' Peggy signalled the waiter.

The idea of a cup of tea was very tempting. Fiona perched on the edge of the chair. Mustn't let herself get too comfortable. Ten minutes and then she would have to get on.

It wasn't long before they were joined by Philippa Western.

'Have you been deserted as well?' Gina asked.

Philippa sank down into the enveloping armchair and raised an eyebrow.

'Fiona was looking for Simon and I said I thought he might be with your husband and some of the others sorting out photos.'

'Oh, I see what you mean.' Philippa barely disguised her boredom. 'I think they all went to Austin's room, although they were talking of going down to the conference room to try them out on a big screen.'

'I must say, I do love that perfume you're wearing, Philippa. It's very distinctive.' Undeterred by Philippa's offhand manner, Gina seemed determined to try to ingratiate herself.

'Mmm. It is nice, isn't it? Daddy bought it for me a few weeks ago when he was in Paris.'

Fiona finished her tea and put down her cup. 'If you'll all excuse me? I must go and check that everything is ready for tonight.'

Peggy looked at her watch. 'I'll have to make a move soon too. I'm planning on a nice lazy soak in the bath this evening before I get changed for dinner.'

'See you all later.'

As she made her way out, Fiona passed Dee and Hazel sitting at a nearby table.

'Did you enjoy today?'

'Very much. Thank you, Fiona,' Dee replied. 'Help yourself to a chockie. We couldn't resist buying a few boxes at the chocolate factory. They were supposed to be taken home as presents, but we both decided we really ought to test them first.'

'You did that at the factory!' Fiona remonstrated with a laugh. 'They plied us all with enough free samples.'

'That's the trouble. Hazel here is a chocoholic, aren't you sweetie? Once you start, you can't stop. Go on, Fiona, do have one.'

'I need to think about my weight,' Fiona protested. 'The trouble with my job is that all this rich hotel food tends to pile on the pounds.'

'Rubbish! You've got a lovely figure.' Dee put a hand on her arm and lifted the box. 'I'm not letting you go until you've taken one.'

It was the last thing she fancied after her post-lunch excesses earlier, but she could hardly refuse. As she bit into the enormous praline, Fiona glanced across at Hazel. Dee might be full of bonhomie this evening, but there was a flash of pure hatred in her friend's eyes before she managed a somewhat fixed smile.

The conference room was on the first floor and Fiona headed for the stairs. Although there were signs of activity inside as the waiters prepared the tables for dinner, the doors to the Baudouin Restaurant were still closed. There were no guest rooms on the first floor, the other rooms being either conference suites or offices, so she was not surprised to find the corridor deserted. It felt strangely eerie as she turned the corner after all the bustle and noise of the ground floor that she'd just left. She could hear her footfalls even on the thickly padded carpet.

It occurred to her that the door might be locked for security reasons and it was a relief to find it open when she got there. The blackout curtains had been drawn and the room was in pitch darkness. She fumbled a hand on the wall by the door trying to find the lights. The first switch operated the rear bank of lights. It was enough to see that most of the tables had been removed and stacks of chairs had been brought in and placed against the wall ready to put out. A long cable lay coiled on one of the tables plus a small flexible-arm lamp, but unsurprisingly, no expensive portable equipment. The room would not be needed for at least a couple of hours, so there was no need to go chasing anyone to get everything sorted.

She was about to leave when she spotted what, in the half-light, looked like a pair of glasses on the floor beneath the front table. Best to pick them up before they were trodden on.

They were much further under than she first thought. It was no good; she could not reach them. She would have to get down on all fours and crawl under. It was very dark under the table with the bulk of her body cutting out the poor illumination from the back row of long-life bulbs, which were taking their time to warm up.

The sound of the door opening made her jump and she banged her head. It must be Simon and the others. She began to back out as the footsteps approached.

'Is that you, Si . . .'

She turned her head and caught sight of something fast approaching before she felt the blow.

Chapter 24

The ground beneath her was soft but it felt strange and itchy on her cheek and palms. A dusty, woolly smell drifted into her nostrils. All sorts of voices seemed to be jabbering away all round her. All at once. Urgent. Insistent. But she couldn't understand what they were saying. Too much effort.

Her eyelids began to flutter, and she was aware of the blurred dark green shape of a figure kneeling alongside her, but the light hurt her eyes and she needed to concentrate on the dull pounding behind her temple. She dragged her hand over the carpet towards her and lifted it to her head. Her hair was wet and sticky. Gently but firmly, a hand took her wrist and moved it away and probing fingers began feeling through her hair pressing lightly into her scalp.

She groaned.

She felt something slide under her cheek and several pairs of hands took hold of her limbs.

'Un, deux, trois.'

She felt herself being lifted and slowly rolled over, only to be laid on her back on another yielding surface.

Someone gave a plaintive whimper. Perhaps it was her.

'Un, deux, trois.'

She felt herself hoisted up into the air, followed by the sickening sway of movement. She wanted to tell them to stop. Just to leave her there. Why wouldn't they let her sleep? The last thing she wanted now was to be jiggled and jolted by marching feet.

The siren broke into her dreams. Did it have to be so loud? That penetrating two-tone whine was making her head hurt. She tried to move, to protest, but strong arms held her down.

Someone tried to put something over her nose and mouth. She struggled violently and tried to push the culprit away. Were they trying to smother her?

'Shush. Shusssh.' A hand took hold of her hers and a soft voice whispered, 'You're safe now.'

She clung onto it gratefully. Bill, her dear dependable husband. Now he was here everything would be all right.

Voices. Soft but urgent. Ignore them and perhaps they'll go away.

Her whole body felt heavy and leaden. And so unbelievably weary. Her head hurt. Not a sharp, stabbing pain but a dull, incessant pounding that blotted out everything else. It was as if her heart had been moved to the right side of her skull, each pulse resonating inside her temples.

It was dark. Pitch dark. And cold. A shudder ran through her whole body. There was a sudden scraping sound beside her. No. No. No. It couldn't be happening again. She tried to cry out but all she could manage was a high-pitched whimper. A hand was gently laid on her arm.

'Shussh. Go back to sleep.'

She did as she was told.

When she woke again, the drumbeats in her head had eased to a more bearable throb. She did not have to open her eyes to know that it was still dark. Why was she lying on her back? She always slept on her side. It was much too much effort to roll over. She sighed. A low, weary moan.

There was a sudden movement beside her. She stiffened.

'Fiona.' It was barely a whisper.

She relaxed again. Slowly she let her eyes open, just a fraction, letting them adjust to the poor light; allowing the swimming sensation and the nausea to subside. Through her half-closed lashes she could sense rather than see the dark shape of someone leaning towards her. He was still here. Everything would be all right now. She could go back to sleep. Her lips parted in a smile.

She felt the backs of his fingers gently brush down her cheek. Instinctively she lifted her hand to take his. Their fingers entwined and he gave hers a gentle squeeze.

'Love you.' Her voice was barely a whisper.

Why didn't he answer? He always said, 'Of course you do.' Perhaps he hadn't heard her. Dear, darling Bill. Her rock, her strength.

She felt the soft brush of his lips on her forehead.

Moments later, she drifted back to sleep.

Day 9 Saturday, Leuven and Mechelen

This morning we take a short journey to the small historic Flemish town of Leuven, famous for its university and its brewing industry. The university, founded in 1425, is one of the oldest and most important in Europe and its historic college buildings dominate many of the town's squares and streets. Its famous alumni include Erasmus, the founder of humanism; the great mapmaker, Mercator and Adrianus VI, tutor to Charlemagne, who became the only pope from the Low Countries.

After our tour of the town to see the Oude Markt (Old Market), the magnificent St. Pieterskerk in the Grote Markt (Main Market), the Stadhuis (Town Hall) and the peaceful Groot Begijnhof, which is a UNESCO World Heritage site, we will visit the Stella Artois Brewery.

After lunch, we will enjoy the quiet charm of Mechelen which was the former capital of the Low Countries under the Burgundian Prince Charles the Bold. The small town has a rich past and its heyday marked the change from the Middle Ages to the Renaissance. It is the seat of the Catholic Archbishop of Belgium and the city centre boasts eight Gothic and Baroque churches dating from the 14th to the 17th centuries, including the magnificent St. Romboutskathedraal with its splendid 97-metre-high tower.

We will return to Brussels in time for some last-minute shopping before we travel back to England tomorrow.

Super Sun Executive Travel

Chapter 25

It was the nurse, pushing open the door, who woke her. Light was streaming in through the windows. Fiona looked around the small stark room and the array of equipment beside the bed. Why was she in a hospital? The dull ache at the back of her head brought it all back.

'How are we feeling?'

We? Fiona had to smile. It sounded so stereotypical, exactly like a character from one of those old British comedies. Perhaps that was where the girl had picked up the idea this was how English nurses always addressed their patients.

'Much better, thank you.'

'Do you remember what happened?'

Fiona gave a rueful smile and put her hand to the egg-sized bump behind her ear. 'I don't think this is going to let me forget in a hurry.'

'Pardon?'

'I remember being hit from behind, but nothing much after that. I vaguely remember receiving some kind of treatment in an ambulance, but I don't think I was a model patient somehow?'

The nurse was too busy taking Fiona's temperature, blood pressure, pulse and heaven knows what else, to try to make sense of Fiona's babbling.

'All the results are back to normal,' the nurse said with a smile as she entered the figures on Fiona's chart.

'Excellent. Does that mean I can go soon?'

The nurse looked up sharply. 'Certainly not.'

'But I need to get back to my passengers.'

'The doctor will be doing his ward round soon and once he has seen you; he will let you know when you can go.'

She felt a rising panic. 'I need to ring my driver.'

'Would that be Mr Taylor?'

Fiona nodded.

'He telephoned first thing this morning to ask how you were. He left a message to say that everything has been taken care of and that you are not to worry. The company has been made aware of the situation and everything is in hand.'

Fiona had to smile. Typical Winston. She should've known he would have sorted things out.

'He said he would come and visit you when the party returns to Brussels this afternoon, but I told him there is a possibility that you might be back in the hotel by then.'

'That is good news.' She had fears of having to stay for at least twenty-four hours. Clearly her injuries were not considered serious if they didn't even want to keep her in for observation.

The nurse replaced Fiona's hospital file in the pocket at the end of the bed.

'There are two policemen waiting outside to speak to you when you feel up to it.' Seeing the look on her patient's face, she gave a conspiratorial grin. 'Shall I get you a coffee first?'

'I'd love a cup of tea.'

The two policemen came in almost as soon as the nurse had collected her breakfast tray. Not that she had managed to eat more than a couple of bites of toast. Even a few sips of tea had made her feel distinctly nauseous. The nurse assured her that it was only because of the drugs and that she would soon recover her appetite once the effects wore off.

'You cannot identify your assailant?' The younger officer asked after she'd told them all she could remember of the attack.

'I'm afraid not.'

'Was it a man or a woman?' He stared at her disapprovingly.

'I have no idea. I heard the door open, but I was still picking up stuff from under the table, so I didn't see who it was. They came up behind me and as I turned my head, I caught sight of something swinging down towards me. I was too busy trying to avoid whatever they were wielding to take a look at their face.'

'You were fortunate that it was only a glancing blow. A reading lamp was found on the floor beside you.' The older of the two men was far more sympathetic. He gave her a friendly smile. 'It was tested for fingerprints but the crinkled plastic covering the flexible arm meant that the results were badly smudged and incomplete.'

'That's a pity.'

He smiled. 'As a means of identifying your attacker quite possibly, but it did absorb most of the impact. According to the doctors, had the arm been solid, you could have been killed or, at best, seriously injured. It is good also that you were found so soon. You are a lucky lady.'

She gave him a rueful smile. 'I can't say I feel that lucky at the moment.'

'Have you any idea who might want to harm you?' The other officer, who appeared to be the more senior, was keen to get on with his questions.

Had Robert's murderer suspected that she was close to sussing him out? The last thing she needed right now was to give them a lengthy explanation of all that had been going on. She shook her head. Not a good idea. Her head began to throb, and she felt dizzy.

'How long were you in the room before your attacker came in?'

'Not long. A matter of minutes.'

'You were not aware of anyone following you?'

'No. the corridor was deserted when I went up.'

'No one could have seen you go in there?'

'I don't think so.'

'Who knew you were going to the conference room?'

'No one.' The man's constant staccato questions, barely giving her time to think were confusing her. Fiona thought for a moment. 'I may have mentioned it when I was in the lounge. But I can't see Peggy, Gina or Philippa doing anything like that. And what possible reason could they have for attacking me?'

'Did you go straight from the lounge to the conference room?'

'Yes. I . . .'

The door opened and the nurse was back again.

'Mrs Mason needs her rest now. Perhaps you gentlemen could return later.' As she had spoken in English, her comment was obviously intended for Fiona rather than the policemen.

The officers must have decided that there was nothing more of value to discover and left with a parting shot that they would probably be in touch when she returned to the hotel.

From the deference shown him by the nurse, Fiona judged that the spotty-faced youth who entered sometime later must be the doctor. Not that she was unduly surprised. Recent years spent back and forth to the new University Hospital with Bill had taught her that junior interns invariably looked to her like Year 13 schoolboys let out on work experience. Not that this was a problem. She was far from at death's door and now fully recovered, the sooner she was allowed out of the hospital to some semblance of the mad existence she was now learning to call normality and back to the hotel, the better.

He took the chart the nurse handed to him and the two rattled off a lengthy conversation that went far beyond anything Fiona could understand. She may have managed to scrape a pass at French O'level, but that was a long time ago and despite her recent attempts to brush up on the language for her new job, anything more than the basic vocabulary needed to get by, eluded her. Apart from which, it was all far too much effort.

The doctor came over to the bed and taking a small torch from his pocket, proceeded to shine it into each of her eyes, his cheek only inches from her own. From his smile when he stood up, she gathered that all was well. He gabbled away again at the nurse.

Once he'd finished her notes and returned the folder to its holder at the bottom of her bed, Fiona asked, 'When will I be able to leave? I really do need to get back to look after my passengers.'

He frowned and shook his head. His English may have been as limited as her French, but he clearly understood.

'In cases of concussion such as yours we do like to keep patients under observation for twenty-four hours,' the nurse translated.

'That really isn't necessary in my case. I lost consciousness for a few minutes at most. I distinctly remember coming round while I was still lying on the floor. I was a qualified nurse. I assure you should any symptoms arise, I will seek professional medical help immediately.'

Once again, the doctor and nurse spoke rapidly to one another. Eventually, the nurse turned back to her.

'The doctor says he is going to send you for a CT scan and providing there are no complications, he is prepared to discharge you.'

'Excellent.' She turned to the doctor. 'Thank you. Merci.'

'Still looking at Fiona, he rattled off something in French.

'The doctor wants to know when you are intending to travel back to Britain.'

'First thing tomorrow morning; all being well.'

He did not wait for a translation. 'You fly travel?'

'No. By coach across to Calais and then the ferry.'

He frowned. At first, she thought it was because he had not understood her reply but when his torrent of French was translated, Fiona appreciated there was a problem.

'Normally after such an injury, the patient would be asked to report to their own doctor in a day or two, but because you will be travelling such a long way and it will take a long time, the doctor would like you to return to the hospital before you set off.'

'Is that absolutely necessary? There really is nothing wrong with me now. I'm perfectly fit to travel, and we are leaving very early, straight after breakfast.'

Fiona's wheedling made no impact.

'We make early appointment.' The doctor smiled and made his exit.

She must have dozed off again because when she opened her eyes, Peter Montgomery-Jones was standing at the foot of her bed.

'Good morning, Fiona. How is the head?'

'Fine. They want me back for a check-up first thing tomorrow before we travel back to Britain but after my scan, I should be able to go.'

'So I hear.' He raised an eyebrow and with mock severity said, 'I understand that you have not been a model patient.'

She gave him a suitably chastened expression. 'He did say I should take it easy for the rest of the day.'

'That sounds eminently sensible.' He moved the chair to her bedside and sat down. 'I understand the police have already been to take a statement?' Was he about to make her go through it all again?

'Not that I was able to tell them very much.'

'So, I understand.'

That explained why he hadn't bothered to interrogate her. He'd spoken to them already.

'Why the frown?'

'I was just wondering how my group were getting on. I

have rather left poor Winston in the lurch. Some of my passengers can be a little demanding.'

Montgomery-Jones raised his eyes heavenwards. 'Mr Taylor was most insistent that I should tell you that he is more than capable of looking after everyone for the day. He said that your job was to rest and to take your time getting better.'

'Good old Winston. He really is a treasure. I'll give him a ring when I'm allowed to use the phone.'

'Your sons might also appreciate a call. I have let them know that you are out of danger and about to be discharged, nonetheless, I expect they will be anxious until they hear that directly from you.'

'Mr Montgomery-Jones!' She stared across at him in disbelief. 'You didn't phone them?'

'I am afraid I had no choice. They are your next of kin. I appreciate that you like to maintain the fiction that the worst thing that happens on any of your tours is having to deal with the odd awkward customer, but there was no way of knowing how serious your injuries were.'

'What did you tell them?'

'Only that you received a bad blow to the head. I may have given them the impression that you may have fallen and because you were knocked unconscious, it was thought prudent to bring you to hospital to check that there was no permanent damage. Your eldest son has rung several times. He was most insistent on knowing all the details.'

'You didn't let him know I was attacked?'

'I implied that I was not aware of the details.'

'Thank you for that at least. If either of them have the least suspicion that working as a tour manager is anything but the opportunity to have a constant string of free holidays, they will insist on my giving up the job. Adam in particular has never approved of me working for Super Sun; or working at all come to that. He doesn't seem able to accept that I am not an old lady incapable of making sensible decisions for myself. I can't seem to make him understand that I need to be doing something useful with my life, not just sit by the fireside knitting.'

'If you want to be useful, there is one thing you can do for me when you have a moment. I would like you to write down everything you have learnt about each of your passengers.'

She stared at him, appalled at the enormity of the task. 'All of them!'

'Perhaps not all.' He had the grace to give her an apologetic grin. 'Start with the three women you were talking to in the lounge before your attack. Anything about their past. Things that might have happened in the last few months you have heard about.'

'I'm not sure I understand.'

'Take Philippa for example. How well does she get on with her father? Has anything unusual happened in her life recently? It may seem a strange request, but I want to build up as accurate a picture of each of these people as I can.'

'Philippa! But I thought you . . .' Her voice faded away.

'You thought what?'

She felt the colour rising to her cheeks. 'She seems an unlikely suspect, that's all.'

His knowing smile indicated that he knew exactly what she'd been thinking. She could only hope that he didn't think she was jealous. Which of course she wasn't. Why should she be? Just because he had seemed attracted to a beautiful woman, and there was no denying that Philippa Western was the sort of woman that made every man and not a few women in the room turn and look at her, was no concern of hers.

'Just because a woman is blessed with good looks and an attractive figure and can afford to dress in such a way as to show off those features to their best advantage does not make her the type that all men find appealing. In my estimation, whatever Philippa Western's good qualities, and I do not doubt that she has many, she is, nonetheless, a woman whose own self-interest will always be paramount.' Before she could fully digest the implications of what he'd just said, he asked, 'What can you tell me about her?'

Fiona sighed and after a moment's thought, told him about the encounter she witnessed on the first day. 'I am certain Robert had some sort of hold over her. I'm convinced that it was at Robert's insistence that she persuaded her father to invite some of his influential friends, people who might be useful to advance his ambitions, to her dinner parties. I saw how she and Robert reacted to each other when they thought they were alone and to say she was not predisposed to doing him any favours is an understatement. She loathed the man and it was all she could do to be civil to him in public. According to Peggy Brent, before Robert became a frequent visitor, such occasions only involved the Western's close friends and were much more friendly, purely social affairs.'

'Have you any idea what that hold might be?'

'I thought at first, it was because she and Austin Pilkington were having an affair and Robert had threatened to tell her husband, but now I'm not so sure.'

'You do not believe they are?'

'There's little doubt! It's an open secret. They barely try to hide it. Bernard is no fool. He knows exactly what is going on. For what it's worth, I think, not only does he condone it, he seems happy to encourage it. The price of having such a much younger trophy wife. Besides, Austin is like a son to him, so he is more than happy to go along with the arrangement. I can only assume it's his way of ensuring that he can keep a hold of her.'

'If it was not an affair, then what might Heppell be using against her?'

She shrugged and shook her head slowly. 'I wondered if it was something in her past. She didn't give any details, but Olive happened to mention some scandal in Philippa's student days. I have no idea what it was, but her father had to hush it up.'

'Interesting.' He stirred his coffee, looking thoughtful. 'How did Heppell get to hear about it, I wonder?'

'Through Olive, I have no doubt. She's the type who listens at keyholes. It wouldn't surprise me if she made it her mission in life to ferret out all sorts of secrets to pass on to Robert. The poor woman was totally smitten with the man. In her eyes, Robert was a god who could do no wrong. I'm convinced she would have done anything for him.'

There was a knock at the door and the nurse came in with a porter with a wheelchair.

'We are ready to take you down for your CT scan now, Mrs Mason.'

Montgomery-Jones insisted on taking her arm and helping her into the chair, gently tucking a blanket around her legs.

'I feel such a fraud. I really am fine now. I'm sure I could walk there.'

'Even if that were true, I am not sure that it would be quite proper for you to wander round the building dressed only in a hospital gown.' He turned to the nurse. 'Would you be good enough to telephone me when Mrs Mason is ready to leave the hospital in order that I may drive her back to the hotel.'

'But I can easily . . .'

He held up an admonishing finger. 'Do as you are told.'

She pulled a face. 'Yes, sir. Thank you, sir.'

'Less of your cheek, madam. And do not forget to telephone your sons.' With that he was gone.

Chapter 26

The man who had introduced himself as Inspector Mertens, led Philippa down the corridor behind the hotel reception desk with the short, pudgy-faced man in plainclothes bringing up the rear. He pushed open a door, stood back and motioned her inside.

The small cramped office, its walls lined from floor to ceiling with shelves heavy with box files on one side and filing cabinets on another, had been set up for an interview with a table and chairs in the centre. The atmosphere was claustrophobic. It didn't help that there was only one small window set high up on the wall so that all one could see outside was a few white billowing clouds against a pale blue sky.

'I don't understand why you've dragged me away from the rest of the party. I have already told you I know nothing about the attack on Mrs Mason.'

'Please sit down, Mrs Western.' The two men took their places opposite her. 'As I have already explained, you were one of only three people to whom Mrs Mason mentioned where she was going after she left the lounge.'

'So what? It doesn't mean that one of us followed her. Why would we? None of us had a reason to want to harm Fiona.'

'Can you tell us exactly what you did after Mrs Mason left?'

'I sat talking with Peggy and Gina for a while and then I went up to my room to get changed for dinner.'

'You were the first to leave I understand?' She nodded.

'Exactly how long did you spend talking after Mrs Mason's departure?'

'I can't remember. Five minutes. Possibly ten.'

'Did you walk up the stairs or did you take the lift when you went to your room?'

'I used the lift.' She was beginning to get annoyed. 'I went straight up to the fourth floor. I did not see Fiona; I did not attack Fiona and I have no idea who did. I have absolutely no reason to want to hurt the woman. I cannot help you, so can I go now?'

As she moved to get to her feet, the short, round-faced plainclothes man who had so far remained silent waved her back down. There was a long pause. He pushed his rimless spectacles further up the bridge of his nose, then leaned forward, folding his arms on the table.

'Tell us about your relationship with Mr Heppell.' There was no trace of accent in his voice. He could almost be English.

'What has that got to do with the attack on Fiona?'

He ignored her question. 'You must have every reason to feel considerable relief at the man's death.'

'I beg your pardon?'

'Robert Heppell was blackmailing you.' It was a statement, not a question.

'That's ridiculous!' She gripped the edge of the table with both hands and leaned forward, a look of fury in the dark eyes. 'If you are suggesting I paid Robert . . .'

'Not for money admittedly, but it was at his insistence that you invited your father and several of his associates to dinner parties at your home when Mr Heppell was a guest.'

'I have no idea what you're talking about.' Her cheeks were burning, and her mouth had gone dry. 'This is all nonsense!'

'Did he threaten to tell your husband about your affair with Mr Pilkington if you didn't persuade your father to pull a few strings for him?'

'How dare you!'

'Or was it in return for keeping quiet about what you got up to in your student days? Did he find out about your extra-curricular activities? I expect it all seemed wildly exciting at the time, but it would be acutely embarrassing if the story was to come out now.'

Philippa inhaled sharply and her eyes widened.

'Oh yes, Mrs Western. We know all about Ms Stein and her escort agency. It must have been quite a catch for her to have a young woman who was not only stunningly beautiful but well-educated and sophisticated in her stable. Exactly what she needed for her high-class, high-paying clients.'

Philippa's jaw tightened and she swallowed hard. She picked up the glass of water and stared at him over the rim taking small sips as she played for time.

'It would have caused quite a scandal if Heppell were to make public the fact that the daughter of a prominent city financier had worked as a call girl. Especially, when her clients included magistrates, politicians and leading businessmen. Such a revelation would seriously jeopardise your father's chances of his name being put forward for a knighthood.'

White knuckles gripped the edge of the table. 'I don't know what you're talking about.'

'Your father sometimes brought a Member of Parliament to your dinner parties. Was Tom Moorhouse ever a guest when Heppell was also present?'

'Of course not!' she snapped. 'Robert was a dyed-in-the-wool Tory; he would never give the time of day to a man like Moorhouse.'

A slow smile spread across the man's face. 'You admit your father and his guests were present at Mr Heppell's request.'

How had she let herself fall into his trap? 'I'm admitting nothing.'

'Then perhaps it might be best if we continued our discussion at the station.'

'No! I can't. We're leaving for Leuven in half an hour.'

'Not to worry Mrs Western. We will inform your husband and Mr Taylor that you will be joining them later. Assuming of course, we have no cause to detain you.'

It was no good. She couldn't put it off any longer. But she would tackle the easier option first. Fiona punched in Martin's number.

'Hi, darling.'

'Mum. How are you?'

'I'm absolutely fine. It's all been a lot of fuss about nothing.'

'What happened? The chap who rang said that you'd had a bang on the head and had been knocked unconscious. He couldn't give us any details, but said you were taken to hospital as a precaution. Adam's been in a right flap. He must have rung me three or four times since last night. Have you spoken to him yet?'

'It's only six o'clock in the morning over there!'

'I honestly don't think he'd mind. He woke me at some ungodly hour. Let him have a taste of his own medicine.'

'That's not very brotherly.'

'You know how he fusses. He insisted that I drop everything, collect you from Brussels and bring you back straight home. He also said that this job of yours is obviously much too much for you and if I can't persuade you to give it up then he was going to ring the tour company.'

'Did he now?'

'Don't worry. I told him he was being a prat. I started reading him the riot act and telling him you were perfectly capable of making your own decisions. He's calmed down a bit now. Apparently, Kristy had already torn him off a strip, telling him much the same thing. That woman must have the patience of a saint living with a man who turns everything into a major drama. What was this accident then?'

'I banged my head that's all.'

'How for goodness sake?'

'I crawled under a table to retrieve something and banged my head when I got up too soon. But I'm fine now. Look darling, I must go. I'm not really supposed to be using my mobile in the hospital; you know what they're like.'

'You're still there. I thought you'd been discharged.'

Damn, damn, damn. Why had she said that? 'I have. I'm about to leave any minute.'

'You're not going back to work?'

'You sound like Adam. No, the coach driver has already taken my party out for their excursion, so I've got nothing to do for the rest of the day. Must go, darling. Mr Montgomery-Jones will be waiting to take me back to the hotel.'

'That's the chap who phoned me, isn't. Who is he?'

'Just someone I work with. That's all.'

'He sounds a bit upper crust for a Super Sun employee. Is he a tour manager like you?'

She laughed. 'No. He's not.'

'So?'

'It's a long story. I'll tell you all about it when I see you. Now you take care. Speak to you soon, darling. God bless.'

'Bye, Mum.'

Chapter 27

Montgomery-Jones had missed most of the interview by the time he arrived back at Brussels Station Headquarters shortly before noon. Not that it would have been appropriate for him to be involved in the actual questioning, but he would have liked to watch Philippa Western's reactions through the observation window.

'Have we learnt anything more?' he asked Ferguson who was back in the incident room.

'She still adamantly denies attacking Mrs Mason, though she has admitted Heppell was blackmailing her into inviting her father and various other people to her dinner parties. She claims that although she tried to persuade her father to help Heppell, she let him think it was as a kindness to a friend. According to her, Heppell never attempted to blackmail Ensley directly.'

'Ensley knew nothing about it?'

'It would appear so. But Ensley was never in the frame for Heppell's murder, was he? He was hardly likely to come hightailing over to Belgium, brick clutched in his hot little hand, on the off chance of catching Moorhouse in the back of beyond somewhere.'

'Do we know the grounds for Heppell's blackmail?'

'Salmon asked her directly if it was because of her student activities as a prostitute, back at the hotel before he brought her in. She was in a bit of a state by the time they got here. Even so, it took a while before she admitted it. After that, it all came pouring out. Give him his due, Salmon is a good interrogator. He knows exactly when to probe and when to keep his mouth shut.'

'Did you seriously think he was not? He would never have risen to his present position on a whim.'

Ferguson pulled a face. 'Suppose not. He just brings out the worst in me. His high horse attitude gets under my skin.'

'It works both ways. The more you try to annoy him by playing the unsophisticated upstart risen from the ranks of some second-rate Secondary Modern, the more officious he becomes.'

Ferguson grinned. 'Point taken.'

'Has Mrs Western said anything else useful? What about her father's associates and his connections with Truelove?'

'Unfortunately, she wasn't much help. Although she and her father are close, she claims she doesn't know much about his business affairs. Which is probably about right. Not the type to bother much with anything that doesn't directly concern her. As far as she knows, he hasn't had any recent dealings with Moorhouse, not since he abandoned The House six months ago and became a full-time protester at Anti-Austerity demos. She gave us a few names of her father's closer friends, people that Ensley invited to his country house down in Surrey or plays golf with on a regular basis. No one who stands out particularly. Salmon's on the phone to Cumming to get his team to check up on them, just in case. Seems he has been spending a lot more time with Truelove lately, but she doesn't know if that's merely social or because they're both involved in some project or other.'

'Interesting.' Montgomery-Jones looked thoughtful. 'Did Salmon question her about her time as an escort?'

Ferguson chuckled. 'And how! In the end, he managed to get her to provide quite an interesting list of clients.'

'It would be too much to hope that Tom Moorhouse was one of them?'

'Too right. But she did admit that she was introduced to

him when he was still at the Treasury. She accompanied her father to one of the Lord Mayor's Banquets where all the great and the good were gathered at Mansion House to listen to the Chancellor's annual speech on the state of the economy. Claims he was very charming.'

'Was that their only meeting?'

'She says yes, but there's something going on there. Salmon thinks so and so do I but getting it out of her is going to be tricky.'

'What is happening now; is she going to be released? I would not have thought there was enough evidence to charge her.'

'There isn't. But she is still the most likely suspect in the attack on your Mrs Mason. Salmon has arranged for lunch to be brought in for her. He's happy to let her stew for an hour or so in the hope she'll be a bit more co-operative when he goes back in. We'll have to wait and see.'

It was almost lunchtime before the doctor had checked the results of her scan, signed her discharge papers and the medication had arrived from pharmacy and Fiona was ready to leave the hospital.

Montgomery-Jones led her across the car park, adjusting his lengthy stride to match her own. He held open the passenger door of his car, allowing her to slide onto the soft creamy-tan leather seat. As he walked round to the driver's side, she reached for the seatbelt, feeling more exhausted by the short walk than she cared to admit.

It was pleasantly warm as the sun streamed in through the windscreen as he drove out onto the main road. She closed her eyes and settled back into the luxurious comfort of the perfectly contoured seat.

'Tired?'

'A little. Although, apart from some very vivid dreams, I slept pretty well last night all things considered. Things are still a bit fuzzy. It's probably the effect of all those

244

tranquillisers they pumped into me. According to the doctor, sleep is the best thing to let the body recover after a bang on the head, which no doubt explains why I still can't remember much about what happened.'

'It will not take long to reach the hotel and then you will have all afternoon to rest. But first, some lunch. You must be hungry. Apart from yesterday's roll at lunchtime, you cannot have eaten a proper meal since Thursday. One of my colleagues recommended a decent restaurant which is not too far out of our way.'

'But I can easily get something at the hotel,' she protested.

'Strange though it might seem, Mrs Mason, I also have to eat. And I am ravenous. You are not the only one who missed dinner last night.' His heartfelt retort brooked no argument.

This was not time to tell him she still felt slightly nauseous from the medication she'd been given in the hospital.

It was no surprise to discover that the restaurant was decidedly upmarket, but then Peter Montgomery-Jones was evidently used to the best of everything. She had rarely seen him in the same suit twice and he probably spent more on his ties in a year than she spent on her whole wardrobe. Now she was being foolish. It was only because she felt so inadequately dressed, especially in yesterday's clothes, for such an establishment.

Despite her insistence that she did not feel hungry, the Fillets of Sole Veronique that he ordered for her were delicious and before long she had cleared her plate.

'Are you sure I cannot tempt you to something from the sweet trolley? Belgian desserts are exceptionally good, especially the chocolate ones. This may be your last chance before you return to England.'

Fiona shook her head. 'Thank you but no. Just coffee will be fine.'

He sat back in the chair and looked at her, his face serious. 'Assuming you go back tomorrow, of course.'

'What do you mean?'

'Until we have identified your assailant, you are still in danger. There is no way that I am going to allow you anywhere near any of your party until he or she is arrested.'

'But . . .' She could not deny his logic. With all that had been going on this morning plus a very fraught long-distance phone call to Adam that had drained every last drop of her energy, she hadn't had time to consider what might happen next.

'As I told the policeman this morning, I have no idea who attacked me.'

'None at all?' He glanced across at her as though he thought she was keeping something from him.

'I would tell you. I presume whoever did it was worried that I must have worked out who killed Robert.'

'That would seem a reasonable assumption.'

'But I don't *know* who killed Robert! I've told you about everyone who I thought might possibly have a motive, but we've more or less ruled them all out.'

'I would not say that.'

Fiona sat lost in thought as the waiter arrived and Montgomery-Jones ordered coffee for them both.

Once they were alone again, he asked, 'Were you able to give any thought to my request this morning?'

'I've jotted down all I can remember about the people who Robert might have had some sort of hold over. But they are just my impressions and I've nothing to back them up. Most of the other stuff is only hearsay and knowing the people spreading the gossip, probably wildly inaccurate.'

'No matter.'

She took out the sheets of paper from her shoulder bag and handed them over. He glanced through them, his face expressionless, before folding and tucking them away in an inside pocket of his jacket.

'Thank you. This is exactly what I need.' A slow satisfied smile spread across his face.

'Does that mean you have a definite suspect?'

His smile widened. 'Let us just say that Philippa Western is helping us with our enquiries.'

It came as a surprise when Montgomery-Jones drove into the small car park.

'This isn't my hotel,' she protested.

'True. However, as I said before, I have no intention of allowing you to return until this whole matter is settled. Although I very much doubt that your attacker would make a second attempt, I am not prepared to take that risk. If it is any consolation, I feel certain that an arrest will be made shortly, so it should not be for long. I am confident you will be back in your own room by this evening.'

They took the lift to the fourth floor. He led her along the corridor to a room at the far end. Taking a key card from his pocket, he unlocked the door.

'My goodness me,' she said as she looked around. In addition to the customary unit of drawers, fridge and bar with a large plasma screen on the wall above, there was a long settee and two deep armchairs arranged around a sizable coffee table in front of a large picture window leading to a balcony.

He led her through a large archway, to the bedroom area. 'You should be able to relax here without any worries about your safety.'

'I suppose I should be grateful you haven't insisted on giving me a bodyguard.'

He gave a low chuckle. 'I did consider it. The hospital let you out only on condition that you have complete rest. I thought having a police officer sitting out there might inhibit your ability to drop off to sleep.'

'Too right!'

'However, should you have any concerns at all, just press this bleeper and someone will be with you in seconds.' He laid it on the bedside table.

She frowned. 'This is your room.'

'It is, but as I said earlier, you should be back in your hotel in time for dinner this evening. Feel free to make use of the facilities. I will leave you to get to bed. Do try and get some rest. I will be back in a few hours. You have my number, so ring me if you need to.'

As he was walking to the door, she said, 'Before you go . . '

He turned. 'Yes?'

'Philippa Western. She's not your suspect?'

'She was there when you said where you were going, and she left the lounge minutes after you. I cannot divulge what it is, but she also had a strong motive to kill Heppell. Plus, she has no alibi for the time of his death.'

'But it can't have been her who attacked me.'

'Oh?' He walked back and sat down on the bed next to her.

'Philippa wears a very distinctive perfume.'

'I have noticed it.'

'If Philippa had come up behind me, I would have smelt it.'

'Are you sure? As you said, everything happened very quickly.'

'True. But she also wears several jangly, gold bracelets. I'm sure I would have heard if not seen them as I was struck. They make such a racket.'

He sat there looking at her thoughtfully.

Philippa Western looked up as Salmon entered the stark interview room. He took his time placing the A4 folder on the table and pulling out the chair before settling himself comfortably.

From the observation window, Montgomery-Jones watched her expression carefully. Although she was doing her best to give her inquisitor a dignified disdainful stare, he could tell from the white-knuckled grip of her clasped hands that she was nervous.

'If you are going to interview me again, shouldn't I have a

solicitor present?'

Salmon looked at her for the first time. He gave her a pleasant smile.

'This is not a police station, Mrs Western. And I am not a policeman.'

'Then you have no right to keep me here.'

She was halfway out of her chair before he said, 'I do as it so happens. A man in your group has been murdered and another person attacked.'

'As I've already told you, that has nothing to do with me.'

'Sit down, Mrs Western!' Surprised at the sudden barked command, she dropped back onto the chair. 'The sooner you stop prevaricating and answer my questions, the sooner you can go.'

'This is ridiculous.' Her voice failed to carry the conviction of her words. For the first time, she looked wary. Almost afraid.

'You will be pleased to hear that Mrs Mason is now awake and has been able to talk to us.'

'In which case, she will have told you that I was not the one who attacked her.'

Salmon shook his head. 'Unfortunately, Mrs Mason did not see her assailant so there is no proof either way. The problem is, Mrs Western that, as we have already established, you do have a good motive for killing Robert Heppell.'

'No, no, no!' Her voice rose to an exasperated wail. 'I didn't kill Robert and what possible reason could I have to want to hurt Fiona?'

'If you didn't kill Robert Heppell, who did?' He leant forwards, arms on the table, his eyes locked on hers.

'How, in heaven's name, do you expect me to know that?'

'Did your father know Heppell was blackmailing you?' The questions came thick and fast, giving her little time to think.

She put down the glass, sat back and folded her arms across her chest. From the glare of pure hatred in her eyes, it was obvious that she had no intention of answering any more questions.

'Or perhaps I should ask did he know the real reason he was blackmailing you?'

There was a barely perceptible twitch of her eyebrows, but she said nothing.

'Not exactly a forgiving man, your father, is he? I can just imagine the explosion when he found out.'

She gave a derisive snort. 'What are you suggesting? That my father came all the way to Belgium to murder Robert? You really must be desperate to suggest something as idiotic as that!'

'Tell me, Mrs Western, was Robert Heppell connected with Tom Moorhouse?'

'No.' Tricked by the unexpected change of tack, she blinked back angry tears and looked away from the penetrating gaze. 'I don't know. How would I know? I had as little as possible to do with the man.'

'Which man? Heppell or Moorhouse?'

'Both,' she snapped, banging her fists on the table.

He gave a slow smile. 'You admit to knowing Tom Moorhouse.'

'I meant,' she snarled, 'that I do not approve of his politics or the way he conducts himself.'

'But you do know the man. As I understand it, the two of you were very friendly at one point. Before you deny it, Mrs Western . . .' He opened the folder in front of him and flicked through the pages. 'It says here that you attended the Mansion House Dinner where he was the keynote speaker.'

'That was over twenty years ago! And besides, there were hundreds of guests at that event.'

'But after the formalities, you made a point of introducing yourself. You must have been quite taken with the man because you spent the rest of that evening talking with him. And you left together.'

'It was not what you're implying! He offered to drive me back to the hotel. That's all. We did *not* spend the night together.'

'If you say so. He was the rising star of the government. The man of the moment. You were flattered by his attention.'

She gave a snort of derision. 'I hardly think so. I'll admit he could be quite charming and entertaining with a wicked sense of humour, which is more than could be said for all the other boring old farts at that banquet, but he was an arrogant self-publicist on the make even back then.'

'Then why go on seeing him? That meeting at the Mansion House was not the only occasion you got together, now was it?'

Her eyes narrowed. But before she could deny it, Salmon continued, 'We've been speaking to one or two of your old student friends.'

'All right! I talked him into inviting me down to Cowes one weekend with a group of his friends.'

'And?'

'We ran into each other a few times at various social events and I had dinner alone with him once. But that was it. We never had an affair if that's what you're trying to insinuate. I wanted to persuade him to introduce me to some people, but I haven't seen him or spoken to him since then. Not since I left Kensington.'

'Which people?'

'Influential people. People I thought might prove useful.'

'Useful to you or your father?'

She glared at him for a moment or two before she snapped, 'Both.'

'Did your father ask you to?'

'Of course not!' She was almost shouting as her anger began to spill over. She made an effort to keep herself in check. 'I wanted to help him. Mummy died just after I got my place at Imperial. Her death hit Daddy hard. He threw himself into his work. I thought if I could arrange a meeting with Tommy it would open all sorts of doors for him.'

She sat back in the chair and folded her arms across her

chest.

'No doubt, your father was grateful.' Salmon smiled and removed his glasses and leisurely proceeded to polish them with a handkerchief. Once he'd replaced them, he looked across at her and continued, 'After all, it was the start of a very profitable relationship for them both.'

'If you say so.' She shrugged her shoulders. 'I know absolutely nothing about my father's business affairs.'

'Really? Such a pity that the East European Agricultural Project they promoted collapsed so spectacularly. Especially as they both worked so hard to recruit a vast number of investors. Though, as I understand it, they both managed to get out in time to protect their investments. In fact, though a great many people lost their life savings, your father made a great deal of money.'

'Just what are you implying?'

He held up his hands to placate her. 'Only that he was an extremely fortunate man.'

She banged her fist on the table. 'I resent your insinuations and if you have no further questions, I'd like to return to my hotel.'

'One more question, Mrs Western. When is the last time you had any form of communication with Tom Moorhouse?'

'I've already told you, I haven't seen or spoken . . .'

'That's not what I asked,' he said fiercely, leaning across the small table until his face was only inches from hers, 'I'm talking emails, texts or even an old-fashioned letter.'

She visibly swallowed but recovered quickly. 'I've given you my answer! I have had absolutely nothing to do with the man in seventeen years.'

They sat glaring at each other for a whole minute. Suddenly, Salmon snapped the folder shut and got to his feet.

'All right, Mrs Western. We'll take a break. I'll get someone to bring you a cup of tea.'

Chapter 28

'What do you think?' he asked Montgomery-Jones when the two men returned to the incident room. 'It's like pulling teeth from an elephant. We keep going over the same ground and getting nowhere fast.'

'It might be slow going, but we now know she was responsible for introducing her father to Moorhouse and that it was at her instigation, even if she knows nothing about what they got up to together.'

'If you can believe what she says.' Salmon sounded dubious.

'I think I do. She is her father's daughter. Hard-headed, and knows exactly what she wants. Her interest in Moorhouse was as a means to an end, to help her father. There is no evidence that she had any more involvement with him or the deals that brokered between him and her father.'

Salmon sighed. 'We're going to have to let her go, aren't we? She's definitely hiding something, but if we keep her any longer, we're going to have to charge her with something.'

Montgomery-Jones looked thoughtful. After a long pause, he said. 'Let me have a word with her.'

Salmon raised an eyebrow.

'I appreciate that I said before that I thought it better if I were not involved in the interview. She thinks I am simply a friend of Mrs Mason and for the moment I would prefer to keep it that way. However, it might be worth a try.'

They walked back along the corridor to the interview room

and Salmon opened the door.

'You have a visitor, Mrs Western.'

'Philippa.' Montgomery-Jones smiled as she looked up at him. 'I have come to take you back to the hotel.'

As Montgomery-Jones walked towards the table, Salmon quietly closed the door, leaving the two alone.

'I have just been talking to Mrs Mason. She is convinced that you were not the person who attacked her,' he said as he took the chair opposite.

Hope blazed in Philippa's eyes. 'Then I really can go.'

'Finish your tea first.'

'That man said Fiona couldn't identify whoever it was?'

'That is true. However, she is adamant that you could not have been that person.'

'Thank goodness it's all over.'

'Let us hope so. Although I should warn you, the police remain unconvinced.'

'Did you know Robert was murdered?' Her bottom lip trembled as she gave him a wide-eyed look. 'It wasn't an accident and they think Fiona was attacked because she found out who did it. Whoever attacked Fiona must have been the killer.'

'Mr Salmon thinks Robert was blackmailing you.'

'He didn't tell you why?' Her face fell.

'Some of it.' He leant across the table and took her hand. 'But it all happened a long time ago.'

'It's all such a mess.' The tears began to fall, and she pulled away to bury her face in her hands.

'We all do stupid things when we're young. Things we regret,' he said quietly.

It did not take long for her to pull herself together.

'I must look a sight.' She picked up her handbag from the floor beside her and pulled out a tissue, scrubbing the running mascara across her cheeks as she wiped away the tears. 'It wasn't for me. I only did what Robert asked to stop him ruining Daddy's chances. He so wants to be Lord

Ensley. But I didn't kill Robert, Peter. Honestly I didn't.'

'I believe you.'

She dissolved into tears again.

Eventually Montgomery-Jones's gentle voice broke the silence.

'You love your father very much; I can see that.'

'Of course, I do.'

'You are lucky. I was never very close to my father. Much of the time I was away at boarding school and I never saw much of him in the holidays. He was always at work. There never seemed to be time for me.'

She smiled. 'It was like that for me too.'

'It must have been worse for you. After your mother died, I mean. He may have loved you, but I imagine he was so wrapped up in his grief, there was not much room for you was there? You must have felt neglected. Where was he when you needed him most? I expect he buried himself in his work and there was hardly any time left for you. Is that how it was?'

She nodded and gave a deep sigh, looking down at her hands restlessly scrunching up the tissue in her lap. 'Something like that. Looking back, I suppose that's why I joined the Escort Agency. To shock him into giving me some attention.' She looked up, her eyes almost pleading with him. 'But it's not like that now. We're very close.' She swallowed. 'At least we were, until recently. We haven't spoken for a few weeks.'

'Why is that?'

She managed an exhausted smile and tried to avoid the question. 'Don't be so nosy.'

'Did your father think that it was Moorhouse who introduced you to the woman who ran the agency?'

'Of course not!' She shook her head violently and her eyes narrowed. For the first time, she was suspicious. 'What makes you think it was Tommy, anyway?'

'You told Mr Salmon that Moorhouse introduced you to all sorts of people, I simply assumed she was one of them.'

'It wasn't like that. Lavinia happened to be one of the crowd we met up with at Ascot. He didn't suggest I become an escort. Tommy didn't know anything about it.'

'I am sorry if I upset you.' He reached forward and put a hand on her forearm.

She flinched in pain and snatched her arm from his grasp. Her elbow caught the glass of water, knocking it over.

'Now look what you've done!' She dabbed ineffectually at the sodden sleeve of her turquoise silk blouse with a tissue.

'Here, let me help.'

Montgomery-Jones got to his feet and walked round to her side of the table. He took the handkerchief from his top pocket and refolded it lengthwise. He pulled down her bracelets, wrapped it over her sleeve, unbuttoned the cuff, and rolled back the wet material in the dry handkerchief up to her elbow.

'That should help dry it out and stop it feeling so uncomfortable.' He held onto her wrist and frowned as he stared at the jagged red welt running almost the length of her forearm. 'What have you done to yourself?'

'A car accident. It looks worse than it is.'

'What happened?'

She gave a huge sigh. 'I was upset. I'd just had the most horrendous row and I was driving much too fast along a country lane. I didn't brake early enough for the corner and went straight on into a tree.'

'You poor thing. It sounds as though you were lucky not to be seriously hurt.'

She gave a mirthless laugh. 'I came off a lot better than my poor car. It was a write-off.'

'With whom did you have the argument?'

'None of your business.' The obvious tension in her whole body belied the attempt at a light-hearted putdown.

'Was it your father? Is that why the two of you have not spoken in weeks?' He waited, but she made no comment. 'It must have been serious if he failed to get in contact after your accident.'

Her jaw tightened, but she remained stubbornly silent, looking down at her injured arm now cradled across her chest.

'Philippa?' His voice was soft. Full of sympathy.

'He tried.' Her voice was barely a whisper. 'He came to the hospital, but I refused to see him. He'd said some unforgivable things.'

'It must have been some argument that you are still so angry with him.'

'He threw me out! Said he never wanted to set eyes on me ever again.'

'What?' Her answer took him by surprise.

Tears were running down her cheeks. 'It was his birthday. I'd bought him this lovely little Lladró figurine for his collection. I spent hours choosing just the right one. We were supposed to be going out for a celebration lunch, just the two of us. We were having a drink before we set off and then it all went wrong. I've never seen him so angry. He went berserk. He picked up the china shepherdess and smashed it against the wall.'

She covered her face in her hands.

'What was he so angry about?'

She shook her head then dissolved into tears.

He put an arm around her shoulders. She leant into him, still sobbing.

'Did he find out that you had been seeing Moorhouse?'

At first, she did not answer, but as they slowly separated, she nodded. 'It's so stupid. That time we first met at the Mansion House Dinner, Daddy was furious that I'd spent the whole evening with him even though I explained that it was only because I thought he would make a useful contact. Back then, Tommy was a Junior Minister at the Treasury, the up-and-coming man in politics. I thought he'd be a valuable asset, someone who would be able to put a word in the right ear when contracts were being awarded.'

'But your father did not see it that way?'

She gave a bitter laugh. 'You wouldn't think it now, but back then Tommy had a bad reputation as something of a gigolo. Daddy forbade me ever to see him again. It was all so silly because the two of them have been involved in all sorts of business deals ever since.'

'Your Father knew nothing of your outings together?'

She shook her head. 'But I never lied to him. I told him I was going out for the day with a group of friends. And that was true. I just didn't tell him that Tommy would be there too.'

'I can understand that he might not be too pleased when he learnt how you had deceived him, but surely that was all a very long time ago. Why did he get so irate with you recently?'

'It wasn't just . . .' She stopped abruptly, putting her head in her hands. When she spoke again, her voice was so muffled, the words were barely audible. 'I let it slip. I wasn't thinking.'

'Let what slip?'

She shook her head, staring down at her feet. He put a finger under her chin and slowly raised her head. Big brown eyes looked up at him and she said in a little-girl voice, 'Can we go now?'

He smiled. 'Of course. Let us get you back to the hotel. The coach will be returning with the rest of your party in an hour or so.'

'I ought to phone Bernard. He'll be worried.'

'A good idea. I am sure he will be relieved to know that you have been released. Would you like me to give you a few minutes in private?'

Salmon was waiting for him in the corridor, a smile on his round face.

'Any idea what that trigger might have been.'

'Not a clue but there can be little doubt that it was something which involved Moorhouse.'

258

'Agreed. Which means that Ensley has to be our man. I've already phoned London. Cumming's team are stepping up the checks on recent communications to see if he had made any contact with our gun-for-hire suspects. We've already established Ensley was too clever to withdraw a large sum from his legitimate accounts, but they are still trying to see what can be done to get hold of the details of some of the offshore ones. Not that I think we'll get much joy there.'

'I concur. At least, not in the immediate future.'

'He's under observation, but that's unlikely to give us much at this stage. As soon as Cumming can establish anything that can even remotely link him with this whole affair, we'll bring him in for questioning. I'm going back to London now. This is one interview I want to do personally.'

'Ensley is a cold, ruthless player. If anyone can break him, I feel sure you can. For what it is worth, I think he may have one Achilles' heel, his daughter. Speaking of whom, I must get Mrs Western back to her hotel. I doubt I will be able to persuade her to give any other useful information at the moment, but I will obviously keep you informed.'

Chapter 29

Fiona sat curled up on the king-sized bed, cocooned in one of the thick, fluffy bath robes she'd found hanging up in the bathroom, flicking through the television channels. Two televisions in one hotel room seemed an extravagance, but then she had never spent time in a suite as grand as this before. Peter Montgomery-Jones certainly didn't stint himself when it came to the best.

Not that she objected to making use of such luxury. The long, lazy soak in the almond and magnolia bubbles had been just the thing to ease away the worst of the aches and pains and even more importantly, the pervading sense of muzziness and the vaguely disconnected feeling she'd been experiencing since waking up this morning. The only thing missing had been a book to read. Not that she seemed to have much time for such indulgences as a leisurely bath with a book or even without one these days. Certainly, not in those last years when she was nursing Bill or in the year since he'd died. Now, her life was busier than ever. Back in the days when the boys were toddlers and Bill was not on call at the hospital, her Sunday afternoon bath time had been sacrosanct. Her me-time. For a brief hour, she could escape to the bathroom with not only her latest novel but a mug of coffee and a bar of chocolate. Those were the days!

Time to get dressed. The thought of having to put on yesterday's clothes was not conducive to action, but she couldn't lie here reliving old memories any longer.

She had barely finished getting dressed when she heard a gentle tap on the door.

'Who is it?'

There was a chuckle followed by, 'Whom are you expecting?'

She opened the door and gave him a broad smile. 'Hello, Peter.'

'I was not sure if you would still be sleeping.'

'Wide awake.' She laughed as he sank down in one of the armchairs, stretching his long legs out in front of him and closing his eyes as he laid back, 'Though I'm not sure you are.'

'I confess, after all the excitement of the last twenty-four hours, I am feeling somewhat weary. Perhaps some tea would help.' He reached back, picked up the phone on the wall table behind him and rang for room service.

'How goes the enquiry?' she asked.

'We have interviewed Mrs Western, but she was not charged. She denies the attack on you, which we are inclined to believe. Plus, she would have had to have been extremely lucky for the time she claims to have been shopping on her own to have been sufficient to race to Leopold Park, find and murder Heppell and return to her friends for lunch.'

'All a waste of time then?'

He shook his head and gave a slow smile. 'I would not say that. She gave us some valuable information pertinent to our investigation into the Moorhouse assassination.'

Fiona knew better than to ask.

There was a knock at the door. A trolley, complete with silver teapot and bone china cups, a plate of daintily cut sandwiches and another of small cakes was wheeled in. It was only after the waiter had left that they were able to return to their discussion.

'I suppose that means having lost your prime suspect, we're back to square one again?'

'Not you too!' he said almost to himself, looking pained.

'Everyone seems to be talking in clichés today.'

She suppressed a giggle. 'I'm sorry. I should know by now how much that irritates you.'

'I am the one who should apologise. I must be more tired than I realised. However, this situation is no joke, Fiona. Until we can identify whoever attacked you, you are still in danger.'

'Assuming that whoever tried to silence me murdered Robert, it would help if I were to know which of my passengers had no alibi for the time of Robert's death.'

He took a small notebook from an inside jacket pocket and flipped over the pages until he found what he was looking for. 'Those whose alibis cannot be corroborated except by their partners are Noel Appleby, Patrick and Joan Cahill, Dee Foley, Simon and Gina Lithgow, Felix Navarre, Olive Scudamore, Hazel Tonkin and Philippa Western. However, we can rule out Appleby and Simon Lithgow. They were with Austin Pilkington sorting out photographs at the time you were attacked.'

'Several people saw the Lithgows having lunch in one of the restaurants in the Rue des Bouchers.'

'I appreciate that, but at least on paper, one or another had time to kill Heppell and return to the City Centre by one o'clock, which is around the time they were seen.'

'So, presumably Robert was murdered some time between the rioting after Tom Moorhouse was shot and when his body was discovered?'

'Not quite. It may have taken place before the shooting. Heppell left the rest of your group when everyone came out of the Hotel de Ville at around a quarter past eleven. It would have taken at least twenty-five minutes at a brisk walk for him to get to where his body was discovered at twelve fifty-seven, which is the time the police received the call.'

Fiona did a quick calculation. 'Which gives a window of an hour and a quarter or so?'

'Exactly.'

'I remember Robert setting off almost as soon as we came out into the Grand Place. Nearly everyone else milled around for a few minutes deciding what to do. I don't remember seeing anyone following him. I seem to remember hearing Peggy invite Olive to go for a coffee with a group of the other older members, but I think she wandered off in the other direction. Apart from the fact that she doted on Robert, I doubt she had the strength to bash him on the back of the head so I'd hardly put her on the top of the list of suspects. There's been a great deal of gossip flying around about various members of the Association, but I've never heard a whisper against Felix. The Cahills aren't even members of the Swanley Association. They'd only met Robert the day before and unless you've discovered some past connection, I can't see why they might want him dead.'

'True. However, Dee Foley and her friend Hazel Tonkin had known him for less than twenty-four hours and yet a great deal of hostility had developed between them.'

'Not enough to kill surely?'

'They were also in the lounge. Miss Tonkin left moments after you and Miss Foley approximately five minutes after that. Is it possible that they may have heard you mention you were going to the conference room?'

'It's a possibility, I suppose.'

Fiona poured out another cup of tea for each of them, picked up hers nursing it in both hands as she sat back in the deep armchair, sipping it slowly, lost in thought.

'Do we know what time Dee was arrested?'

He smiled. 'The police van arrived in the alley at 12:14 according to the log. Time enough to kill Heppell and get to the far side of the park.'

'But how could she know where he would be? Or that he was coming to the rally at all, come to that?'

'Perhaps she chanced across him once the stampede began and seized the opportunity. Though I confess how she managed to fight her way back against that wall of people to end up on the other side of the park I cannot fathom.'

'We're getting nowhere fast here, are we?'

He gave her a rueful smile. 'That, Mrs Mason, has been the problem all along.' He put down his cup and eased himself forward to get to his feet. 'And it also provides us with another. With Mrs Western released and no credible suspect, it looks as though I will need to go and book you a room here for tonight.'

'Wait!' She put up a hand then continued less peremptorily, 'I'm not so sure that's such a good idea. I think it might be best if I returned to my hotel.'

'I refuse to allow . . .'

'Please, Peter. Hear me out. I appreciate you're concerned for my safety, but if we are going to catch Heppell's murderer, there really is no other option. First thing tomorrow morning, the Super Sun coach will be returning home. Even if the police or British Secret Services had the power to prevent that, which – with no useful evidence – I doubt, have you any idea of the total furore that would cause? Twenty irate passengers, a very annoyed Super Sun Head Office, rebooking hotels and a ferry etcetera. The only chance of finding the culprit is tonight. To do that I need to be there to smoke him out. And if that's another cliché so be it.'

'Be that as it may, putting yourself in danger is not an option.'

'I am not suggesting for one moment that I act as some kind of bait. All I propose to do is see the reaction I get when I go back. I would imagine that at this moment the culprit is nervous and once they see I'm no longer at death's door they might well give themselves away.'

The grim expression on her face was matched by his. For a long moment, they stared at one another. Both determined not to give way. In the end, he was the one to capitulate.

'All right. I will allow it, but on one condition: that you are under surveillance at all times and that you carry an alarm.'

'That's two conditions and while we're at it, Mr Montgomery-Jones, may I remind you that *you* are in no position to dictate what I can and can't do.' She pulled a face at him to show there was no animosity. 'Though I would be grateful if you would be kind enough to run me there.'

He had the grace to smile. 'May I finish my tea first?'

An hour later, Montgomery-Jones decided to drop into Brussels Station Headquarters on his way back to his hotel. Fergusson looked up from his desk.

'Thought you were done here for the day.'

'I am. I need to collect some papers.'

'How's Mrs Mason?'

'Sufficiently recovered to be her usual stubborn self. I have just taken her back to her hotel. She insisted.'

Ferguson raised an eyebrow. 'Isn't that a bit risky?'

'You try telling her,' Montgomery-Jones said with a rare flash of emotion. 'Do you think you could arrange some discreet protection for her as soon as possible? Nothing obvious.'

Ferguson picked up his phone. 'Consider it done.'

Montgomery-Jones busied himself at his desk sorting out the papers he needed and putting them in his briefcase.

'Salmon has left already I take it?' he asked when Ferguson replaced the receiver.

'Yep. Gone back to his hotel to pack his things. There's a Eurostar at 17:56 so he's hoping to be in London soon after seven. If he misses it, there's another an hour later.'

'Let us hope that Cumming's team will have something more concrete by then.'

'Do you think Salmon will keep us in the loop now he's back at Thames House?'

'I would think so. We will have to make sure that he does.'

Chapter 30

Fiona took her time getting ready for dinner. She had promised Montgomery-Jones that she would stay in her room until he had had time to put his security arrangements in place.

She stared at her reflection in the mirror and picked up her hairbrush. Although the blow she'd received had broken the skin, it was not serious enough to need a dressing. But it was sore. It would be several days before she could brush her hair properly. As she gently cradled her fingers over the lump it felt the size of an egg, but twisting her head at all sorts of angles, she could see no obvious signs of swelling under her fluffed-up hair.

Winston would probably be worrying about her. She glanced at her watch. The coach should be back by now. Retrieving her mobile from her bag, she dialled his number.

'Sweetheart! Is you okay?'

'The doctors have pronounced me fit and well and I'm back in the hotel reporting for duty.'

'The nurse said they'd let you out on condition you go straight to bed. Tha's why I din't ring before.'

'How did it go today? I was supposed to take everyone on a guided walk in Leuven. I hope they weren't too disappointed.'

'No probs, sweetheart. I rang the tourist office and they arrange for one of their guides to do it so the passengers didn't miss out. She also gave them all a folder with maps and lots of info so they was all happy.'

'Excellent. Then they got a much better deal than if I'd been there.'

'I wouldn't say that, sweetheart. They all missed you.'

'I'm sure. Did the men enjoy the beer tasting?'

'The ladies too by all account. Anyways, they was all smiling by the time I brought 'em back.'

'I'm sure they were. You're a star, Winston. What would I do without you?'

'We's a team, aint we? I's cleaning the coach right now, so you get lots of rest and I'll see you later.'

'Bye.'

Apart from a fleeting thought when she realised she would not be back in time to accompany the day's tour, she had not given a thought to her passengers all day. She found herself smiling. Perhaps, at long last, she was finding that sense of perspective that her fellow Super Sun staff were constantly urging her to develop instead of feeling responsible for them every minute they were in her care. Then again, it probably had a great deal more to do with the fact that she'd had far more important things to worry about than their welfare in the last twenty-four hours.

She sat down on the bed with a sigh. Having spent the best part of the day doing nothing, the last thing she wanted to do was sit around idly. Her mind was far too active to concentrate on reading her book. The sooner she could get on with the task in hand the better. Surely, Montgomery-Jones could not object to her going down to the lounge. As long as she stayed where there were lots of people around nothing could happen to her.

She waited until she heard voices in the corridor outside her room, then stepped out behind them. The two German-speaking guests nodded a greeting as they all got into the lift and then resumed their conversation. Even without the steady flow of people returning from their afternoon's activities, there was always a couple of staff behind the reception desk. Feeling self-conscious, she crossed the foyer to the lounge. Despite her resolve, she was not sure she was ready for all the attention her return would attract.

'Fiona!'

Emerging through the glass entrance doors, Eleanor Prior followed by her little coterie came bustling towards her.

'How are you? We thought you'd still be in hospital. They said you were attacked.'

'I'm fine.'

'What happened?'

'I got a knock on the head. That's all.'

'Someone said they had to carry you out to the ambulance on a stretcher.' Eleanor shook her head.

'It's good to see you're fully recovered now, Fiona.'

'Thank you, Glenda.'

'You wouldn't believe the kerfuffle after they took you off in the ambulance. We all had to be interviewed by the police.' Eleanor Prior's voice rose to a near shriek. 'Was it a burglar? Really, you're not safe anywhere these days. Did he take much? We never carry much money in our bags when we're on holiday.' She rushed on, not waiting for answers.

'Best to leave all your valuables in the safe,' added Glenda Diamond, not wishing to be left out. 'Have they arrested anyone yet?'

'The police haven't told me.' At least that much was true.

'What with one thing and another, Brussels doesn't seem like a very safe city to be in right now.' Eleanor pursed her lips. 'Perhaps it's a good thing we're all going home tomorrow.'

'When the driver told us they were keeping you in hospital we all feared the worst.' Jeffrey Prior looked at her suspiciously. 'You don't look as though you were badly hurt.'

'They wanted to run some tests, but as you can see, I'm back now. I hope my not being there didn't spoil your visits today.'

'No, it was fine,' said Glenda. 'Winston gave us a running

commentary and pointed out the main buildings as he drove us around. He's a great character, isn't he?'

Fiona smiled. 'I wouldn't do a tour without him.'

'We need to get this stuff to our rooms,' muttered Aubrey Diamond to no one in particular with a sniff. He juggled the various carrier bags he was holding in order to fish a handkerchief from his pocket.

'Oh dear, Aubrey. Your cold still not any better?'

'It's hay fever. Brought some tablets from home, but they aren't doing much good.'

Fiona was relieved when all four of them ambled off to the lift. She needed to sit down. Perhaps she still wasn't quite as up to power as she thought. It was a relief to see only strangers in the lounge. She was able to take herself to a quiet corner table and sat with her back to the wall so that she would be able to see everyone who came in.

Her eyelids were beginning to droop, and Philippa was halfway across the room before Fiona saw her approaching.

'How are you?'

Fiona gave a weak smile. How many times would she have to answer that question and go through the same saga this evening?

'I'm glad I've caught you on your own. I just wanted to say how grateful I am to you for what you said to the police about being certain it wasn't me who attacked you. I seriously thought they were going to arrest me. I don't think they were too happy to let me go. If it wasn't for Peter, I think I'd still be there. I don't understand why they thought I of all people would want to harm you.'

'I gather they think the person who attacked me also attacked Robert.'

Philippa frowned. 'They said much the same thing to me.'

'Why would they think you killed Robert?' Fiona hadn't really expected an answer and she didn't get one. 'I'd only met him briefly, but I have to say he wasn't the easiest passenger I've had to deal with.'

'He upset a great many people. He could be a very difficult man, but I find it hard to believe anyone would actually want to kill him.'

'Quite. The police seem to think Robert's death was connected to the assassination of that MP for some reason,' Fiona said, picking her words carefully. Philippa gave her a quick glance, her expression wary. Doing her best to sound casual, Fiona asked, 'Did they mention him to you at all?'

The silence seemed to drag on. Eventually Philippa nodded.

'I wonder if they knew each other.'

Philippa shrugged. 'No idea. Robert never mentioned it and he liked dropping names into the conversation. Liked to give the impression he was hobnobbing with the well-known and powerful.'

Fiona laughed dutifully. 'I can imagine. Didn't you say you knew Tom Moorhouse?'

'Did I?'

'Or perhaps it was your father.'

'Daddy worked with him some time back, but they haven't seen each other in years.'

Much to Fiona's surprise, Philippa's eyes began to brim with tears. She took a tissue from the evening bag dangling on her wrist and blew her nose.

'Is there something wrong?' Fiona asked.

Philippa waved away her concern. 'Sorry. It's nothing. I think it's all the shock of being treated like a murder suspect.' She blinked away the last of the tears, folded her right arm across her chest and began to rub it with her left hand.

'Philippa! What is it?' Fiona was genuinely worried.

Philippa shuddered, as though pulling herself back to the present. She glanced down at her arm as though she had no idea of what she'd been doing then looked directly at Fiona.

'Did Peter tell you?' Her voice was barely a whisper.

'Tell me what?'

'About the row with my father.'

Fiona shook her head. 'Peter is nothing if not discreet.'

Philippa let out a long sigh. 'I had a god-awful row with my father a few weeks ago about Tommy. We haven't spoken since and I . . . It's upset me more than I can say. We were so close.'

Fiona resisted the urge to prompt when Philippa lapsed into silence.

'I'm frightened Daddy might have done something very silly. He's not a very forgiving man. He knows people. People like Karaseiwicz.'

Philippa took out a handkerchief and blew her nose.

Fiona knew it would be a mistake to press her.

'Fiona, Philippa!' Peggy's face was all smiles as she approached.

The moment was lost.

Once Peggy was comfortably ensconced and Fiona had assured her she was now fit and well and that the rumours of her near-death experience had been greatly exaggerated, Peggy turned to Philippa.

'And how about you? Bernard said you had one of your bad migraines.'

'I'm much better now, thank you.'

'You still don't look your usual self. I think both you ladies should get an early night. There's nothing quite so tiring as travelling and we've got a long journey ahead of us tomorrow.'

At the first opportunity, Fiona found a quiet spot to phone where she was certain she could not be overheard. For once, it was a good half minute before he answered her call.

'Montgomery-Jones.' His voice sounded strange. As though she'd just woken him from a deep sleep.

'It's Fiona. I've just been talking to Philippa. She said the two of you had talked about the row she had with her father.'

'Yes.' His voice was wary.

'She didn't mention the details, but she said it was about

Tommy and I presumed she meant Tom Moorhouse. It may all be nothing but . . .'

'Go on.'

'She said she's worried about her father. She thinks he may have done something rash. Does the name Karaseiwicz mean anything to you? He's some sort of associate of her father's and I get the impression he is a dangerous man.'

'You were right to let me know.'

Fiona slipped her mobile back into her shoulder bag and turned to go back towards the restaurant. Her heart skipped a beat. A man was standing at the end of the corridor.

She put her hand in her pocket, finger poised on the alarm button. He walked towards her and as he passed, said very softly, 'Stay with the crowd.'

Relief flooded over her as she hurried back to the corner. Not an attacker. Just one of her minders.

Chapter 31

Fiona had nursed a faint hope that she might learn something from the immediate reaction of her suspects when they realised she was back in circulation. As things turned out, by the time everyone came down to dinner, word had spread throughout the party. Any chance of a surprise encounter was lost.

Even as she turned the corner, she could see a small group waiting outside the doors to the restaurant. Eyes lit up, there were squeals of joy and within seconds she was surrounded by well-wishers. By the time she managed to get inside, half the party seemed to have gathered.

Even once she'd sat down, each of the new arrivals came over to express their pleasure at her return and to ask how she was. At least she was saved from having to go through endless repetitions of what had happened, but all the attention was proving exhausting.

The noisy chatter stopped, and all eyes turned to the entrance. Fiona turned to see what they were all looking at. Barbara McArdle was standing in the doorway holding an enormous basket of fruit. Several of the Super Sun party got to their feet to see better as Barbara processed across the room to Fiona's table.

'A small gift from us all to wish you a speedy recovery, or I suppose I should say to welcome you back.'

As Fiona got to her feet to accept it, clapping broke out. Those not already standing got to their feet.

Fiona looked around. 'Thank you so much everyone. This is so very kind. I don't know what to say.' She felt a decided lump in her throat.

'There's a card as well and we've all signed it.' Olive presented her with an enormous envelope.

The picture on the front other card was of a cute bear with a bandage around its head holding a large bouquet of multi-coloured flowers and a balloon floating above with the words, 'Remets-toi vite!' written on it. The inside covered with goodwill messages.

When all the commotion died down and everyone had resumed their places, Fiona was left wondering what to do with her newly acquired gift. There was no room for it on the table. She beckoned to one of the waiters.

'Would it be possible for you to find somewhere to put this until I've finished dinner?'

'Certainly, madam.' He gave her a charming smile.

'We chose fruit because we thought you'd still be in hospital and they don't allow flowers on the wards these days,' said Gina who was sitting next to her.

'It was a good choice anyway,' Fiona assured her. 'It might have been a touch tricky travelling back tomorrow with all the wet stems.'

Fiona glanced around the table at her fellow diners. She had not had a great deal of choice of where and with whom to sit when they had eventually moved into the restaurant. She had been hustled along in the general melee. It had been Charlotte Appleby, now sitting opposite her who had firmly suggested she needed to sit down and take the weight off her feet. Apart from the Lithgows and the Applebys there were Peggy on her immediate left and Felix Navarre sitting across the table next to Charlotte.

Chance had provided her with the opportunity to get close to two of her suspects, but would the opportunity to quiz them arise, even assuming she could think of suitable questions to ask?

'What have you enjoyed seeing most on this holiday,' Fiona asked as the soup dishes were cleared away.

'It's so difficult to choose.' Peggy started the ball rolling. 'Every day has been so different. I've loved it all.'

Felix gave a broad smile. 'Waterloo wins hands down. I thought it was fascinating.'

'Me too,' agreed Noel.

'Trust the men,' teased Charlotte. 'They love playing soldiers. For me I think it has to be Bruges. It's such a little gem of a town.'

As the rest of the table discussed the various merits of Ghent and Antwerp, Fiona turned to Gina. 'And what about you?'

'Definitely the chocolate factory. That wonderful smell!' She took a deep breath and closed her eyes in rapture.

Fiona laughed. 'I can see where your heart lies.'

Gina glanced around to check that none of the others was listening. 'I'll let you into a secret; I wasn't really looking forward to this holiday very much. From the way Robert described it, it was all much too arty-farty for me. I thought it was going to be traipsing round art galleries staring at pictures all day. Don't get me wrong, I wouldn't wish him dead, but it's been so much better without him. I've loved every minute. I even quite enjoyed some of the art. In small doses.'

'That's good.'

'I don't suppose it's a trip you'll forget in a hurry though, is it? What with Robert's death and you being attacked.' She leant closer, dropping her voice even lower. 'I heard a rumour that Robert's death wasn't an accident.'

'Oh!' Fiona feigned surprise. 'Who told you that?'

Gina tapped her nose. 'Let's just say I overheard a couple of people talking about it this afternoon. They were in the corridor waiting for the lift just as I was coming out of my room. She definitely used the word murdered and he asked if the police knew who'd done it. They changed the subject when they realised I was there, but it had to be Robert they were talking about and it does explain why the police were asking all those questions about where we were on the day he died.'

'Are you sure, Gina? It's easy to imagine all sorts of things when you only hear bits of the conversation.'

'That's exactly what Simon said when I told him, but I know what I heard!' She pouted like a child, indignant that no one would believe her. 'He said I'd been watching too many crime dramas on the telly and that I was mad to even think such a thing could happen in real life. He got really cross with me. Said it was scandalmongering and I wasn't to go spreading such tittle-tattle. But I told him, she definitely said that the police were closing in on the murderer. Simon said that was ridiculous because how would she know that anyway. He more or less accused me of making it up.'

It was obvious that Gina had been stung by her husband's reaction to her sensational news, which probably explained why she needed a friendly ear to confide in now. She had to tell someone who might just believe her story.

'Even if it is true, Simon is probably right about keeping it to yourself, though. I know we're all going back tomorrow, but we don't want to spread alarm, do we? Besides, who would want to kill Robert?'

Gina's expression was set in a childish sulk. 'No one liked him.'

'That's not the same thing though, is it?'

Gina gave a heartfelt sigh. 'I have to admit it's hard to think of any of this lot having the balls to actually stick a knife in him or bash him over the head. Especially when most of the men here wouldn't say boo to a goose. Austin's more of a man and he might I suppose, but he sounded genuinely shocked when Philippa mentioned it so it couldn't have been him.' Nursing her disappointment, Gina appeared to have forgotten that she'd intended to keep her source confidential.

'All the same,' she rallied quickly, 'It's a good job that

Simon and I have a good alibi for when Robert died. We had a coffee and an ice cream then went round the shops for a bit, then took a wander down some of the side roads looking at all the old buildings. We ended up on this street full of restaurants with tables outside and decided to have lunch there.'

Was that all a little too glib? Why else would Gina be so quick to establish an alibi?

'Did you buy anything nice?'

Gina shook her head.

The waiter arrived to take their orders for dessert; a choice of fruit tartlet, waffle soaked in a caramel sauce or chocolate mousse.

'Would you like that with cream or ice-cream, madam?'

'Neither thank you.' Fiona smiled up at the waiter. 'Just the chocolate mousse will be fine.'

As she turned her attention back to her fellow diners, she caught the expression on Felix's face as he stared across the table at Gina. Had he overheard their conversation? Did that frown indicate shock? If so, was that a response to learning Robert was murdered or that the police were about to make an arrest?

When everyone at the table came to leave at the end of the meal, Fiona found Felix had moved to her side.

'Are you coming down to the lounge? May I buy you a drink?'

'That's very kind of you. Thank you, Felix.'

They followed the others out into the corridor. Gina and Simon joined the three older members who had shared the table to wait at the lift.

'It will be a little crowded in there.' Felix turned to Fiona. 'Shall we take the stairs? It's only one floor down.'

Once the two of them were alone, he asked, 'I heard you talking with Gina over dinner. Did she really say that Robert was murdered?'

'You know Gina better than I do, but she does tend to exaggerate things.'

'True but . . .' He sounded thoughtful. 'If he was, do you think it could have been the same person who attacked you?'

'But that was a burglar.'

Felix frowned, slowly shaking his head. 'Did he take anything? Your bag or your jewellery?'

'Well no. Perhaps he didn't have time. I really don't think you need to worry, Felix. I'm sure we are all safe. I expect it was just a coincidence.'

'Maybe, but that's not the point. I think you should make sure you are never alone until we leave. Just in case.'

Was that a concerned warning or a threat?

Chapter 32

The call came through that evening.

'We've got him.' Cumming's jubilation was like a schoolboy's.

Montgomery-Jones smiled. 'That is good news.'

'Definite links between Ensley and Karaseiwicz. It looks fairly conclusive. Ensley must have asked him to find him a gun-for-hire. I doubt we'll ever find our so-called Jean the Gun. Being Belgian, he'd know every Brussels back alley and hideaway intimately. However, now we know what we're looking for, we have enough evidence to request offshore records and it's only a matter of time. By the time Mr Salmon reached Thames House, we had enough to bring Ensley in. Salmon's about to interrogate him. He said to phone you and let you know how grateful he is for the tip-off.'

'We should thank Mrs Mason. She was the one who coaxed it out of Philippa Western.'

'We've still got a long way to go yet before we get a conviction, if we ever do, but Ensley's career is at an end, whatever the outcome.'

'Quite so.'

'How is Mrs Mason? Have you found her passenger's murderer yet?'

'We are still working on it. I am about to go over to her hotel and find out. At least now I can give that investigation my full attention.'

'Well we owe both you and Mrs Mason a big favour.

Anything we can do at this end to help; you only have to ask.'

'Much appreciated, Cumming. Good night.'

Fiona found herself surrounded as she went to sit down in the lounge. The half a dozen or so chairs arranged around the small table were pushed further and further back as the group expanded. Almost everyone seemed to be there, many perched on the broad padded arms of the chairs and three people squeezed onto the two-person sofas.

Everyone seemed to be in celebratory mood, enjoying the chance of a last get-together before the journey home the next day. Fiona glanced around the noisy circle. Olive was looking the most cheerful she'd been all week. Someone had bought her what was in all probability a gin and tonic to judge from her excited chatter and red cheeks. Even the highly-strung Hazel looked relaxed for once and had a smile on her face as she leant forward listening to Liz Kennedy sitting on the other side of Dee.

Fiona sipped her drink and did her best to relax. It was true that she was in no danger amongst this crowd, but the chances of having a quiet word with any of the suspects were zero.

'It's such a pity we didn't get a chance to see the Best Pics of the Holiday slideshow,' Patrick Cahill called out across the circle. 'Any chance of seeing it tonight, Simon? Be a shame to miss it, especially after all the hard work you folk spent putting it together.'

'Oh, yes. Do let's.' Olive clapped her hands like an excited schoolgirl. How many drinks had she had?

'Well, I'm not sure . . .' Before Simon could make any excuses, there were general cries demanding to see the photos.

'I'll have to find out if the hotel will let us use the room.'

Accompanied by Austin, he went to make the arrangements.

Austin returned after a couple of minutes, a big grin on his face. 'Simon's gone to collect the projector and laptop. Everything's fine with the management, but they can't spare a member of staff to set out the room. The chairs are still stacked in there from last night, but I need three or four of you big strong blokes to help me put them all out. Give us ten minutes, folks and then we'll see you all in the conference room.'

Fiona felt unusually weary as she walked out of the lounge into the spacious foyer and even though the conference room was only on the first floor, she decided to join the queue for the lift. Best not to push herself too far in any case.

The lift doors opened and as the small group turned the corner, an arm slipped through hers.

'You sure you're okay with this?'

She looked across at Dee. 'Why wouldn't I be? I'd love to see all the photos as much as the rest of you.'

'I meant, going back into the same place where you were attacked,' Dee said softly, a slight frown on her face.

Fiona laughed. 'With all these people around me, I can't see it happening again, can you?'

'There's no chance of that, but I was thinking more about bringing it all back. Most people would find that far too unsettling.'

Fiona patted the hand on her arm. 'No need to worry about me, Dee. I'm made of pretty strong stuff.'

They walked into the room but before they could sit down Hazel, who had been trotting behind them as they'd walked down the corridor, grabbed Dee's free arm and pulled her away. 'There's a couple of seats over there.'

It was difficult to read the expression on Hazel's face as she glanced back at Fiona. Surely, she had done nothing to arouse the woman's hostility. True, Hazel demonstrated an intense resentment towards any other woman to whom Dee should show even the most perfunctory interest, but surely, she could not believe that Fiona had done anything to seek

Dee's attention?

It was almost half past ten by the time the slideshow packed up. Many of the older members of the party decided to make their way up to bed or to finish their last-minute packing. Fiona would have been happy to lie down too, but the whole point of her insisting on returning to the hotel had been to track down her attacker and to do that she needed to observe these people, even if the chances of the culprit giving himself away by a careless word were looking more and more remote.

The lounge was already busy, and it took several minutes to gather up and rearrange enough chairs to accommodate them all. It was only after Patrick Cahill had taken their orders and left to fetch drinks that Fiona had an opportunity to look around. Montgomery-Jones was sitting at a table tucked up at the side of the bar. He caught her eye and smiled. Was he there to keep an eye on her? He'd already met some of the party earlier in the week so he could hardly expect to go unrecognised. She was still wondering if she should go and talk to him when he got to his feet and came over to join them.

'Fiona, my dear.' He eased his way into the circle to reach her, then bent down to kiss her on the cheek. 'I heard they had let you out of hospital. How are you?'

'I'm fine as you can see. As I've been telling everyone, it was a great deal of fuss over nothing. Do you know everyone?'

The small circle was growing, and Fiona was surprised to see that Olive had decided to join them rather than retreating to her bed. Whether it was the extra wine she had drunk at dinner or Montgomery-Jones's magnetic charm as he took her hand that put the sparkle in her eyes was impossible to gauge. Either way, from the glass now sitting on the table in front of her, there was little doubt that Olive would have the mother and father of all hangovers come the morning. No doubt, a rare experience, Fiona judged, because tonight was the first time that she had seen Olive drink anything stronger than orange juice all week.

Olive was not the only one to be seduced by Montgomery-Jones's bonhomie. All the women, including Dee, appeared to be casting coquettish smiles in his direction and even the men warmed to his easy urbane manner, especially when he bought a round of drinks for everyone.

This was definitely not a Peter Montgomery-Jones that Fiona was familiar with. The somewhat aloof, emotionless, often-patronising character appeared to have disappeared with the change from the formal three-piece suit into the smart casuals he was now wearing. She had always thought of him as a man of few words and it was something of a revelation to see him indulging in the easy banter of social small talk and laughing and joking with the best of them.

Her head was beginning to throb, her limbs felt heavy, and Fiona was grateful when the party began to split up.

Montgomery-Jones glanced at his watch. 'If you will forgive me, ladies and gentlemen, I really ought to be getting back to my hotel. Thank you all for your company. It has been a most enjoyable evening.'

'I think I should call it a night as well.' Fiona got to her feet. 'Good night, everyone.'

Together they walked into the empty foyer.

'Has anything happened?' he asked softly.

'No one's tried to get me in a dark corner, if that's what you mean.' She looked up at him with a teasing grin.

'This is not a joke, Fiona.'

'No,' she sighed. 'And I'm not treating it as one. Having said that, one person did get me on my own, if you can call it that, walking down the stairs from the first to the ground floor. Felix overheard Gina telling me that Robert was murdered at dinner and he was worried that the killer might be the same person who attacked me.'

'How did he manage to work that out?' Montgomery-Jones's forehead creased in a deep frown.

'I didn't have time to ask. I think he was just trying to warn me to take care.'

'And how come Gina knew that Robert was murdered? Presumably, you did not tell her?'

She was too weary to protest at the injustice of his last question. 'She overheard Philippa tell Austin.'

'For goodness' sake! What sort of people do you have on your tours? Do they all go around listening in to other people's conversations; and how come the rest are so indiscreet as to say such things where they can be overheard?'

Fiona had to bite her lip to stop herself laughing out loud at his frustration.

'You have a point. Though it was Olive who surprised me most this evening.'

'Is that the somewhat inebriated older woman dressed like a bag lady?'

'Peter! That's very unkind. I'm surprised at you.'

He had the grace to give her a sheepish smile. 'I am not feeling particularly charitable tonight. Put it down to lack of sleep.'

'She does have a penchant for chunky hand-knitted cardigans I must admit. She was acting out of character this evening. I have the impression that she was upset about something earlier on. Perhaps that's what started her drinking; to steady her nerves.'

'Because you were about to denounce her as your attacker, do you think?'

Tiredness was beginning to take its toll. Fiona sank onto the corner-seating deep in thought. Montgomery-Jones sat down, making no attempt to hurry her.

'I don't think so. She adored Robert. I can't see her hurting him. For all his faults, I think Robert was rather fond of the old dear; saw her as a kind of maiden aunt. He could be downright rude to people, even his wife, but not once did I hear him as much as snap at Olive. In his way, he did look out for her. Of all the people he could have chosen, he made her club secretary quite possibly to give her a bit of status. Even if she discovered he'd been using her, she'd be more likely to collapse in a heap than retaliate violently.'

'Given sufficient motivation, frail elderly ladies might well be capable of surprising feats of strength.'

'I don't doubt it,' she said thoughtfully. She shook her head. 'No. I'm convinced her bitterness at the lack of concern the others showed after his death and her own deep sense of grief and loss were genuine. I doubt she's a good enough actress for it to have been otherwise.'

'I have to agree; it is difficult to imagine Miss Scudamore wielding a brick at a man's head with sufficient force to kill him. You on the other hand would have been a much easier target as you were stationary and already on your hands and knees.'

'I have this strange feeling that there is something hovering on the edge of my recollection about that attack. Something I saw out of the corner of my eye or I heard just before I felt the blow. I had hoped coming back here might help jog my memory. I nearly had it when I walked into the conference room earlier, but someone spoke to me and it was gone.'

Dee and Hazel came out of the lounge and crossed the foyer. As they stood waiting for the lift, Dee turned. Her face lit up and she gave a cheery wave. Montgomery-Jones raised a hand in acknowledgement.

'We have been spotted,' he said softly.

'Mmm,' Fiona replied. 'And Dee appears to have taken your wave as an invitation. They're coming over.'

All smiles, Dee strolled towards them, with a much less happy-looking Hazel dragging her feet following in her partner's wake.

'Did I hear you say earlier that you're going back to London tomorrow too?' Dee asked with eyes only for Montgomery-Jones.

'I do have one more task to see to, but that is the general idea.'

Dee sat down, but Hazel continued to stand.

As Dee and Montgomery-Jones continued to chat away, Hazel began to fidget.

'Why don't you sit down?' Fiona asked her.

Dee looked up. 'Take the weight off your feet, sweetie.'

'We were on our way to our room.'

'If you're so tired, why don't you go on up? I'll join you in a minute.'

Hazel's face crumpled, but Dee had already turned back to Montgomery-Jones to continue her conversation.

'But we were going to get our jackets. It's the last chance for a stroll round the centre when it's all lit up. Just the two of us!'

Dee gave an exasperated sigh and muttered under her breath, 'For goodness' sake!'

'This was supposed to be a romantic holiday to cement our relationship; that's what you said, and you haven't paid any attention to me all week. I might just as well not have come.' Hazel gave one of her little girl sobbing cries. 'And after all I've done for you!'

'You're being ridiculous.'

'I put myself in jeopardy for you!' Hazel was almost spitting in fury and frustration.

'What are you talking about?'

Hazel stood, body slumped, a single tear ran down her cheek.

There was a long silence.

'Hazel?'

It was Fiona who eventually answered Dee's question. 'She took revenge on Robert because he tried to ridicule you in public.'

Dee and Montgomery-Jones turned and stared at Fiona.

Fiona took Hazel's hands and gently pulled her down onto the seat beside her. She slid an arm around the shoulders of the sobbing girl.

'I know you didn't plan to do it.' Her voice was soft and

low. 'You were so very upset after you saw Dee bundled into that police van. It was just by chance you saw him in front of you not long after. There was a brick on the ground, part of the debris the demonstrators were throwing at the riot police I expect. Robert wasn't a big man, not much taller than you. You didn't mean to kill him, but before you knew what had happened, you'd hit him over the head with the brick. Is that how it happened?'

Hazel stared down at her hands, giving the barest nod.

'But why did you want to hurt me?'

Hazel looked up. Tears ran down her cheeks. 'Dee gave you a chocolate.'

'But you put something in my drinking chocolate before that, didn't you? At the chocolate shop. Something to make me sick.'

'It didn't work though, did it?' Hazel stared at her defiantly.

'I only had a sip. It tasted strange. I think you over did it that time. But it worked on the others, didn't it? On Olive, Eleanor, Glenda and Philippa too. And it was you who kept phoning the Westerns' room.'

'But why, Hazel?' asked Dee.

Hazel turned her head to look at Dee. Her bottom lip quivered.

'Because you paid them more attention than you did me!'

'But Dee's not interested in me,' Fiona said softly. 'Or Philippa. Or anyone else for that matter. She loves you.'

Hazel pulled away from Fiona, burying her face in her hands trying to smother the howls of pain.

Dee got up and moved across to sit the other side of Hazel, wrapping her in her arms and rocking her gently to and fro as though Hazel were a small child. When the noisy crying died to a pitiful sobbing, Dee looked up at Fiona and Montgomery-Jones. 'What will happen now? She's always been highly-strung, but she clearly wasn't in her right mind. I should have realised sooner.'

Montgomery-Jones took his mobile from his pocket and

moved off to make the call.

Dee looked up. 'Will they let me go with her, do you think?'

Fiona and Montgomery-Jones watched the retreating car.

'Do you think it will ever come to trial?'

'I doubt it.' Montgomery-Jones shook his head. 'Whatever happens, Hazel will be spending a good few years in a secure institution. The woman is clearly unbalanced.'

Fiona suddenly felt completely exhausted. 'After all that raw emotion, I'm going to break my resolution never to drink on a tour. I think I need a stiff drink. I wonder if the bar is still open.'

They walked back into the lounge.

'How did you work it out? He asked as he put the glass of brandy on the table in front of her.

'The stuff they gave me to make me sleep in hospital left me feeling nauseous when woke up, and it got me thinking about earlier. I thought we had a sickness bug going round the group but this afternoon relaxing in your hotel room I had plenty of time to mull it all over. I realised that all the cases had one thing in common. Hazel. She overheard Olive blaming Dee for making Robert go to the rally and she was near enough to catch Eleanor and Glenda gossiping about the spat which she had with Philippa in the lounge that you witnessed. Seeing Dee laughing with Philippa and then me drove her to jealousy.'

'Adding a laxative or whatever to someone's drink is a far cry from committing murder.'

'True. I know it's a huge jump, but it did make me aware of just how unstable the woman is. You know I told you earlier there was something I couldn't quite remember?' He nodded. 'It was hearing that strange little cry she gives when she's worked up. Half cry, half sob. She did it just now and I suddenly remembered that was what I heard as I lay on the floor. The rest, well that was just guesswork.'

'When we were talking about possible suspects you never

mentioned her name once.'

'Because she was the last person I'd have thought of. She always seemed such a sorry, rather pathetic creature. And there didn't seem to be any motive for her to want to kill Robert. I suppose I should have realised how deeply disturbed she is a lot sooner. She's always been totally obsessive about Dee. Dee's enemy is her enemy. You saw how she was with Philippa that time a couple of nights ago when she found Dee laughing and joking with her. Dee alienated quite a few in the party at the start and ever since that time she managed to get herself arrested, she's tried hard to ingratiate herself with everyone, particularly with me. Hazel was so possessive; things had got to the point that anyone who merited as much as a smile from Dee became a positive threat.'

'Well it's all over now. The case is closed. You can have a good night's sleep with no worries.'

'Talking of cases, how is the investigation into the Moorhouse assassination going?'

Montgomery-Jones smiled. 'Shall we say the end is in sight? We now have our man and now we know exactly what we are looking for, the evidence is steadily mounting.'

'Which means that there is nothing to keep you in Brussels?'

'Exactly. Now your attacker has been identified, I shall be on my way first thing tomorrow. I would go tonight, but you are not the only one who needs a good night's rest.'

They finished their drinks and she walked with him to the revolving glass doors. He bent and kissed her on the cheek.

'Take care. I will be in touch.'

He walked swiftly away into the night.

Day 10 Sunday

Sadly, today we must bid farewell to Brussels and the wonderful mediaeval Flemish towns of Belgium. Once we reach the Eurotunnel terminal in Calais, it will be time for us to wish bon voyage to all our fellow passengers and transfer to the feeder coaches for the last leg of the journey home.

Here at Super Sun, we do hope you have enjoyed your 'Treasures of Flanders' adventure and we hope to see you again soon on another of our exciting tours.

Super Sun Executive Travel

Chapter 33

Her appointment in Outpatients wasn't until eight-fifteen but Fiona arrived early and made her way up to the ward where she had spent Friday night.

'I've brought a card and a little something to say thank you to all you wonderful staff who looked after me so well.'

'Almond biscuits! How lovely.' It was the same nurse who had so gallantly fended off the police until Fiona had had breakfast and a chance to come round from her ordeal.

'I thought you could have them at coffee time.'

'I am about to go off duty. Once the day shift arrives there will be none left by the time I am back again so I shall open the tin and take a couple now, if that is all right.'

'Of course, it is. That's why I came up now. I wanted to thank you personally.'

The night nurse perched on the edge of the desk eating her biscuit. 'Your lovely husband not with you?'

Fiona frowned. 'I don't have a husband.'

'I am sorry. I assumed he was your husband because he stayed by your bedside all through the night. He refused to leave until he was convinced that no serious harm had been done and you would recover fully. We only managed to persuade him to leave once you showed signs of waking up. He went to speak to the two policemen who arrived and then he said he would go back to his hotel for a shower and a change of clothes but would be back later. Did he not return?'

'It must have been Peter. I didn't realise he'd spent the night here.'

She made her way across the busy foyer to collect her room key. The receptionist handed it over, but as Fiona thanked her and turned towards the stairs, she called her back.

'Oh Mrs Mason, someone left a package for you.' The girl lifted the small parcel onto the desk and pushed it across.

'For me? I'm not expecting anything.'

It was definitely for her. Her name and room number were written on a white envelope sellotaped to the top.

'A messenger delivered it about half an hour ago.'

It was about the size of a book but when she picked it up it was much too light to be a paperback. Resisting the temptation to open it there and then, she hurried up to her room. It almost slipped from her grasp as she tucked it under one arm as she extracted her key from her pocket. Whoever had strapped down the envelope had made a good job of the task and she almost ripped it in her excitement.

Inside was a single sheet of paper with the words, "A small gift to show my appreciation for all your help in solving my case. Without your information, we would never have made the breakthrough. I appreciate that you are a reluctant user of modern technology, but I am certain that you will be able to master the enclosed without undue difficulty. It should save you from having to carry a small library and you can download maps for your guided walks. My apologies for not having time to get it properly gift-wrapped. Once again, my sincere thanks. Fondest regards, Peter."

She dropped the note onto the bed and stared at the box. She peeled off the brown wrapping paper and stared at the wording on the box. A Kindle Fire and from all the letters after it, even she could work out it must be a top of the range model. Small it might be, but how could she possibly accept such an expensive present? On the other hand, she could hardly refuse it without causing offence.

His phone went straight to voicemail. He was probably on the train already in the channel tunnel by now.

It was only later that the thought struck her. A red-hot wave of embarrassment swept over her as she recalled that night in the hospital.

That dream she had about Bill. Was it really a dream or had she spoken those words out loud. What on earth would Peter think? Would he even realise that she'd been talking to Bill and not him? Why would he?

She wanted to crawl under the seat. How would she ever be able to face him again? Is that why he'd sent the . . .

Now she was being foolish. Of course, she hadn't said she loved him out loud. His attitude towards her hadn't changed any. He'd always looked out for her, but then he would have done that for anyone in a similar position.

The sudden burble of her phone made her jump. Surely, it couldn't be him?

'Hello.'

'Hi, Mum. How are you? I've been worried about you. You promised you'd ring.'

'I'm fine, Martin. I'm just back from a check-up at the hospital and they have pronounced me fit and fully recovered with no ill effects. We are all off back to England today so I've nothing to do but sit back and enjoy the journey. I shall be back home in Guildford by dinnertime.'

'And then you need to rest up for a good few days. I hope you're not intending to go gallivanting off somewhere else the minute you get back.'

Fiona sighed. 'You are beginning to sound like your big brother. Stop fussing. As it so happens, I don't have another tour booked until next month.' It might be as well not to tell him that she intended to spend the intervening time re-decorating the living-room.

'That's good. How was the trip? Did you see some nice

places? What were the clients like? Any awkward customers?'

'It was lovely. I had a great time.'

Perhaps she should keep a diary. One day she'd let them read it and then the family would realise exactly what adventures she did get up to. But not till long after she'd retired, and she had no intention of doing that anytime soon.

ABOUT THE AUTHOR

Judith has three passions in life – writing, travel and ancient history. Her novels are the product of those passions. Her Fiona Mason Mysteries are each set on coach tours to different European countries and her history lecturer Aunt Jessica, accompanies travel tours to more exotic parts of the world.

Born and brought up in Norwich, she now lives with her husband in Wiltshire. Though she wrote her first novel (now languishing in the back of a drawer somewhere) when her two children were toddlers. There was little time for writing when she returned to work teaching Geography in a large comprehensive. It was only after retiring from her headship, that she was able to take up writing again in earnest.

Life is still busy. She spends her mornings teaching Tai Chi and yoga or at line dancing, Pilates and Zumba classes. That's when she's not at sea as a cruise lecturer giving talks on ancient history, writing and writers or running writing workshops.

***

Find out more about Judith at www.judithcranswick.co.uk

Printed in Poland
by Amazon Fulfillment
Poland Sp. z o.o., Wrocław

60845125R00176